# the popular gir...
## what they se......

Mandy and her friends with their eyes going all black like that. . . . All the elaborate hazing just to be a part of their little in-crowd. I couldn't understand it. The flashes of cold, the uncertainty I felt whenever I was around Mandy. I didn't know what all of it meant.

But I was more determined than ever to find out.

"Hip, modern Gothic. Lindsay is a wonderful heroine—strong and smart." —Kelley Armstrong, *New York Times* bestselling author of *The Summoning*

"Imagine 'Gossip Girls' with a Gothic twist. It's hard to tell who's scarier—the queen bees or the evil spirits—in Nancy Holder's clever, creepy boarding school snarkfest." —Nina Malkin (*Swoon*)

"The poor little rich girls of Marlwood Academy will scare the devil out of you." —Marlene Perez (*Dead is the New Black*)

"Nancy Holder pens a riveting tale of teen angst and insanity, love and overpowering fear as she explores the dark depths of the human soul." —Debbie Viguie (*Wicked* series)

"Nancy has created the most evil clique since the witches in *Macbeth*." —Paul Ruditis (*DRAMA!* series)

# POSSESSIONS
## NANCY HOLDER

razOr
bill

Possessions

RAZORBILL

Published by the Penguin Group
Penguin Young Readers Group
345 Hudson Street, New York, New York 10014, U.S.A.
Penguin Group (USA) Inc., 375 Hudson Street, New York, New York 10014, U.S.A.
Penguin Group (Canada), 90 Eglinton Avenue East, Suite 700, Toronto,
Ontario, Canada M4P 2Y3 (a division of Pearson Penguin Canada Inc.)
Penguin Books Ltd, 80 Strand, London WC2R 0RL, England
Penguin Ireland, 25 St Stephen's Green, Dublin 2, Ireland (a division of Penguin Books Ltd)
Penguin Group (Australia), 250 Camberwell Road, Camberwell, Victoria 3124, Australia
(a division of Pearson Australia Group Pty Ltd)
Penguin Books India Pvt Ltd, 11 Community Centre,
Panchsheel Park, New Delhi – 110 017, India
Penguin Group (NZ), 67 Apollo Drive, Rosedale, North Shore 0632, New Zealand
(a division of Pearson New Zealand Ltd.)

Penguin Books (South Africa) (Pty) Ltd, 24 Sturdee Avenue, Rosebank,
Johannesburg 2196, South Africa

Penguin Books Ltd, Registered Offices: 80 Strand, London WC2R 0RL, England

10 9 8 7 6 5 4 3 2

Library of Congress Cataloging-in-Publication Data

Holder, Nancy.
Possessions / by Nancy Holder.
p. cm.
Summary: When Lindsay Cavanaugh transfers to the prestigious Marlwood
Academy after recovering from a breakdown at her previous high school, she discovers
that there is something strange going on involving a clique and some unsavory activities
from the school's little-known past.
ISBN 978-1-59514-255-9
[1. Supernatural--Fiction. 2. Boarding schools--Fiction. 3. Schools--Fiction. 4. Cliques
(Sociology)--Fiction. 5. Ghosts--Fiction.] I. Title.
PZ7.H70326Po 2009
[Fic]
2009010627

Printed in the United States of America

To those who walk in darkness.
There is light. I promise.

# October:
# The Search

*All our possessions are as nothing compared to health, strength, and a clear conscience.*

—Hosea Ballou

*The man who seeks revenge digs two graves.*

—Ken Kesey,
*Sometimes a Great Notion*

# one

**October 28**
**possessions: me**
    Tibetan prayer beads
    Mem's UCSD sweatshirt
    used black leather boho bag (thrift shop in Poway)
    Converse high-tops (from Target)
    Dad's socks (too big, but they're his)
    tattered jeans (origin forgotten)
    tortoiseshell headband (plastic)
    NO makeup
    five single-subject notebooks
    regulation Marlwood Academy planner
    ditto binder
    six #2 pencils, one missing eraser (panic attack)
    pens (unlimited)
    cell phone (no bars, no reception here AT ALL)
    Jason's St. Christopher medal (thanks, Cuz!)
    me, Lindsay 2.0 (or so I hope)

*haunted by:* my past

*listening to:* my heartbeat—too fast again! *don't forget to breathe.*

*mood:* frozen to death (not a mood?!)

**possessions: them**

oh.

my.

God.

is there anything they DON'T have???

*haunted by:* not seeing any haunting

*listening to:* each other

*mood:* excited? they can pay for any mood they want.

---

**Fog had crawled** up the mountain, like a wounded animal on pine-tree claws, and bled all over the campus. I stopped and squinted at my map with its handy printed stats—a hundred developed acres that included hiking paths and bike trails; thirty buildings, including a brick gym with a plaster frieze, which really needed updating, of ancient Greek athletes (male)—who could also have used some underwear, if I remembered the picture correctly.

The campus was rolling in white mist, and I wasn't sure of the way to the classrooms, which were clustered on the north side of the campus. I had thought there was a shortcut through

Academy Quad, my quad, but it was hard to be sure when I couldn't see more than ten feet ahead of myself.

Then a stiff wind blew, thinning the fog. Sure enough, my building loomed on top of the small hill to my left. Grose was a creaky, scary-looking rectangle made out of brick, with a slate roof. Another dorm, Jessel, crouched at the bottom of the hill like it was waiting to pounce. It was three stories tall with a slight-L-shape, where a back porch jutted out like a hunchback.

Jessel was prettier than Grose. It had towering stone columns on either side of its brightly painted red front door, and four turret rooms, one on each corner, covered in slate shingles. The windows of the turrets were arched, completing the castle-tower effect.

Everyone else in both Grose and Jessel had already moved in, made friends, and started right on schedule—September 5th. I couldn't believe they'd let me start so late. Maybe nervous breakdowns came with benefits.

I was here to reinvent myself in a major way. No one here *knew* I had gone bonkers. No one here knew me at all. I could be anyone—Lindsay Anne Cavanaugh 2.0. I really hoped I would like the remix better. I was optimistic; I had started out well as a person—had normal friends, liked animals, did pretty well in school. I used to kick butt on the cello. Okay, my mom died. And Jane Taylor seduced my boyfriend. In our house. On the throw I knitted for my mom in the hospital.

And yeah, I'd pretended I didn't care. I'd acted like it was no big deal. Because I wanted to be one of Jane's cool chicks.

That was called cognitive dissonance, when you wanted two

opposing things—such as self-respect and popularity. A broken heart and a shot at riding in Jane's limo to Homecoming.

A second chance and all my insecurities begging me to get the heck out of here. . . .

Sometimes, wanting those two opposing things made you fracture, like two tectonic plates crashing together beneath the surface of the ocean.

"So what do you think, Botox? Or a deal with the Devil? I heard Ehrlenbach's sixty-eight." A girl's voice wafted out of the billows of horror-movie white. I placed her at maybe twenty yards to my right—my Jessel side, where a private hedge hid their front yard from view. Dr. Ehrlenbach was our headmistress, and I had yet to meet her.

"Did you spend your summer in rehab? No one does Botox anymore," someone else shot back. "But if she's really that old, my money's on the Devil. My dad would do her in a heartbeat. I've heard him say so. All right, blindfold her."

I blinked. Slowed. Waited to hear more.

"That's too tight. Ow," a third voice protested.

"You know, Keeks, you don't have to do this," the second voice said, but there was a silent *but you'd better* tacked on the end, sharpened with the familiar edge of an accomplished bitch. I knew then and there that I was eavesdropping not only on a mean girl, but a leader of same—a queen bee. I was an expert on queen bees. Unfortunately.

*Nothing to see here, Lindsay,* I told myself, as my face prickled from memories and apprehension. *Move it along. Even better, run.*

They could have their fun. I was not there to have fun of any kind, especially that kind.

"I'm not so sure about this." That was Keeks again.

"Tie her hands." Her Majesty.

*Yow.*

"Maybe we'd better wait." The first girl I'd heard. Not in charge.

"Just do it, Lara. Oh, forget it. Give me the rope and—"

"God, Mandy, chill. I'm on it."

Mandy. How typical. I wondered if Mandy was half as mean as Jane; and if she was, I pitied Lara just for being there almost as much as I pitied Keeks, whoever she was, for agreeing to be blindfolded and tied up in the middle of a fog bank when they should be in class. Obviously, Keeks had to prove herself to get into their exclusive little club. So not worth it.

By then I was at the hedge. *Just a peek*, I told myself, *just to make sure she's okay.*

The privet leaves were wet and small, covering branches that grew together as dense as an actual fence. I smelled wet earth and my own sugar-free cinnamon gum. Wind toyed with my crazed ringlets as I raised myself up on my tiptoes in an attempt to peer out of a thinned-out space above my head. I'm only five-foot-two, and it was out of my reach. I crept to my left, still unable to see anything.

"Let's get started. Breathe in, breathe out, center. We gather to welcome you. Kiyoko, let go, let go of yourself, and become one of us." Nervous laughter drifted from a thinned section in the hedge, a circle of broken branch endings that looked as if someone had clipped them, like wire cutters on a chain-link fence. The opening emitted fog—as if *it* were breathing—and it creeped me out. I hugged my UCSD sweatshirt around myself as I moved in quietly and peered through. My high-tops sank into mud.

"Come to me, come to me," Mandy urged.

The fog rolled and churned; then I saw them. Two girls flanked a third, who was blindfolded. The tallest wore her light, nearly white-blonde hair in a messy bun. She had to be Mandy. Her full lips were curved in a smile I knew well—calculating, cruel, enjoying the distress of her victim.

Maybe-Mandy's neck was fashion-model long, and she was wearing glittering diamond earrings as big as pencil erasers. I assumed they were real. Her clothes were so fine—a long black coat hung open, revealing a knee-length black cashmere sweater-dress over black pencil-leg woolen trousers above high-heeled boots—and I saw a thick gold bangle around her wrist as she smoothed a wisp of hair away from her cheek. Everything looked designer and real.

"Become one of us," Mandy said again, her voice papery, and she exhaled, sending condensed breath all over the blindfolded girl's face.

"Become one of us," the other girl—Lara—chanted. She was grinning like a coyote that had stumbled on a nest of baby rabbits. Her emerald eyes (definitely contacts) gleamed as Kiyoko stood statue-still. Lara was a classic redhead with ivory skin and a few cute freckles, her hair short and her clothes tasteful but boho—a man's plaid suit jacket in olive green and chocolate-brown, an extra-long white shirt, and the skinniest of skinny dark jeans.

Standing blindfolded in the center, Kiyoko's hands were tied behind her back, which was the part that made me extra-uneasy for her. It was going a little too far.

Kiyoko was rail-thin, the kind of thin that was too thin even for a model, and black silky hair cascaded over her shoulders. A gorgeous silvery sweater grazed the thighs of her gray jeans, but it hung too loose on her. Her legs were like sticks. She was chewing her lower lip; her golden-hued features displayed her concentration and eagerness.

"Become one of us," Mandy and Lara whispered together, their breaths spiraling up toward the sky.

Fog rushed all around me, wrapping me up in cold sheets of blank whiteness, and I couldn't see a thing. The chill seeped through my clothes straight through to my bones, and I shivered, hard. It felt as if the cold were creeping under my hair, straight into my *brain*.

I shuddered, and for a few seconds, I couldn't even think. For a quick moment, I thought I smelled . . . smoke? Then the sensation passed. Another strong wind whipped through the fog and thinned it out again—just as Mandy and Lara both stiffened and quickly inhaled. Their faces went slack, with their eyes still open.

I wondered if they were having some kind of infectious seizure. I waited for them to exhale, but it wasn't happening. Then I realized *I* was holding my breath, too, and forced myself to let it out. I felt shaky and weird.

I almost called out to see if they needed help. Before I went nuts, I had done some lifeguarding, and I was still certified in CPR.

Slowly, Mandy turned her head in my direction, as if she knew I was there. Probably not a good thing, spying. Before I realized what I was doing, I stepped to the right, where the branches grew closer together, blocking her view, although I could still see her sick little game.

Mandy's forehead creased in apparent frustration. I squinted as more fog rolled between us; when it wafted out of the way, her eyes looked completely black. No pupils. No white. No color. Just black.

Whoa, how high was she?

"Number Three," she intoned, and her voice sounded different. "Come to me." Higher, shriller, with a little Southern accent. Her laugh was high-pitched, and a tad OOC . . .

"Number three, come to me," Lara added, and her voice didn't sound the same either. Maybe a little lower . . . meaner . . .

"I'm here," Kiyoko murmured. She sounded unsure, more like she wanted to please them than anything else.

A deep chill ran through me, the fog moist and cold on my face. What exactly was I witnessing?

Then someone tapped me on the back, and I gasped and whirled around.

# two

"Oh my God, I'm so sorry," said the girl before me. She had a little gap-tooth grin and I recognized her immediately from the JPEGs she'd sent me. She was my roommate, Julie. Her hazel eyes glittered in her classically oval face; her wheat-colored blonde braid coiled over her shoulder like a friendly snake. She was a couple inches taller than me, and she hunched, round-shouldered, as if to lessen her impact on me. "I didn't mean to give you a heart attack."

"No, no," I assured her. "I'm fine." I moved away from the hedge. I didn't want them to know that I'd been watching them. "So, hi. I'm Lindsay. But you know that." I'd sent her pics, too. But they were pre-breakdown. Maybe I didn't look like any of those pictures. After all, I hadn't been crazy in any of them.

*You are not crazy now,* I reminded myself.

"You must have just gotten in. I dashed to our room to get something during free time and I saw all your stuff," she said, breathy and rosy-cheeked and very, very nice. "So I started looking for you."

"And here I am," I said, smiling as best I could.

"Here you are. C'mon, let's get you settled in. Do you know how to get to Ehrlenbach's? She left a message that she wants to see you. I'll take you there. Then I'll let Coach Dorcas know I'll be late for soccer—I was supposed to start—and I'll meet you back at our room. Do you know how to get there?"

"I think so. And thanks." A beat, and then some of my old snarky self resurfaced. "And tell me that's not her real name."

"Well, *she'd* be happy to tell you that St. Peter raised the original Dorcas from the dead." Julie smiled, then looked in the direction of Jessel. "What's so interesting?"

"Nothing," I said. As we walked away, I felt something like a tap on the nape of my neck, and I glanced back at the hedge. Mandy was standing exactly where I had stood, staring at us. From that distance, I couldn't see her eyes, but I could read her body language. She was on alert, on guard, wondering if we'd seen anything. And I knew then that what I'd witnessed was a secret.

———

**Marlwood Academy** was nothing like the brochure I had snagged in my old school counselor's office back home in San Diego, when they were trying to decide if I was suffering from Post-Traumatic Stress Disorder (verdict: yes) and if I needed meds ("not yet"—that was reassuring). The extremely fancy booklet (eighty-four pages) had featured lots of glossy close-ups of wildflowers and pine trees. There were seventeen dormitories and apparently some condemned buildings that were forbidden territory. Marlwood had three hundred surrounding acres of forest, and a current student population of 201. I had a feeling that extra Dalmatian was me, she who did not really belong here. No matter. I *was* here.

I'd learned a little about Marlwood from emailing and IMing with my roommate-to-be, Julie Statin. She said Marlwood had reopened that year after decades of being closed. Generations of rich Ehrlenbachs had used the extensive grounds as a family retreat, but Dr. Margot had started up the school again for some unknown reason.

Both Julie and the brochure had neglected to mention that the campus was located in the middle of nowhere, surrounded by some seriously eerie woods, or that the headmistress, Dr. Margot Ehrlenbach, looked like something out of a wax museum—at least judging by her photograph on page one. Now I was about to find out.

Julie and I approached the admin building, me watching a cluster of my classmates laughing and strolling to points unknown. They were dressed for a level of upscale success I hadn't dreamed existed outside dishy, trashy websites. I was gawking so intensely that I nearly ran into a big black door, adorned with a circular door knocker clutched in the mouth of a stern lion. Arched windows swagged in dark green curtains looked like eyes; two stone columns propped up lacy iron-work verandas enclosing the two stories.

"I have to leave you here," Julie said. "I'll check in with coach and see you in a few." She patted my shoulder. "Ehrlenbach is freaky, but don't let her get to you."

"Words to live by," I drawled, trying to sound braver than I felt.

"You're funny," Julie said. It was a compliment. "Later."

She dashed off and I went inside.

The scent of ivy seeped through a clogging, old-building smell, and stained glass windows blocked out more light than they let in. It was so gloomy that it took me a moment to see the washed-out receptionist, with gray hair and silver glasses and a gray blouse under a dark green jacket. Dark green was Marlwood's color. She brought the gray to the party on her own.

"Lindsay Cavanaugh," she said. I was a bit taken aback that she knew my name. But of course, I was the only new girl, new defined as starting the semester so late.

"That's me," I blurted.

She didn't smile. "Go down the hall. Her door is on the left. She's waiting," she told me, gesturing. Her nameplate read ANNE SHELLEY.

I passed Ms. Shelley's desk and walked into an even dimmer corridor. At the other end, the marble bust of Our Glorious Founder, Edwin Marlwood, glared at me so hard that I actually took a step back. He had a narrow forehead and a long, hooked nose, and his blank eyes practically narrowed with disapproval. *You*, he seemed to say, *do not belong here.*

Just before I knocked on the heavy mahogany door that said, MARGOT EHRLENBACH, PhD, HEADMISTRESS, Dr. Ehrlenbach opened it herself and invited me to sit down. The office was freezing—even colder than outside—and I was glad I had opted for my high-tops instead of my flip flops. The room was completely bare except for a large cherrywood desk, a bookcase containing a dozen or so thick leather-bound books, her padded leather chair, two upholstered (dark green) chairs in front of it, and some framed watercolor sketches of the Marlwood grounds.

"So. Lindsay," Margot Ehrlenbach said unto me.

My cousin's boyfriend had dubbed her "Maggot" during the endless family debates we'd had about whether it would drive me even crazier to go away to boarding school. I wondered if she kept her office so cold to keep herself from decomposing. I knew she was on the elderly side, but there were no wrinkles on her sharp-featured face. She was wearing an incredible amount of makeup; maybe she had troweled it into all her lines, like grout. Her skin was pulled so tightly she couldn't have smiled if she'd wanted to.

And after seeing me, she obviously didn't want to. I had thought I was all that—proud of my anti-fashion statement: high-tops, tattered jeans, my mom's ratty UCSD sweatshirt, no makeup. And the hair that would not die—my black curls flowing like bubbles over my shoulders, contained—not tamed—by a plain tortoiseshell headband. But it wasn't happening.

"You've arrived," she continued, in a tone that said *We won't make a mistake like that again.*

I had assumed my first stop would be my room, and I had planned to change into a less ragged pair of jeans and maybe even a sweater and Jason's peacoat to meet my headmistress. Instead, Dr. Ehrlenbach's eye-sweep up and down drove home the point that I had blown my first impressi̶o̶n̶ and the silence in the room hung there like a meat cleaver̶.

"And you're ready to get to work," she said̶, skipping the pleasantries. "Because you have a *lot* of catching u̶p̶."

"Yeah, I mean yes. Ma'am," I replied.

She *could* smile, thinly, and arch a brow, doing both as she handed me a schedule, a map, and some syllabi, and then told me all my books had been delivered to my room with the rest of my things.

She said "things" like my things were *things*. Things that should not be there. Things that were suspect, and probably infected. Then she went on to remind me that my room-mate was going above and beyond, because everyone else in my dorm had a single, and Julie Statin had actually *offered* to share with me.

I smiled and at some point I completely fuzzed out and lost track, which is what happens to people with anxiety problems. So I smiled harder and felt sweat icing over my clavicles, and wondered if it was really so bad back home in San Diego.

Big problem: it was.

"So we'll check back in with each other in a week, yes?" she concluded.

"Yes, yes, that would be so . . . yes," I bumbled. I could feel the clock ticking. On your mark, get set. I had seven days to prove myself.

I could see both our reflections on Dr. Ehrlenbach's desk; the room was so cold I could see my breath, too. Each "yes" was like a hiss of steam.

"Then you may go," she said, each word distinct, as if I were either an idiot or couldn't speak English.

She placed her hands on her desk. I swore she had put makeup on them and I tried very hard not to stare. No rings. I was wearing a ring on my thumb. I wondered if that made me look like I was in a gang or something.

I got to my feet, my nerves making me awkward. Or maybe I was just naturally awkward. She cocked her head and I had a crazy (bad word choice, maybe ... "unsettling") moment where I thought she was going to tell me that she'd changed her mind and I couldn't stay. I knew she had protested my admission, and someone on the board had overruled her. I'd heard my stepmom, CJ, talking about it on the phone. I wondered if Dr. Ehrlenbach could tell by looking that I wasn't completely over my nervous breakdown.

*Yes, yes I am*, I told myself.

Then she blew me out of the water. "You know, you have such a pretty face. Maybe with a little grooming . . . " She trailed off.

I knew that one. It was the way people told you that something about your appearance sucked. She could be commenting on my crazy hair, which was a huge mass of ringlets that fell to my shoulders. Or the lack of makeup on my face, which my mom used to say was shaped like a heart. I was born on Valentine's Day. "Grooming" in the current situation probably meant appropriate clothes, though. I felt like such a dork.

"Thanks," I said, which made me feel even dorkier.

Then her face sort of . . . altered, and I couldn't really tell if she was smiling more widely or experiencing intense pain.

I didn't know how to read her, but I had a sinking feeling that she was enjoying watching me squirm. How did a person become the headmistress of a very expensive private boarding school for girls? She had to have a lot of ambition, and cut-throat skills.

I was suddenly very scared of her. We were up here in the mountains and she held my fate in her hands. She could make my life a living hell and—

*Stop it. You are falling into drama mode,* I chastised myself. "All right, then," she said.

I knew I had stayed too long. I turned and fled, forcing myself to walk at a normal pace as I went back down the hall, past the receptionist, and out the front door.

Then I was free, half-stumbling down the brick steps in a mild state of shock, shaking with cold and tension, and wondering if maybe I could whip out the old cell phone and request a rescue. But my dad was probably already halfway to the forlorn little town of San Covino, the closest outpost of civilization to Marlwood. San Covino was two hours away, and the winding mountain road back up to Marlwood had sorely taxed our old Suby.

And I had just spent two weeks convincing him; my step-mom; the administration at Grossmont, my old school; and Dr. Yaeger, my therapist, that I was ready for this fantastic opportunity.

Plus, I had no cell phone reception. No bars. No texting. Just . . . my thoughts.

I was on my own.

# three

**Julie met me** halfway between the admin building and our door. Her cheeks were rosy from dashing all over campus, and I was grateful that she working overtime to make me feel welcome.

"I'm on the red team," she informed me. "In soccer. We're gonna kill the blues. And here we are," Julie announced all in one breath, as she pushed open the door to Grose Hall. The door itself was carved with the Marlwood crest—a capital M surrounded by ivy.

The foyer was dark; on a half-circle table facing us, a foot-high statue of a guy in a robe raised a hand in benediction—speaking of St. Peter—and a jumble of letters was scattered in front of him. He was blessing the correspondence. There was a white board propped beside the statue. It said, *"At Stewart. Ida, eat lunch."*

"Ms. Krige is over at Stewart. There's a meeting," Julie translated. "Ida is one of our dormies."

I remembered that Ms. Krige was our housemother. She had nice handwriting. "Is this a Catholic school?" I asked.

"Not that I know of," Julie said, as she led the way down a hall paneled in nearly-black wood. Small chandelier-style light fixtures hung from the ceiling, which was made of some kind of embossed metal of little rosettes, painted burgundy. The light bouncing off it made Julie's cheeks look sunburned. Or bloody.

There were oil paintings on the walls, mostly of vases of flowers or bowls of fruit, and a few landscapes. The hardwood floor beneath our feet was highly polished, revealing our reflections like a shimmering pool would. I passed a watercolor painting of a girl's head and shoulders. Unsmiling, she had a bizarrely wide forehead and her hair was pulled back tightly in a bun. Her eyes were dark brown, and in the dim red light, they reminded me of Mandy's eyes, back at the hedge.

"I think these are student paintings," Julie said. She made a face. "Not exactly the best advertising for the art department, is it?"

"The eyes follow you." I experimentally moved my head back and forth. Sure enough, Wide Forehead's gaze shifted as I moved. I knew that was a painter's trick. The Mona Lisa did the same thing. But it was still creepy.

We passed several half-open doors—people were trusting there—a couple doors revealing dark, ornately carved beds, each with a different bedspread: sky-blue satin with metallic stars, silky black, hippie swirls of raspberry and yellow. A pair of leather riding boots gleamed dully on a hardwood floor.

"Jessel and Grose are two of the oldest buildings on campus," Julie informed me. "We're Academy Quad. We're the only dorms that have full kitchens. And we have the weirdest bathroom. It's got, like, five bathtubs. Huge ones." She wrinkled her nose. "And ghosts. We're supposed to be haunted."

"Eek," I mocked, ignoring the teeny little shiver that zinged up my spine.

She held up a finger. "Don't be so quick to make fun. This place is bizarre at night. I swear someone keeps walking up and down the hall, but when I go and look, there's no one there."

"Double eek." I didn't mean to sound sarcastic. I just didn't know what else to say.

She huffed but she was still smiling. "Anyway, I'm so glad you're going to share my room. I haven't had a decent night's sleep since I got here."

"Oh." I was a little crestfallen. It hadn't dawned on me that she might have had an ulterior motive for wanting a roommate.

"If you stare at the tiles in the bathroom and say 'Come to me' five times in a row, you're supposed to be able to see a ghost," she went on, scrunching up her face.

"Have you tried it?" I asked her.

"Are you nuts?" she shot back, grabbing her ponytail and making as if to smack me with it. "Jessel's even more haunted," she went on. "It's the most haunted dorm on campus. Also, it's the coolest one. With the turrets. One of them is locked and no one is allowed in."

"That's where Ehrlenbach keeps her coffin," I said.

We both grinned at each other; then she stopped at a door

that looked like all the other doors, except that it was closed. She put her hand on the latch.

"Grose has a very strange layout," she said. "The rooms on our side of the hall have two windows, but the rooms on the other side have no windows at all. They are hideous caves; mushrooms are probably growing in their closets."

"Cool," I replied, and she clicked open the door.

Wow. There was a circular tapestry on the floor, of fat roses and leaves, and a larger version of the chandelier light fixtures gleaming above it. The light bulbs in it were shaped like flames.

Beneath two narrow rectangular windows, two larger-than-twin-sized beds of carved black wood were placed on either side of a common large nightstand made of dark wood inlaid with what looked like mother-of-pearl. Each bed had another, smaller stand on the other side; these were a little plainer, as if they hadn't been part of the original grouping. One bed was covered with a very thick pink satin quilted bedspread with fist-sized ivory tassels. I could tell just by looking at it that it had been very expensive. If my family had ever hoped to have things like that, the hope was gone. My dad was still paying off my mom's medical bills.

A stuffed unicorn sat on top of a stylish trio of velvet pillows in three different shades of pink bordered with soft gray fringes. The unicorn was lavender with metallic silver hooves and a matching silver horn, and its black curled eyelashes were very long. It looked amazingly cheap, compared to the bedspread and pillows.

Julie saw me looking at it. Her cheeks went pink as she

crossed to the bed, picked it up, and waggled it at me. "Are you going to mock me for having a stuffie?"

"Only if he has friends," I said, trying to make a joke. Then, gazing at the oversized trunk at the foot of her bed, I added hastily, "Unless he really does. In which case, I apologize."

"No. Caspian is my one and only transitional stuffed animal."

She started to put the unicorn on her bed, then picked it up and cradled it against her chest. She made his front right hoof wave at me. "And he is very happy to meet you."

*Okay, that's going a little too far*, I thought, but I said, "Same here, Caspian."

The other bed—mine—was covered with a brocade tapestry bedspread. The circular rug tied in with it, but didn't quite match it. It dawned on me that these were real antiques, one-of-a-kind items. That was what forty-one thousand dollars a year for tuition and room and board got you. Plus a thousand for fees and a thousand for books. All of which I was getting for free.

My cheesy brown polka-dot suitcases and plastic bins from Home Depot were grouped around the footboard of the tapestry bed and on top of a study desk with turned legs. A two-shelf bookcase sat beside the desk. There was a row of what appeared to be textbooks lining the top shelf. My chair was wood, with dark green upholstery, and a bazillion levers to adjust the height and such. I also had a dresser, with four drawers, and an oval mirror atop it. The mirror had a grayish tint, as if it were very old, and the frame was carved. Roses.

My room at home was a jumble of non-matching furniture

I had tried and failed to coordinate with purple-and-green drapes, some matching throw pillows, and a lamp with a purple lampshade I had decorated with silver and green beads. My throat tightened for a second with emotions I couldn't begin to name, even if Dr. Yaeger had been there with his collection of happy, sad, pissed-off, and depressed faces to give me clues.

Until then, I had assumed the pictures in the brochures were exaggerations, and my bed would be a metal frame and a mattress. I'd imagined a stained mattress at that, and a sort of set of cubbies where I would stash my clothes.

My clothes. My unbelievable rags. What had I done?

"I think our room used to be two rooms," Julie went on as I moved on to the textbooks and began examining them one by one. I half-expected them to be written in a secret private-school code, or for each page to be covered in footnotes referring to things I'd never heard of. They looked like regular schoolbooks, nothing too beyond me, and I exhaled with relief.

"To explain the two windows," she said. "Two rooms. But they'd have been about as big as prison cells. I mean, this one is pretty cramped as it is."

I glanced up from my brand new Spanish book. Was *she* nuts? Her room—our room—was huge.

"We can see Jessel," she said, crossing to the windows. "They hardly ever close their drapes. Mandy Winters lives in Jessel. Mandy came late, too, but not as late as you."

Mandy's last name was Winters. It sounded vaguely familiar. I remembered her black eyes as I came up beside Julie and gazed down at Jessel. The turrets really were amazing. We had a great view of one of them, although the curtains were closed.

"That's Mandy's room," Julie said, following my line of vision. A beat. "You've *got* to know who the Winters are . . . "

I made a little face.

"Oh my God. They live in the stratosphere of richness. Their maids have maids."

"Do you hang out with her?" I asked.

She shook her head with a faraway look. Her earrings were tiny enamel daisies.

"I had a horse at the same stable as Mandy for a while but we had to sell him. Mandy never really noticed me. There. Or here." Her voice grew soft. I heard the longing in it, and I did the math: Mandy was on the inside, Julie not so much.

"You had to sell your horse?" I said sympathetically.

She looked down. "We're, um, well, things are a little tight for us. For the moment. Just until the market bounces back." It sounded practiced, as if it were what she and her parents had agreed she should say if anyone was gauche enough to ask her about their financial situation.

*And now you have a roommate.* I wondered if she was getting a discount on her room and board in addition to a human nightlight. Then I felt guilty for being critical. It revealed a lack of self-esteem. Dr. Yaeger and I both agreed on that.

"I hardly ever rode him anyway," she continued. Then, with an air of sadness, she set the unicorn down in the exact center of her bed. "There, Caspi, you stay cozy." She turned with a big smile on her face. "Let's unpack you."

I was as self-conscious of the things inside my suitcases as

I had been of my outfit, back in Ehrlenbach's office. But Julie had already breezed past me with an air of anticipation, and I knew she was going to see everything I'd brought anyway—unless I hid it somewhere and ordered some stuff online with the loaded debit card my dad had given me, for emergencies.

I moved first to my turquoise-and-chocolate backpack and unzipped it. I unwound the Bubble Wrap from my most treasured object—a framed photograph of my parents and me on our trip to Las Vegas. I had been twelve, and it was our last vacation before my mom got sick.

High school had turned out to be my casino, and getting popular was the game I played. I kept on paying with bits and pieces of myself, slowly, before I realized what I was doing. Soon the nice girl I had been had dumped all her old friends, stopped practicing the cello, and spent way too much time obsessing over her clothes. I raised the bar on biting sarcasm and left a path of hurt wherever I swaggered, like a tornado.

But I scored the big prize. In a matter of months, even though I was only a freshman, I was in the coolest clique at my high school; and Riley, my crush, was going to ask me to the winter dance.

Then I lost it all.

My heart began beating too fast. Again.

"That's your mom, isn't it," Julie guessed, examining my picture. "You're so young."

I nodded. "She looks like she was really nice," she went on. "How's your stepmom? Is it weird having stepbrothers?"

"Not really," I said. "They're actually pretty good to me. And CJ's okay. She's just not Mom." It was all true. CJ—Cathy

Jean—and my dad had been married for about a year. I didn't mind. I'd been busy with my own stuff.

Julie looked sad on my behalf for a few moments. Then she brightened as she handed back my photograph.

"Those guys in Jessel, y'know, Mandy? Lara St. Simone lives there, too. I think they have séances. Or something. Maybe you could ask them to contact your—"

I blinked, and she looked flustered.

"Uh, well . . . " She trailed off, grimacing as if she wanted the floor to devour her. "Hey, your picture would look great on our nightstand. What do you think?"

*I think I like you very much*, I wanted to tell her. *I think I really need a friend.*

# four

Julie left to slaughter the blue team, and I finished unpacking less than ten minutes later, even counting the
time it took to hang things in my closet. It was tempting to take
a nap; I was exhausted and I seriously needed to recharge my
batteries. But Dr. Ehrlenbach's pinched-perfect face loomed
large in my mind. I didn't want her to think I was a slacker, so
I grabbed my map and my trendy boho bag and checked my
hair in the mirror. Crazy, yes, but it did have a certain untamed
wildness that looked . . . wild and untamed. Maybe that would
be the new me, too. Wild, and untamed.

All false modesty aside, I did have a pretty face. It was my
mom's face. I pulled my hair back and looked at her big chocolate brown eyes and heavy black eyelashes—so many people
told me I didn't even need to use mascara—her high cheekbones, her wide mouth.

I could almost hear my dad saying, "What's cookin', good
lookin'?" He used to come up behind her and plop his chin
on her shoulder like a big, goofy puppy. She was taller than

me. He had loved her so much. When I was little, I heard him call her "Emmy," her nickname, short for "Emily," and I started calling her "Memmy" instead of "Mommy." Everyone started calling her that, even people outside our family—even her cancer doctor. I knitted her a soft cashmere throw in her favorite color, china blue. And I added an embroidered heart with MEMMY in it.

And that was the throw Jane and Riley rolled all over, when they had sex in my parents' bedroom, and I was in the hall, and . . .

*I'm at Marlwood Academy. I'm safe.* I wiped my sweaty palms.

In the gloom, my face was a pale white heart. We were fourteen hours north of San Diego, high in the mountains, and it seemed that it was getting darker, sooner. The shadows were creeping across the room. I put the photograph on our nightstand.

The curtains in the turret window at Jessel billowed slightly, as if someone stood behind them, watching me as I hovered by my bed and wondered again about what I'd seen those girls in the courtyard doing. Holding a séance?

I walked down the hall, past the bad art, and out the door. I consulted my map and turned to the left. Within a few minutes, I was surrounded by dozens of girls in really, really good outfits on a blacktop path lined with white metal horse heads. The horses held swags of white chain in their mouths, and their eyes were blank and unseeing. The fog washed over and around them, blurring them so that when I looked away, I almost thought they were moving.

I decided that if there were any ghosts at Marlwood Academy, it was those silent sentries. There had to be hundreds of them.

Then I came to Lecture Hall 217, my American lit class-room, and walked inside. The hall was a large, dipping horse-shoe of upholstered seats with pull-down desks. At the bottom of the shoe stood a cherrywood lectern in front of two large, blank whiteboards. About twenty girls were plopped down in random seats. The hall was built for at least three times that, and it had a kind of deserted, melancholy air about it—as if someone had made elaborate party preparations, but no one had showed up. Marlwood had opened its doors for freshmen and sophomores only; the idea was to build up the student pop-ulation over the next two years. The current sophomores—my class—would become next year's juniors. There wouldn't be any seniors until two years from now.

My gaze rested on a thin girl with a retro beehive and large hoop earrings, wearing a charcoal-gray sweater that was even baggier than my sweatshirt, a wrap-around indigo sarong, then another one of wheat-colored fabric over that, leggings, and some kind of floppy boots. From the neck up, she reminded me of Amy Winehouse, from the good days, but the rest of her was bag lady. So, maybe my outfit wasn't the worst after all.

Then I spotted Kiyoko, with her shiny hair and petite shoulders, and her forlorn, beautiful face. Her eyes were almond-shaped. She was seated next to a girl with brown hair. The other girl was holding out what looked to be a protein bar, and Kiyoko was shaking her head. They were dead center in the bottom row of the horseshoe, right up front where good students sat, at least at my old school.

A notebook was flipped open on Kiyoko's pull-out desk

and she was examining a pen, pressing the tip against the page as if testing to make sure it worked. While the other girl unwrapped the bar and took a bite, Kiyoko bent over and studied her handiwork, her dark hair grazing the paper. She laid the pen horizontal to the top of the notebook and carefully tore out the piece of paper she had used, folding it into halves, then quarters, and placing it underneath her notebook. She smoothed the fresh page with both hands.

With a whoosh of air, a door matching the cherrywood lectern opened to the left of one of the whiteboards, and a chubby man with freckly brown skin emerged with a pile of handouts balanced on top of a large hardback book. I glanced down at the prinout of my schedule. His name was Mr. Bhutto.

Kiyoko sat up straighter, giving him her full attention, while most of the others kept chatting.

"All right, ladies, please, settle down," the man said.

I sat down quickly in an aisle seat.

"Today we continue our discussion of Nathanial Hawthorne," he said. "As you know, he was a descendant of one of the original judges in the Salem witch trials. He struggled with an identity crisis, and added the *w* in his name to distinguish himself from his ancestors."

*Wow,* I thought, *Nathanial Hawthorne 2.0.*

"Before we go, I'll put you in pairs for your next project. Here's the rubric. You can also download it and save one of our precious pine trees."

Pairs? Project? *Next* project?

He stepped forward and extended his stack of handouts to Kiyoko. She took one and passed the rest to the girl on her right. When it came around to me, I skimmed. We had to create a presentation that centered on an American short story written in the first half of the nineteenth century. "While you're looking that over, let me introduce our newest student. He paused and looked up. "Lindsay Cavanaugh, please stand up."

And that was the second time that day I realized I should have changed my clothes. I got up slowly and I saw his eyes narrow; then, for some reason, I glanced over at the Amy Winehouse wannabe and she flashed me a huge grin. I wished it would make me feel significantly better, but I only cheered up slightly.

Mr. Bhutto took attendance. I missed the first couple of names on the roll, which went with poised, polished, glamorous girls who looked as if they were models. One of them looked very familiar, and I realized with a start that I'd seen her in a movie. Several, in fact.

There was Charlotte Davidson, kind of an upscale goth, slightly overweight; and a few others, but not many, who didn't look like they were going to a fashion show. The beehive girl who had smiled at me was named Rose Hyde-Smith. Kiyoko's friend was Shayna Maisel. Kiyoko was the very last. Yamato.

"All here, which is no surprise," Mr. Bhutto said flatly. "Lindsay, you'll be expected to attend class unless you're in the infirmary. Open your text books, please."

Call it wacky, but that was the moment I fully grasped that I was at a boarding school. That I'd eat all my meals with the girls I went to classes with; that I'd go to bed and wake up with strangers, and walk to my classrooms with girls who tied each other up behind hedges. Suddenly, I felt a little panicky. I had left everything behind. No one even knew I'd left to come here, except for my father, my stepmom, my two stepbrothers, my cousin Jason, and his boyfriend, Andreas. I hadn't even said goodbye to Heather Sanchez, who had once been my best friend, back before I turned into a popularity addict.

I was crazy to think I could do this. I'd only made it in because of my killer personal essay on the application, and my extreme need to get out of town.

Mr. Bhutto explained the project in greater detail. I tried to focus, but it felt like everything was sliding away from me again, all the bits and pieces of the universe suddenly having not much to do with me. My heartbeat picked up.

Again.

Mr. Bhutto started calling out the pairs. I concentrated on my breathing and brought myself under control. No one could tell, of course. The turmoil was all inside.

"Susi Mateland and Gretchen Cabot . . . Rose Hyde-Smith and Charlotte Davidson. Shayna Maisel and Aliya Rashid . . . " There didn't seem to be a pattern. It wasn't alphabetical or anything.

"Lindsay Cavanaugh and Kiyoko Yamato."

"Huh," I blurted, hopefully too softly for anyone else to hear. Kiyoko jerked up her head from her book and gazed around the room as if she had absolutely no idea who any of the people in the room were. I held up a finger. Kiyoko's wandering stare landed on me and she nodded once, then returned her attention to Mr. Bhutto.

"Please join your partners," Mr. Bhutto said.

Kiyoko glanced at me, obviously expecting me to move. I had a rebellious moment where I thought about digging in and making her come to me. *Come to me, come to me* . . . I felt a chill just remembering Mandy's chant earlier that morning. But curiosity overcame me and I went to her.

"Hey," Kiyoko said as I sat down in Shayna's vacated chair. I felt a little awkward—after all, I had spied on her just a couple hours ago—but I managed a half-smile, half-nod in return. Her notebook was open; she'd taken extensive notes, and her handwriting was amazing. She had a French manicure. My nails were jagged, my cuticles even worse.

"I'm Kiyoko," she said, shaking her silky black hair off of her shoulders.

"Lindsay." But of course she knew that.

"So we need to pick a story for the project," she said, moving on from the pleasantries. "What about this one?" She flipped the pages. She had the most delicate fingers I'd ever seen, like a pianist's. "'Young Goodman Brown.' What do you think? It's about a Puritan man who meets Devil worshippers in the woods."

Before I could reply, she went on. "We're supposed to use the story as a springboard for a project with more scope, right? So I was thinking we could do a report on the history of satanic rituals in America. Or is that too weird?" Her dark eyes widened.

I was amazed. She was like a machine; I had never met any-one who was so . . . linear.

A little shadow passed across her angular face, but just as quickly, she was smiling again. "Hey, we can watch *The*

*Crucible* with Daniel Day Lewis together."

*We can?* I was caught off guard. I'd expected her to be cruel, like Mandy. Guilt by association—I'd been nice, too, before I started hanging out with Jane.

"We can probably download it. How about tonight after dinner?"

"I guess," I finally said. This was all happening very fast. Then I realized how lucky I was to be her partner. There was no way she was going to allow us to get a bad grade.

She was quiet for a moment. Then she touched her finger to the corner of her mouth, and looked at it, as if she were checking her lipstick. She dropped her hand to her lap and turned, facing me squarely.

"Listen," she said. "I . . . I think someone should, you know, *help you out*." She looked at my hair, then at my clothes. "This is a very good place to be, Lindsay." She flushed and reached down to a beautifully tooled shoulder bag. She pulled out a tissue and tapped her finger against it.

"Our parents, and the people they know . . . you can make connections that will get you anything you want."

She searched my face. "I don't know why you showed up so late. How you got in, no offense. Maybe somebody dropped. Someone I don't know."

*Someone unimportant. Someone beneath your radar*, I filled in, but I was listening.

"So . . . you need to make an effort." She took a breath. "And here's the dealio, Lindsay. I'm good to know, but Mandy Winters is even better."

*Whoa*. I had not expected that.

"It's *incredible* that Mandy Winters is here." She searched my face. "Her parents know presidents and kings. And rock stars. Mandy had lunch at the White House two days before she showed up here."

"Wow," I said. Julie was right: the stratosphere of rich.

Sensing that she had my attention, Kiyoko leaned toward me. "She has a driver. She can ask her father for the *jet*. Her mother got her old boyfriend into Harvard on a phone call."

"Yeah, and got him booted when they broke up," Shayna declared, swinging her head around from a chair nearby.

"She did not," Kiyoko said, but her voice was less firm.

"Whatever. She's another rich you-know-what, but I can't say it because my father is a rabbi."

Shayna stretched her arms overhead and dropped them to her sides. "So, Lindsay, hi. Scholarship, huh?" She gave me a fakey wink. "Don't freak. Everybody knows. Everybody knows everything. Including why Mandy's here instead of that so-posh school in London." She wrinkled her nose. "Marlwood is significantly closer to home. San Francisco."

"We don't know that," Kiyoko said quickly.

"Mandy Winters and her brother Miles were found in bed in the Lincoln Bedroom at the White House. Together." Shayna snorted and rolled her eyes. "So they sent Mandy here, in case they feel like checking in on her. And they sent Miles back to rehab. *Again*."

"That is not true," Kiyoko whispered, as she touched the corner of her mouth.

A chime sounded. I jerked. Kiyoko reached into her bag with a shaking hand and took out a bookmark, laying it over the page and smoothing it as if it were very precious and valuable. Smoothing it again. It was made of red cardboard with raised black lettering and a pentagram. *RUNES,* it read. *San Francisco's Premier Occult Bookshop.* I thought again of the weird ritual I'd seen her doing this morning with Mandy and that other girl, Lara. Were they some kind of coven? Cult?

She pressed the book closed and started packing up. She was one of the most elegant people I'd ever seen, but kind of robotic.

"That was the dismissal bell," Shayna told me.

"Thanks," I shot back, and got to my feet. She moved out of my way, and I scuttled back to my chair. There was a lot of energy in the room, and some laughter. My fellow students were moving to the rhythm of academia and their already-established friendships. I wondered how many of them had been to boarding school before. And how many of them were dying to be friends with Mandy Winters.

---

**I met my dorm mates** at dinner. They were all very nice: Ida, who was Iranian; and Claire, very tanned—her mom owned half of Maui; and Julie of course. And April and Leslie, our soccer jocks. Haley wanted to study opera, but for some reason, everyone called her Elvis. And last was Maria del Carmen, who went by Marica. She was wearing huge emerald earrings, despite the fact that the Marlwood booklet had said to leave valuables at home.

Their interest in me totally peaked when they found out I was going to Jessel to watch a movie. Julie was especially wide-eyed, and I wanted to tell her so many things that I had learned the hard way. Such as: avoid the home of the cool girl. Avoid it like the plague.

"I'll steal you a souvenir," I promised her, and she blinked, looking a tad hurt.

Before I knew it, we had left the commons and my dorm mates were forking right, toward Grose, while I started down the hill, toward Jessel. Elvis was singing "Blue Hawaii" at the top of her lungs. Marica's emeralds glittered in the light.

I walked alone through the falling darkness and the blowsy white, past more silent horse heads, to Jessel's front porch. I could see myself in the leaded glass windowpanes of the door as I knocked and folded my arms, trying to look casual. But in the dark, with only moonlight shining on my skin, my reflection looked like a ghost.

I was about to knock again when the door creaked open. Mandy, not Kiyoko, stood in the doorway, in her ebony sweater and trousers. She had swapped out her more stylish city boots for hiking boots.

As for the rest of her, if she'd had to make an effort to look gorgeous, it didn't show. Her white-blonde hair had been rearranged into a sleek ponytail held in place with a jet clasp; and her skin was flawless. Mandy was the kind of girl who would become a beautiful woman and stop aging at some point. She would always look great, and she would moisturize with stuff that cost a thousand dollars for a quarter ounce and make sure she got plenty of sleep by hiring other people to run her errands and organize her fabulous life.

"Oh, hi," she said, as if we knew each other.

Surrounded by shadows, her head seemed to float by itself. She took in my appearance; the right half of her mouth drew up in a smile as she cocked her head, gazing at me as if there were something wrong, like I had food caught between my teeth or something.

"Hi," I replied, since it was such a startlingly original thing to say.

"You have amazing eyelashes. We're opening wine. Are you good with red?"

"Sure," I said, even though wine was forbidden. Maybe they were bribing their housemother to keep quiet, or maybe they were really good at sneaking around. But more likely, the rules just didn't apply.

"A girl after my own heart," Mandy approved. "You've got potential."

*I really don't*, I wanted to tell her. *I don't care about coming to your dorm. I don't care if you notice me, or if you can change my life with all your money and your connections.*

But my cheeks warmed at the compliment.

Then she opened the door wide. Beyond her, the room was pitch-black, and for a second, I had a strange feeling that I shouldn't go in there. Into Jessel, the most haunted dorm at Marlwood.

But I didn't put much stock in strange feelings.

So I ignored it and walked on in.

# Five

## Jessel.

For a moment, I just stopped and stared at the interior. *This* was a dorm? The foyer was enormous, with a cathedral ceiling that rose at least twenty feet straight up, to a larger, fancier chandelier than the one in Grose. Swags of black-and-silver bat decorations were wrapped around the varnished oak banister of a staircase that ran along the far right side of the room, a balcony jutting out into the space, overhanging the back of the room.

The dimly lit living room was crowded with Victorian antiques—ornate sofas upholstered in burgundy velvet with black fringes, overstuffed chairs in black and gold, elegant ferns splayed from ceramic pots, and ivory columns. I saw a half-opened cardboard box revealing what appeared to be bloody hands and feet. There were more boxes, all marked M. WINTERS, JESSEL HOUSE, MARLWOOD ACADEMY. Dozens, actually.

"We're the haunted house," Mandy explained. "For the Halloween carnival. What are you guys doing?"

"I don't know," I said. *I just got here.*

"Well, the haunted house is the centerpiece of the whole carnival," Mandy declared. "My dad gave me a budget of fifty but I said, 'Hello? What can we do with *that*?'" Without missing a beat, she added, "You're Lindsay Cavanaugh."

"Yes." Fifty *thousand? Dollars?*

Kiyoko, in black pants and a sweater, was placing candles in white ceramic candleholders arranged on a grainy carved fireplace mantel. Black oil lamps flickered, etched with red roses.

"Well, it's looking good," I admitted.

"Oh, please. We haven't even started," Mandy replied, with a patronizing toss of her blonde head.

I became aware of a clock ticking as our three shadows splashed across the brick wall fireplace, joined by a fourth that crossed over mine. I turned to see Lara's vibrant red hair tied in an expert knot with loose strands; she was rubbing her pale, freckled arms, looking cold in a dark blue cap-sleeve blouse top over a jean miniskirt.

"Lara, get the wine," Mandy said, as Lara reached forward and moved one of the skull candleholders.

"But . . . " Lara began, glancing at me as if to say, *In front of her?*

"It's *fine.*" Mandy picked up the candleholder. "I liked it where Kiyoko had it. Keeks has great taste."

Lara huffed and sailed out of the room, disappearing through a doorway.

"I swear, you can't get good help these days," Mandy said. Kiyoko only half-smiled, and I didn't smile at all.

As if by unspoken agreement, we moved from the mantel. Beneath the overhanging section, a huge plasma screen TV faced two of the overstuffed sofas and a couple of big chairs pushed together. Beyond, a panorama window revealed the stars, the mountains, and the inky blackness of Searle Lake. I knew that Lakewood Preparatory Academy for Young Men was located on the other side of the lake. Three things were forbidden on Marlwood soil: cheating, drugs and alcohol, and boys. I thought about the Lincoln Bedroom at the White House. I could totally believe that Mandy had stayed there. I wasn't so sure about the part with her brother, Miles. It boggled my mind.

I looked around the room at the beautiful furnishings. On one of the sofas, I spotted a skein of amazing yarn, soft enough to be butter, in shades that ranged from silky white streaked with crinkle-leaf brown to burnished gourd to deep burgundy. My knitter's fingers longed to touch it.

Lara reappeared with a silver tray bordered with silver rosebuds, containing four glasses of red wine. She set the tray down on a table kind of like the nightstand in my dorm room. She grabbed a glass. Then she walked to the panorama window and took a long, thoughtful swallow as she stared at the darkness.

"It's cold out," she said. "Foggy. Maybe we should call it off."

*Call what off?* I wondered.

Mandy didn't respond. She handed me a glass and got one for herself. Clinking glasses with me, she said, "Cheers." She sipped. "We have a little thing to do tonight. In fact, we should get to it."

I went on red alert. A little thing? I glanced at Kiyoko, who left the mantel and walked toward the hall tree, loaded with coats and jackets.

"Lara's right," Mandy said. "It's cold out. Kiyoko, get Linz a jacket, too."

*Linz.*

Kiyoko nodded to show she'd heard, piling outerwear in her arms, including a large black leather jacket. Mandy said, "Ha ha, Kiyoko."

"It was the first thing I saw," Kiyoko said. "You never wear it anyway."

Mandy considered. "I guess it's okay."

Then Kiyoko bent down and slung on a sleek navy blue backpack with *Kiyoko* embroidered on the back.

"What's going on?" I asked, as Kiyoko handed me the black leather jacket without making eye contact. I had never felt anything so luxurious in my life—well-worn leather, lined with satin.

"It's going to be fun," Mandy said.

I stood my ground. "Tell me what we're doing."

"Kiyoko has something to do," Mandy said. Her smile was kind and reassuring.

"I didn't check with Mandy before I scheduled our movie. We'll see it soon. I promise," Kiyoko told me. Her face was pale and she touched the corner of her mouth—a nervous habit, I realized.

"Come on, Linz, we want you to be with us," Mandy said, and I could feel the warmth radiating off her. She had charisma; I'd give her that. I tried to remind myself that she was exactly the kind of girl I should stay away from, but there was something about her . . . something I couldn't explain, that urged me to give her a chance.

Maybe *they* could get in trouble, but I was there on scholarship. I couldn't risk getting caught doing . . . "a little thing"—at least, not if it was against school rules. So I got ready to give them a "thanks anyway" speech as we all picked up our wineglasses—I hadn't touched mine—and walked down a hall and into the kitchen.

Lara grabbed the wine bottle beside a stainless steel refrigerator, unslung her mannish jacket from the back of a barstool at the white-and-green tiled breakfast bar, and slipped it on. Lara brought the bottle with us as we tiptoed out the kitchen door and down a path covered with pea gravel, Mandy and Lara first, then Kiyoko, then me. Kiyoko looked over her shoulder at me, put her index finger to her mouth, and pointed to a room jutting from beside the kitchen. Lights were on. I heard a TV.

"Housemother," she whispered.

"We think she's deaf," Mandy said, her nose crinkling with pleasure as we scurried past their building.

"I haven't even seen mine yet—I think my dorm mates killed her," I shot back.

She snickered.

Our shoes crunched over the gravel as we walked down a slope, then onto another blacktop path lined with more horse heads. Mandy's ice-blonde hair glowed in the darkness ahead. Fog swirled around my ankles. An owl hooted, and I smelled pines.

As wind caught at my crazy hair, I took my first sip of wine. It was very bitter, and I tried not to make a face. I was tightly wound, very nervous. These people weren't my people. I thought about the scene at the hedge that morning. They'd called Kiyoko Number Three; my guess was that Lara was Number Two, and Mandy, of course, was *the* One. I knew I shouldn't be there, and that I had succumbed, yet again, to peer pressure. I quickened my pace to catch up with Mandy, who was rounding a large boulder and a stand of trees with brittle leaves that seemed to collapse off the branches as she passed.

"So, what's going on?" I asked loudly.

"It's for fun," Mandy said, obviously amused. "Just trust us."

"Why should I?" I said. I thought I heard Kiyoko gasp.

I turned my head to look back at Jessel, and I felt a little shock because I couldn't see it anymore. All I could see were enormous granite boulders and tall pines rising up around us, seeming to suck up the sound of my high-tops, my breathing, my heartbeat. We were cut off, alone.

I looked back at Mandy. "Just do," she replied, raising her chin. She looked amused.

"God, it's cold." Lara wrapped her arms around herself, her very pale, exposed legs shook a little under her bulky jacket. I jerked; her voice seemed so loud in the empty woods.

"Wait until November," Mandy said, also in a normal tone, as if she knew we were far enough away that we wouldn't be heard. "I heard it snows up here."

"I have great snow boots," Lara crowed.

"I'm sure you bought them at some men's store," Mandy said, rolling her blue eyes. Blue, not black. Normal.

Just then, we stepped out of the trees onto a cliff over the lake. Far below us, black dots and points of light skittered beneath the moon, clumping at the water's edge.

"Everyone finish your wine," Mandy ordered. I had two choices: dump it out or chugalug it. I went with number two, and it hit me, hard. Then Lara gathered up our glasses, opened the backpack on Kiyoko's back, and wrapped them in white linen napkins. She zipped the backpack and gave it a little pat.

Mandy walked along the lip of the cliff and grabbed onto a leafy bush. She found a foothold and grabbed an outcropping of rock. Lara followed after, and it was obvious to me they'd gone down here many times before.

"Here," Kiyoko said, reaching into her pocket. "She told us to bring flashlights. I—I won't be needing mine."

"Why not?" I asked her.

She tried to smile, but she didn't make it.

"Because it's . . . my turn."

A clatter of falling rock echoed through the blackness.

"Careful," Mandy called back to us, "it's slippery. Let's not have any sacrificial offerings tonight."

Kiyoko started down the cliff face, giving it her full attention. I followed after, the last of four, wondering why on earth I was doing this. We had a ten o'clock curfew, and before then we were allowed to go either to another dorm or the library.

We sure weren't allowed to go down to the lake.

But I kept going. After all, I didn't know how to get back.

---

It took us a while to climb down, but we finally stepped onto grainy earth. There was a ripple through a milling crowd of maybe ten girls as we approached, Mandy first, like the Homecoming Queen, then we three, like her royal court.

I saw Julie with two of my new dorm mates, Ida and Claire. Ida had great highlights, and at dinner she'd told me the movie star I'd seen in lit class was Chyna Loftis. Of course. Ida's father had something to do with the San Francisco Opera but I wasn't sure what. Ida wanted to go Harvard Law. Claire from Hawaii was bronzed all over, even her "area" and her "chi-chis," Julie had informed me, rather scandalized.

Julie had stuffed her hands in the pockets of her peacoat, and she rocked back on her heels when she saw me, her eyes spinning with excitement. I had the feeling she hadn't known about this little trip at dinner. But she was there now.

I smelled the lake water—mossy, with a slight undercurrent of rot. The moon glittered on the vast, black surface. Flashlights bobbed as the girls stood beneath starlight and moonlight, waiting, like me, to see what was going to happen next.

Then, at the very edge of the shoreline, Shayna from our lit class shifted her weight. She was dressed in gray sweats and a navy hoodie, holding a folded blanket in her arms.

Kiyoko saw her, stopped, and said, "I brought a towel, Shayna."

"This is stupid," Shayna hissed. "I can't believe you're doing it. That you didn't tell me."

"This is why, Shay," Lara said. "You're embarrassing her."

Lara took hold of the backpack and slung it off Kiyoko's back. She unzipped it and pulled out a coil of white nylon rope. She dropped it to the sand and showed the end to Kiyoko. Kiyoko took a deep breath and took off her jacket. Then she pushed her skinny pants down over her ankles and stepped out of them. She was wearing a red-and-black bikini bottom that was practically a thong. On her, it wasn't very sexy—she was skin and bones.

I had a feeling I knew what was going to happen, and I didn't like it. As Kiyoko snaked her sweater over her head, the top of her bikini stretched over her almost-flat chest confirmed it. She was going to swim in the freezing cold lake.

Lara handed the coil to Mandy as Kiyoko wrapped the other end around her waist. I could see Kiyoko's breath as she looked out at the lake. Her shoulder blades looked sharp enough to cut steak.

"It's good and strong," Mandy confirmed, testing the rope between her hands. "But the ghost of the lake is very lonely. She will try to untie it, and keep Kiyoko with her."

Nervous laughter greeted her announcement. I puffed air out of my cheeks and shifted my weight. I couldn't believe Kiyoko was going to willingly jump in the lake. Correction: I could. I would have done it, if Jane had told me to.

"Just more one thing before you go in," Mandy went on, giving Kiyoko a once-over. "No suit, sweetie."

Kiyoko blanched; beside her, Shayna shook her head disapprovingly. "You didn't say anything about that," Kiyoko murmured.

Mandy tsk-tsked like some melodrama villain. "I said 'no clothes.' That means . . . no clothes."

"It's freezing in there, Mandy," Shayna protested.

"Then it won't matter if she's wearing a bathing suit or not, Shayna," Mandy said. She turned back to Kiyoko. "You don't *have* to do it."

I knew then that Kiyoko's fate was sealed.

"All right," Kiyoko half-shouted. She grabbed the blanket out of Shayna's hands and wrapped it around herself. Then she snaked her left hand up and grabbed her suit strap, giving it a tug down her arm. Some of the girls closest to her began to hoot and applaud.

"Take it off, baby!"

"Go, Ki-yo-ko!"

She moved and shifted inside her blanket; about ten seconds later, her suit dropped to her ankles.

Mandy lifted a brow. "Check the rope. We want you to be safe. Lara?"

Lara pulled some plastic glow-in-the-dark necklaces out of the backpack. She broke the liquid inside and they started to glow green, pink, yellow. She looped a few over Kiyoko's neck. They rattled on her collarbones.

"Her ankles and wrists, too," Mandy said.

"This is stupid," Shayna hissed, as Kiyoko stuck out her right arm and Mandy wrapped one of the glow-necklaces around it.

"No one is forcing her," Mandy reminded her. She smiled at Kiyoko, whose blanket began to undrape; Kiyoko turned her back, holding the blanket between her teeth as she tried to maintain her modesty. Her rounded shoulders and back looked bluish-white beneath the alien green and pink of the glowing necklaces.

Then she walked to the edge of the lake, black and deep. I couldn't imagine how cold it was. Despite the heavy leather jacket I was wearing, my teeth had begun to chatter.

"Drop it!" Lara called.

A few took up the chant. "Drop it! Drop it!"

And she did. She dropped the blanket, revealing her scrawny, naked backside to all of us, and placed one bare foot in the water. I saw her jerk to a stop, as if she were shocked by icy pain. Then she took another step, and another. Girls were laughing, cheering. They didn't care how loud they were. They didn't have to. We were a long way from our housemothers.

She kept going. I felt sorry for her and mad at her; I didn't want to watch, but I had to. I was afraid for her. I knew I would go in after her if she got in trouble, but I didn't want to.

*Mandy's got hold of the rope*, I reminded myself, checking to make sure. Mandy and Lara were standing together, shrieking with laughter.

But I didn't know if Mandy would keep holding the rope. I didn't know her at all. And I liked her less.

Kiyoko went in to her knees, and started to back out. She stopped herself and staggered forward, up to her thighs, then her bottom, and then she pushed off and started to swim.

Flashlights trained on her like searchlights. I saw her glow-sticks above the waterline, and the occasional flash of neon green around her wrists. She started to splash the water with opened palms. Did she even know how to swim?

Mandy cupped her hands. "All the way under!" she yelled. "Get your hair wet!"

Kiyoko started coughing. Her leg kicks were random.

"No, get out now," I said, but no one could hear me.

As her head went under, the applause was thunderous. Cheers bounced off the lake.

I watched, counting *one, two, three . . .*

*four . . .*

*five . . .*

She didn't come back up.

The applause ebbed; the cheers began to fade.

The lake was still.

And I began to think the unthinkable, because bad things really did happen. People really did die.

# six

"Kiyoko?" Shayna called. "*Kiyoko?*"

Shayna bolted into the water. I flew in after her. Mandy tried to grab my wrist as I darted past; I shook free and kept going—

—just as Kiyoko breached the surface, screaming.

"Something grabbed me!" she shrieked, shooting out of the lake and barreling past me, her tiny breasts bouncing. The rope was still around her waist, and her wrists and ankles glowed. As I turned around, she dashed onto the shore in a blur, hysterical, racing past Shayna and into the darkness.

Then there was a flash and I turned in its direction. Mandy had taken Kiyoko's picture with her cell phone.

"And off to Lakewood," she said gleefully.

"You bitch! You unbelievable bitch!" Shayna shouted, heading for her.

"It was the ghost!" Kiyoko cried.

Mandy's cell phone flashed again.

Then, suddenly, a second figure shot out of the water, and everyone screamed and scattered.

As terrified shrieks bounced off the lake, I crossed my arms and watched a guy in a body-hugging wet suit and scuba gear rise from the water, his dark face shining wet in the moonlight. Floodlights erupted from a rowboat, and two guys started laughing their butts off. Scuba guy had obviously swum from the boat, tracking Kiyoko via her glowing necklaces and bracelets, all to scare the wits out of her.

Julie rushed over to me, grabbing my arm like a little girl, and I slowly shook my head at the intense meanness of it all. Shayna was shouting and Kiyoko was crying and almost everyone else who'd been watching now loitered on the outskirts by a cluster of tall pines, gossiping.

I narrowed my eyes at the scuba guy, who was pulling off his hood. Skin like mocha cappuccino, eyes like dark chocolate, and more ringlets than even I had. Mega-cute.

"Hey," he said, looking through me, "this wasn't the way you said, Mandy."

Mandy swirled around me and walked toward him, stopping short at the water's edge. She was laughing so hard she couldn't talk.

"*Hey*," he said again, unhooking the tether around his waist and tossing it behind himself as he sloshed through the water toward her. He was wearing swim fins. "This is not cool."

She kept laughing, and a wild, crazed impulse came over me to push her in the lake. As if Julie sensed what I was thinking, she tightened her grip on my arm.

Shayna stomped over to Mandy and held out her hand. "Give me your cell phone. Give it to me or I'll tell Dr. Ehrlenbach."

"Hey," Mandy said, wiping tears of laughter from her pale pink cheeks. "I didn't really send it to Lakewood. How could I? I don't have any reception."

"You lied to Kiyoko," Shayna said. "You said all she had to do was go under the water. You didn't say anything about skinny-dipping or guys!"

The scuba guy looked at Julie for a full, measured beat. She blushed. Then he turned his gaze to me.

"You're wearing my jacket," he said.

And I couldn't believe, given the circumstances, that he would either notice or care. So I said the first thing that came to mind: "You're a jerk."

"Lindsay," Julie murmured under her breath. "He didn't know."

Mandy burst into fresh giggles. All the drama and anger were making her high. "You want it back?"

He narrowed his eyes at her. "Yeah. Maybe I do."

I looked from him to Mandy to Kiyoko, tear-stained and hiccupping, wrapped in the blanket Shayna had brought her, like a true friend. I grabbed the jacket sleeves, my trembling hands clumsy as I eased out of it and held it out to him.

"That's actually mine," Mandy said, reaching for it. "I won it in a poker game."

As her fingers brushed the right sleeve, I let go of it, and it tumbled into the lake.

"Whoops," I said coldly. Then I turned my back.

Mandy was quiet. Then she started to laugh again, cackling like a wicked witch.

———

**Apparently,** a bottle of some tequila was also in the backpack, and Mandy opened it and passed it to only a select few: Lara; the swimmer, whose name was Spider; the two other guys; and Kiyoko, who had calmed down a little. In fact, she saluted me with it before she drank.

Then Mandy passed it to me. We were all gathered at the base of the cliff, sitting in a circle, huddled under our sweatshirts.

After she changed back into her original clothes, Kiyoko took the bottle again and slugged back three big gulps. She was so thin I figured it was enough to get her really drunk. She laughed and tossed her hair like a superstar. Then she caught sight of Shayna, who was watching in silence with the other spectators, and hesitated.

For a minute, I thought she would pass the bottle to Shayna, in a gesture of friendship. Shayna straightened her shoulders and waited; then Kiyoko handed the bottle back to Mandy.

Shayna pursed her lips and turned away.

I wanted to strangle Kiyoko. I knew she'd made her choice. I'd done the same thing. Heather Sanchez had stuck by me all the months—*years*—of my mom's terminal illness. Maybe that was the real reason why I had dumped her. She had known me when. But what I'd told myself at the time was that she just wasn't cool enough.

Ida and Claire left shortly after the alcohol came out. Ida

gave me a little wave as if to say, *No harm no foul, catch ya on the flipside.* I liked her more than ever. Then the boys rowed away shortly after that, disappearing back into the night. Julie loitered with three girls I didn't know. I knew I didn't have invitation rights, so I couldn't call her over. But there was no way I would dis my roommate the way Kiyoko had dissed Shayna. So I left the territory of the charmed ones and walked over to her. She knew what I was doing, and I could see the warmth and gratitude in her eyes.

"That was . . . " she began.

"Insane and mean?" I finished for her.

"Kind of extreme," she allowed.

"If someone had pulled that stunt on me, I would've been gone in a hot minute," I declared.

*Not back when you were playing the game,* I reminded myself. *Then you would have done it. And stayed and laughed over it, even if twenty boys saw you naked.*

"We'd better go," Lara said, as she knelt and repacked the now wet nylon rope into Kiyoko's backpack. "Ms. Meyerson might actually notice we're gone." She took the dark green booze bottle from Mandy's outstretched hand.

"Okay," Mandy replied, as if doing Lara a favor. "All right, ladies. Show's over. We'll be here all semester."

Good-natured chuckles accompanied her lame joke as everyone got up and dusted the sand from their clothes. Everyone who'd come to watch imagined they had a bond with Mandy Winters now. To prove it, we would all hike back together—although no one would dare approach the inner circle of Mandy and her friends. I marched with the rest of the not-so-cool, determined to keep as much distance between Mandy Winters and myself.

It turned out there was an easier route back to our quad, on a blacktop road. From there, the lesser beings could hike back to their own uncool dorms. The return took a little longer, which was probably why we had defied death to climb down the cliff. It was also how the outsiders had arrived ahead of us to watch the fun.

Mandy came up beside me, carrying the stinky wet leather jacket. I grimaced.

"Sorry," I gritted.

"It's forgotten," Mandy promised, and then she chuckled. "Well, maybe not by Spider."

"I'll be happy to replace it," I said stiffly.

Mandy blinked at me; then she began to laugh. My face burned. I knew it had to be expensive. I didn't know it would be hilariously out of my reach.

"You didn't approve of our little prank," she said, changing the subject.

"Lindsay's a lifeguard," Julie piped up loyally. Mandy and I both looked at her, and she turned ten shades of scarlet. I knew those words had cost her, and I wanted to hug her sweet little fifteen-year-old self. "Lake. Night. Dangerous."

"Oh." Mandy made a show of tapping her chin. "Gosh. You're right."

*Back off,* I wanted to say, but Julie laughed pleasantly.

"Only, not so much, because I had the rope." Mandy gestured to the wet backpack hanging from Kiyoko's thin shoulders.

"Ropes untie," I said, more to side with Julie than argue with Mandy.

We walked a few more feet; then Mandy zipped in front of me and circled around to Julie's other side. "I heard you had to sell your horse," she said. "Pippin's her name? That is so wrong."

Julie swallowed and twisted her wheat-blonde ponytail. "Pippin's a boy. The new owner said I could ride him, but . . ."

"Dixie told me." Mandy pulled a very sad face. "Pippin's new owner hasn't shown since he bought him. Pip's still being boarded at the stable." Her frown turned upside down. "Maybe I could pull a few strings."

"Oh." Julie's eyebrows shot up. She looked like a little kid sitting on Santa Claus's lap. "Wow, thanks." It was clear she wasn't sure which strings Mandy was referring to. But strings at all were good.

"Spider asked me what your name is," Mandy continued. "He said you were a hottie." She almost winked at Julie.

I nearly gagged.

"He's cute," Julie murmured, blushing again.

Mandy smiled at her. And the thing was, I knew Mandy was up to something, but I found myself smiling faintly, too. It was so weird; it was as if I couldn't stop myself.

We walked on. Those who were not worthy kept their distance, but I watched them watching Julie and Mandy. As we climbed the hill, Lara and Kiyoko chatted as if nothing unusual had happened; then gradually, they clumped up with

Julie, Mandy, and me, until we were five.

I looked down at the lake, wide and dark. I shivered, trying to imagine what it must have been like for Kiyoko. Scary. Freezing. And she'd been a terrible swimmer.

Lara walked up close beside me as Mandy and Julie drifted along, talking about horses some more. I could smell tequila on Lara's breath. "There are all kinds of stories about that lake. Some girl got pregnant and drowned herself. And there's supposedly a school bus down there. It was carrying a bunch of kids home from a field trip and the driver lost control. It sank right to the bottom. It rolls around in the current. The water's so cold no one decomposed, and if you go diving, sometimes you see them."

"That doesn't make any sense," I said. "That's a *lake*. It doesn't have a current."

She picked up a pebble and turned it over in her hands. "If you stare into it long enough, you'll see . . . things." She stared out at the lake. "Like when you stare into the darkness. Shapes start to move. You think it's a pile of clothes, but it's someone sitting in your chair. Someone dead. In your room. Watching you sleep.

"Or you're half-asleep and you hear something under your bed. You think it's your cat . . . except, maybe, your cat ran away . . . "

I knew she was trying to scare me, but I didn't scare easily. She thought I was just like all these other girls who would let themselves be spooked, so Mandy could have her fun. I was so past that.

After all, I'd watched my mom die.

"Thanks for the warning." I smoothed my hair out of my eyes as the wind batted at it. "I'll be sure not to look."

"Some people can't help but look," Lara said. "Like when there's a car accident. They slow down to gawk."

"Okay, this is about as morbid as I can—"

She dropped the pebble on the ground. Looked at me.

"Mandy likes you," she said.

"That's great." I tried not to sound snippy. Because it actually warmed me a little bit inside. *No. No, no, no*, I told myself. *Danger. Been there.*

"So it's all settled," Mandy herself said in a loud voice. I turned back, to see her clasping Julie's hand and swinging it back and forth as they strolled. Julie looked like she was about to wet her jeans.

"What?" I asked.

"Julie's helping us with a prank tomorrow night. How about you, Linz? Are you in?" She fake-batted her lashes at me.

I looked at Julie. She smiled at me *please, please, please?*

And suddenly I knew that San Diego had accompanied me to Marlwood. What was the saying? *No matter where you go, there you are.* I had a choice, here and now, to place another bet at popularity roulette or stay well away.

"Can I watch?" I hedged. That would get me there, so I could make sure they didn't kill Julie, but I wouldn't be an official participant. Kinda in, and not out.

"Yes. You can be our safety monitor," Mandy told me grandly. "Make sure we don't harm any animals." She tousled

Julie's hair. "Or roommates."

Lara snickered.

"I'm sure it will be superfun," I snarked, sounding a little edgier than I'd intended.

Mandy's grin practically split her face. "You are such a freak," she told me.

"Just give us the deets," Julie said. Then, uncertainly, "Details."

"You got it, toots," Mandy replied, fixing her attention on Julie.

Canary, meet cat.

---

**Alone in our room,** we got ready for bed—I wore a long T-shirt and a pair of socks—and it took me awhile to settle down. "Everybody thinks it's funny until it's their turn. But when you're singled out by the clique, it hurts worse than it feels good," I warned her.

"*O-kay,*" Julie muttered, clearly not interested in my lecture. In a few minutes, she was snoring lightly, and I remembered how I used to beg my mom and dad for a little sister. They discovered my mom's ovarian cancer when she had a miscarriage.

I began to drift, and dream, and somehow, in that way that people doze, I thought I felt . . . not felt . . . it was nothing physical . . . I sensed that someone was *there* . . . and I heard myself whisper, "Mom?"

# seven

**I couldn't move** and it was coming and it was here.

I was panting, screaming, clawing.

Sweat rolled off me. The back of my neck was cold but my forehead . . . my forehead, oh God. I couldn't move and it was crawling toward the bed; one hand was on the mattress oh—

Come to me come to me come to me come to me come to me.

It was on my chest, it was pressing down—

"God!" I screamed, and sat upright.

The light flashed on. My shoulders heaved. I gathered up my damp hair and tried to catch my breath.

"Lindsay?" Julie said.

"Bad dream," I mumbled. "I'm sorry." I couldn't seem to catch my breath. I put one hand over my forehead and one hand over my heart. I was afraid I was going to have a heart attack.

"What was it?" she asked me. "What did you dream?"

My mind was fuzz. I shook my head. "I don't know."

And I didn't want to know. I was so scared I was afraid I was about to throw up. But the thought of getting out of bed and going into the bathroom—

*Come to me. She said it five times and so that means—*

I licked my lips. "I'm okay," I said.

*Bodily cavities . . .*

But I wasn't.

# eight

**October 29**

Cat, canary.

Moth, flame.

Antelope, Serengeti: that was me, racing to catch up in every single class. I already knew that high school was designed to cull the herd: cut out the dopers, the surfers, and all the other varieties of losers, so the rest of us could become productive citizens and keep the world turning. But at Marlwood, the "losers" were doing better than the top of my previous heap. I had extra assignments and those assignments had assignments.

As I tried not to panic, everyone else talked about tonight's big prank, the one featuring Julie as a big helper. It was going to be a showstopper. Seemed that there was a whole other Marlwood at Marlwood: at least a dozen buildings that were off-limits to us. They were condemned as unsafe, boarded off, locked up tight. In other words, forbidden fruit.

So, of course, they were supposed to be haunted.

And rather than blow her entire budget of fifty thousand

dollars on the "regular" haunted house for the school carnival, Mandy Winters had seized possession of one of these buildings, and refurbished it for major scares. Julie got the downlow, including the names of the victims: two of the *other* richest girls on campus. Alis DeChancey and Sangeeta Shankhar.

"It's going to be a Chamber of Horrors," Julie said in a gravely, creepy voice as we staggered out of Tuttle Hall after last period, weighed down by names and dates of the American Revolution. Tuttle was one of the four brick buildings where we had classes. The gym was on our right; the naked Greek athletes gazed down at us with their blank stone eyes.

At my questioning look, she went on, "The prank will be in this super-ultracondemned building that used to be an insane asylum. It's the most haunted building on the campus."

"I thought Jessel was the most haunted," I said, as I felt a flutter of panic. Not because of the chills and thrills, but because I really didn't have time to go watch a prank. I couldn't remember the name of George Washington's wartime aide-de-camp, and if Jefferson or Jackson had owned Monticello. "And this place was never an insane asylum. It was a family retreat." I tried to remember the history of Marlwood. "And a girls school a long time ago. During the American Revolution," I added lamely.

"*After* the Civil War. So they *said*." Julie wagged her brows. "But *we* know different. It was a loony bin."

*We.* I suppressed a sigh. I wanted to remind her that she was the one who was so afraid of Marlwood's ghosts that she had gotten a roommate.

Sneaking out when you lived on campus wasn't much different from sneaking out when you lived at home. It turned out that Julie and I were supposed to show up at ten, giving me lots of time to study. The prank was scheduled for midnight and everyone knew about it. Half our dorm was planning to watch. The other half was too afraid they'd get in trouble. Smart girls.

Julie helped me arrange pillows on my bed to look like I was sleeping. She was so excited and nervous that she was shaking.

We tiptoed past our housemother's door. Ms. Krige was not very motherly. Her TV was on, and I hoped for the best. We opened the front door very, very slowly . . . then we flared out into the bitterly cold night. In sweaters and coats, me in my high-tops and shredded jeans, we crossed our quad, darting past Jessel's privet hedge, and dashed into the woods.

Lara was waiting for us. She was dressed all in black and carrying a black hood. She said, "Just you two, right?" and craned her neck around us. I was willing to bet Claire and Ida were back there, probably Elvis and Marica, too. They weren't allowed to show up until later. We two were the only Grose-ites privileged to see things up close and personal. But I let Julie do the nodding, and Lara seemed satisfied. She turned and walked us into a thick stand of redwood trees. Leaves rustled. I heard organ music.

Then we stepped out of the shadows into a moonlit clearing. The hair on the back of my neck rose as I stared through a chain-link fence with a large sign that read DANGER! KEEP OUT! CONDEMNED. Veils of mist shifted and trailed over a decayed two-story building with a jagged rooftop of chimneys and gables jutting over the upper floor. Ivy trailed down the brick exterior, and at least half of the structure had collapsed into piles of rubble. Cobwebs stretched over mounds of broken bricks and rusted metal. I spotted an eyeless baby doll and a rotted satin slipper.

Lights flashed on in the arched windows, revealing faces in the broken glass—blurry white circles with blackened eyes and mouths opened in silent screams.

"Wow. This is pretty incredible," I said.

"Isn't it cool?" Julie nudged me. "Can you believe they did all this and Ehrlenbach doesn't have a clue?"

No, I couldn't, actually.

In front of the house, the mist thickened. I heard a scream, and then the whole house went dark and silent.

"Okay, good." Mandy's voice blared over a PA system. "Take a break."

Then the rotted front door creaked open, and Mandy stood in the frame, wearing a white robe that covered her straight shoulders and plunged to the ground. The Bride of Frankenstein.

"You're la-ate," she said to Julie in a singsong voice. "Lara will have to cut off your head for that." She smiled at me. "Hey, Linz."

"Are we really late?" Julie fretted.

Lara rolled her eyes and dropped her black hood over her head. Then she scooted past Mandy and went inside.

"That's a good look for you," I told Mandy, trying to sound cool and unfazed. But seriously, all this for a *prank*? What was the other, "official" haunted house going to be like?

She raised a brow as if giving me points for trying. "Just think, all this could be yours." She smiled lazily and gestured for both of us to follow her in.

"So what was this building?" Julie asked her, as we went inside.

"Library," Mandy said.

"Oh. I thought it was an insane asylum."

"Nope," Mandy replied. A beat. "The entire campus was an insane asylum." She grinned over her shoulder at Julie.

"Rock," Julie enthused. "Cool." I wondered if what Mandy was saying was true.

"Where's the electricity coming from?" I asked. "I'd think they'd be worried about the whole thing burning down."

"That's where the fifty grand went," Mandy said, looking mildly impressed that I'd think of such a thing. "We're using special effects lighting. Lots of batteries."

"I'll bet," Julie said, and Mandy chuckled affectionately. The floor was littered with dirt, paper, a crushed Coors can, some broken glass. Some girls I didn't recognize stepped from the shadows. They wore white. They had on white Latex gloves.

"This place is gross," said the middle one.

"Some of our ghosts," Mandy told Julie and me. "It's so hard to get good ghosts these days." She flicked on a flashlight. "Come into my parlor."

We turned left and walked into a cavernous room. Bulbous lamps provided dim light, revealing bookcases that reached into the gloom. They were clogged with moldy books. Some of the titles were still visible. *Female Behavioral Reformation. Neurological Science. Psychology of Hysterics.*

"This really was a library," I said. All the books seemed to be ancient psychology volumes. It certainly lent weight to the theory that Marlwood really had been an asylum for girls, rather than a school. Some kind of reformatory. The idea gave me the creeps.

"How did you get access to this place?" Julie asked, enthralled.

Mandy shrugged, miming ignorance. Then she took the end of Julie's ponytail and ran it under Julie's chin, pulling it upward, like a noose.

"If I told you, I'd have to kill you," Mandy said.

I remembered her black eyes, and I wanted to grab Julie's ponytail out of Mandy's hand. I had started to let go of that memory, deny I'd seen what I'd seen—the same way I'd pretended that I didn't know Jane was having sex with Riley.

I shivered. What was I doing here? What was Julie?

"We have to get you into costume," she told Julie. "You're going be a headless Frenchwoman. You'll chase Alis and Sangeeta in, and when it's over, then you'll chase them back out."

"No," I said, but it was too soft for them to hear.

"Cool," Julie said. "What about Lindsay?"

"Crowd control," Mandy said.

She headed toward the door, taking her flashlight. Julie fell in behind her, and I trailed behind as the dark got darker, the lamps dimming. I turned around one last time.

A ghostly apparition appeared, see-through, standing in a long white dress. Her long, crazy hair—kind of like mine—hung in her face, and her head was bowed. Slowly, she began to raise her head. . . .

. . . And for some reason I couldn't explain, I didn't want to see her face. I caught up with Julie and Mandy as they left the room; then, on the threshold and a little braver, I looked over my shoulder.

She had shifted her position, and she was staring straight at me. Her face was chalk-white and her eyes were black—black like Mandy's, back at the hedge.

I felt a chill. *It's just a girl, a student, someone who's in on it*, I reminded myself.

But she kept staring at me.

"Okay, where's my costume?" Julie asked, and the girl disappeared in a blink.

"Linz, could you go outside now and keep the animals calm?" Mandy asked sweetly, and I realized I was being booted.

"Julie," I said, wanting a moment with her. Wanting to tell her that I had a funny feeling—make that a creepy feeling—and I thought maybe she should bail. But she was already flitting down the hall with Mandy, arm in arm, heads pressed together.

"Julie, " I said again.

I started after them, but Lara stepped into the hall. She was still wearing her hood, her brilliant red hair peeking out the edges. Soundlessly, she raised an arm and pointed toward the door.

I went outside and looked at the house. A crumbling brick

chimney hunched between two broken sections of the house like a knobby backbone. Sitting atop it all was a bell tower shaped like a tulip, with curved slate sides, and the bell still there.

There was no moon; except for the lamplight, it was very dark. Skeletal trees stood frozen and unmoving in the frigid night. The windows flashed on and off with their parade of white faces. The face of the dark-haired girl with the black eyes appeared in the window directly across from me. I waved to show that she wasn't getting to me. She stared.

My unease grew. I stood in the shadows and glanced up at that strange, white face. Instead of Julie, I was the one being singled out. I was sure of it. I just wasn't sure why.

# nine

**Girls started showing up** at about eleven-thirty. Ida and Claire came over to me, all shushes and giggles. Shayna was back for more punishment. Quite a little mob scene of at least two dozen Marlwoodians gathered for Mandy's version of a good time. Elvis and Marica wore sleek swing coats and leather jackets, cute knitted caps and charm bracelets. Another girl was wearing a white fur coat. I was staring at thousands and thousands of dollars in clothes.

"Oh my God, that house is so scary," Ida said shrilly.

It was, even without any of Mandy's help. Whole sections of the walls had fallen away, leaving gaping holes where fog swirled in and out.

"*Come in,*" echoed a low, evil voice. "*Come in and die, Alis and Sangeeta.*"

"Bwahaha," Claire murmured.

We found a rock and a tree stump to sit on. The Amy Winehouse chick, Rose Hyde-Smith, bounded through the underbrush and plopped down on a log. Waving at us, she sat with her legs crossed, in her beehive and a short denim skirt and orange tights with big yellow polka dots on them. Her boots were chunky leather rectangles.

She looked me up and down, at the remnants of my jeans, my high-tops, and my sweatshirt—advertising just how much I didn't belong there, like her. We looked like escapees from the circus, or a shelter.

"Hey, I'm Rose. From our lit class."

"I know." I grinned, but then tensed up again, wary of what was about to happen.

"Here they come," Ida whispered.

I craned my neck and saw a bunch of white blobs emerging from a stand of pine trees about twenty feet away. As they approached, they grew more distinct: Lara and Kiyoko walked on either side of tonight's two victims, Alis and Sangeeta.

Then a tall, headless woman dressed in a shredded white poof-skirt ball gown burst from the trees and bobbed after them. Julie, of course. Blood pumped from the stump, which Julie must have been wearing like a hat, and sluiced down the low-cut bodice onto the gown.

"Heeeee!" the woman shrieked.

Alis and Sangeeta whirled around, saw her, and screamed. Kiyoko and Lara boxed them in as Julie started herding them toward the front door. Sangeeta pushed against Alis, who started laughing. The house erupted into flashing lights and organ music, and just as abruptly stopped.

"Holy cow," Ida murmured.

Lara handed the girls flashlights. The two flicked them off and on, testing them. They entered the condemned building.

Julie ran after them into the house staggering a bit. Alis raised a hand as if she were waving to us onlookers, and a couple of girls cheered.

"And they were never seen or heard from again," Claire intoned.

"Except in the bathroom," Rose put in, "if you say, 'Come to me, come to me, come to me, come to me, come to—"

"Stop," Ida pleaded.

"Mmmm . . . " Rose teased. Ida batted her arm and Rose shook her head and rolled her eyes.

The building came alive. The lamps flashed, creepy organ music cascaded out the holes in the walls, and crazed laughter echoed over the dark hills and pine trees. Someone shrieked. A second scream joined the first; then the screaming was a crescendo falling over itself like a waterfall.

"What's going on in there?" Ida asked me, and I understood the genius that was Mandy. She'd shown me just enough to make me something of an insider. I could share information. But I didn't have all of it, so I couldn't give away all the surprises. Only Mandy's chosen few—and her victims—would have the 411.

"I know not," I assured her.

"Did you get to go in?" Claire asked me.

"Yeah, but I didn't really see anything," I said. They both eyed me dubiously. "It smelled like rotted books."

"So there're books?" Ida asked. "What kind of books?"

"Rotted books," Rose said.

The music blared; the screams became real.

"It sounds like they're *dying*," Ida said.

I got the feeling that someone was watching us, the watchers.

On a rise to my left, pine trees swayed and moved in the night wind. A figure stepped from their bobbing branches. His hair was dark and bedroom-tousled, his eyes deep-set in a tanned face. He was cut—broad chest and muscular shoulders encased in a hoodie that read *LAKEWOOD*.

I stared at him for another heart-stopping moment. He was *hot*. He was rock-solid, wearing faded jeans that molded to long legs and athletic thighs. As the organ music tumbled note over note over note, I thought he was staring at me, too. Then he stepped back into the shadows.

"Guys," I said. "There was a—"

"I heard Alis and Sangeeta have to get to the bell tower and flash their flashlights on and off in Morse code," Claire said, "to spell out 'come to me' five times."

" . . . Meeeee," Rose finished.

"No!" Ida cried, batting Rose's arm.

"Listen, there's a guy here," I said.

Ida and Claire turned to look. "A guy? Like that guy from last night? That diver guy?" Claire asked. "Corbin Bleu looka-like? He thinks Julie's cute."

"A different guy," I replied.

"Ooh. Does he have a chainsaw?" Claire asked.

"You're evil," Ida said.

Claire struck a pose. "That's why you love me."

Sangeeta appeared in the bell tower. Alis popped up next. A cheer rose up from the spectators as the two girls hopped around in a victory dance, then pointed their flashlights down as Mandy strode stick-legged out of the house and turned around and faced them. Kiyoko appeared in a white hospital nightgown, and Lara still had on her hood.

"We did it!" Sangeeta declared. Her voice echoed; it was very cultured British. "Might we come down now?"

"You need to do the code!" Lara called back, lifting her hood up from her mouth. "Flash us, honey!"

"Please! We are freaking out!" Sangeeta protested, swirling her flashlight overhead.

"Do the code!" Kiyoko shouted.

"Do the code! Do the code!" The chant was taken up.

They flicked their flashlights in a rhythmic pattern.

"Come to me," Mandy called through her microphone.

They did it again.

"Come to me." Lara and Kiyoko sang along with Mandy.

The flashlights went on, off, on, off, on, off.

"*Come to me.*" The girls around me took up the chant. Rose rocked back on the log and pounded it with her open palms. I couldn't bring myself to join in.

"*Come to me, come to me!*"

And that strange coldness crept into my head again. I jerked and touched the back of my neck. Was it wet?

"Okay, you can come down," Mandy informed Alis and Sangeeta.

They cheered and disappeared down some stairs. "Hey," I said to Rose, "is my neck wet?"

"Huh?" She got up to check, pulling down my jacket and my sweater. "Ewww."

"Ewww what?" I cried.

She snickered. "Oh my God, you're easy. There is nothing on your neck."

"Here they come," Mandy announced. A cheer rose up as Alis and Sangeeta barreled out of the house just as Headless Julie ran up behind them. Mandy, Kiyoko, and Lara threw their arms around Alis and Sangeeta. They turned to the rest of us and bowed. People started applauding and cheering. Then they moved to the right, into the shadows. Around me, the girls started heading out, in a rush to sneak back into their dorms. The lights in the house went off. Poof, just like that.

Julie swayed forward, then stopped. She looked confused.

"Hey, Julie," I shouted, waving my hands.

"Ju-lie! Ju-lie!" Ida and Claire chanted.

Julie started toward us. The stump and the torso shifted forward, throwing her off balance, and she stumbled, ran-walked, and stumbled again.

Then Julie tripped on something. She flew forward and landed in a ball-gown heap on the ground.

I got up and hurried to her. Rose, Ida, and Claire jogged behind me. Julie looked pretty bizarre, headless and all, as the last of her fake blood poured onto the ground. Rose and Ida started pulling apart the Velcro strips that held her neck-stump together. It split down the middle like she was hatching her own head. She was sweaty and flushed.

"I—I tripped on something." Julie groaned. "Ow! It *hurts*!"

"Look." Claire shined her flashlight on a blob of white gleaming in the moonlight. It was a human head made out of glass—maybe porcelain. The brain was showing and it was divided up into sections with numbers painted in black.

"What the heck is that?" Ida said.

"It's Julie's missing head," Claire informed her.

"No, it's like a chart. Like a cut-by-numbers. Oh my God, did they do brain surgeries out here?" Ida made a face.

I gently touched Julie's ankle. She sucked in her breath.

"Ouch, no," she said. "Oh, it really hurts." She looked off to the left, where Mandy's group had gone.

"Can you stand up?" Rose asked.

Julie groaned. "I don't know." Ida loosened the torso section of the costume, and Julie pulled out her arms. She was wearing a simple white T-shirt and a jog bra underneath. Her ball gown was gathered around her hips, the torso and stump sticking straight out from her stomach. The pumping mechanism had shut off.

"We need to get help," I said. "Maybe someone's cell phone works up here. We can call security."

Ida and Claire both grimaced; Julie shook her head. And Rose said, "Let's think that one through, okay? It's one in the morning and we are out here." She looked around. "Maybe Mandy's got an idea."

"Go ask her," Julie begged. "And tell her I'll be right there, okay?"

Rose bounded away.

"I think I broke her costume," Julie told me under her breath. She sounded very young and scared. I felt for her. She'd been so excited to be included.

"Well, she's lucky you don't sue her," I replied.

"We could sling our arms under her shoulders and walk her back to the dorm," Claire suggested.

"No, it's almost a mile," I argued. "Rose will come back with Mandy."

But Rose jogged back empty-handed, shaking her head.

"They're gone."

"Oh, great," Julie moaned. I could hear the hurt in her voice. They hadn't waited for her.

"Hey," said a deep masculine voice.

Two hiking boots were planted in front of me. Two long, muscular legs, in jeans. I gazed up to see the guy from the pines, tousle-headed, bedroom eyes . . . gazing directly at me. He caught my gaze and held it. All that was very nice . . . *very* nice . . . but it was his smile that mesmerized me. Sweet and kind of innocent. It actually made *me* smile . . . and tingle, and look down for a moment, to catch my breath. Then I looked back up.

"Chainsaw guy," Ida breathed.

"Hi," he said to me. "Need some help?"

# ten

He stood in front of us, gazing down, his dark hair curling around his face, his eyes warm and deep blue. He had the kind of mouth that looked great when he smiled, with dimples on either side. His nose was straight, then a tad bit turned up, very adorable. His Lakewood sweatshirt clung to a fantastic chest and good arms. Jeans and boots finished it off. He smelled like wood smoke. It was a good smell for him.

"I saw you fall," he said to Julie. He jerked his head in the direction of the pine trees. "I've got a car," he said. "I can drive you back to Marlwood. Maybe you should go to the infirmary." He looked at me again, as if he saw something he wanted to keep track of. Riley used to look at me like that.

There was no way Riley was going to share this moment. *None.*

I couldn't seem to make my brain connect to my mouth. After an extended silence, I said, "Cool."

That was brilliant.

"Can you get us close to our dorm instead?" Julie asked him.

"We're in Grose." Julie looked quickly at me before continuing. "We can wait until morning to get it looked at. I'll say I slipped on my way to breakfast. That way we won't get in trouble."

"No," I said, picking up the layers of her dress and running my flashlight the length of her leg. Her jeans concealed her injury. "I say better a little bit of trouble now than, I dunno, gangrene setting in."

"It's just a sprain," Julie retorted, but her voice was shaky. "And I don't want to be in trouble, even a little. I want to go back to Grose." Julie looked at the guy. "Please?"

"Sure," he said, overruling me. "There's a hole in the chain-link fence," he told us. "You'll have to crawl through."

"I can do that," Julie said.

He caught his lower lip and scratched his nose. He had dark eyebrows and just a hint of a five o'clock shadow. He was wearing a ring that caught the light. "You haven't seen the hole yet."

He looked at me, and my knees wobbled. "I'm Troy, by the way," he told me. "Troy Minear."

"Lindsay. Cavanaugh."

We stared at each other for a second, and I felt something pass between us. It was physical, but it was more than that. After Riley, I thought I was over guys forever. One of the most appealing things about Marlwood was that it was an all-girls school. But now I was trying very hard not to drool.

"I could carry her," he told me, pointing to Julie. I was normally a feminist type, but his heroic offer was seeming really hot right now. "Or two of you could let her sling her arms over your shoulders ... what?" He cocked his head at me.

"Nothing. Sorry." I had just been wishing I was the one hurt. I definitely wouldn't mind being carried. I looked at Ida and Claire. "Are you guys in?"

"Yeah." Ida bent down and picked up the weird porcelain head. "Is this what you tripped over, Julie?"

Julie nodded. "I want to keep it." She reached out her arms. She looked guiltily at me. "If it's valuable, I'll give it back."

"What is it, a head?" Troy said. "I'll carry it for you." He took it from Ida, wrapping his big hands around it as if it were a football. My imagination suited him up in shoulder pads and a helmet. Or maybe a basketball uniform. He was very tall, maybe too tall for football. If I ever tried to kiss him, I'd have to use a ladder.

*Stop.* But my heart was skipping beats. He was too, too hot.

And he was rescuing us—well, Julie, anyway.

Troy and I eased Julie to a standing position while Ida and Claire pushed down her costume. Rose folded it up.

"Can you put this in your trunk?" she asked him.

"Don't put any weight on your ankle," I told Julie, as she slung her arm over our shoulders and we started walking. Poor Julie moaned and hopped along. It was awkward in the extreme.

"Nice, kiddo," Troy said. He was very gentle with her. "You look like a quarterback coming off the field."

We reached the chain-link fence. Ferns and ivy braided the diamonds. Ida shone her flashlight along it, and we saw the jagged gap, which, luckily, was flush with the ground. Troy went through first, crab walking, then grabbed the top links of the hole and tried to stretch them upward. Each of us squirmed through; part of my mom's sweatshirt caught on the broken fence, tearing the arm.

I helped Troy pull Julie through next. Julie sucked in her breath a lot, but we took our time. My fingers brushed Troy's. I was hyperaware of touching him.

At last, the six of us stood on a rise. A hill spread below us, and there was a dark shape in the trees. His car. He fished in his pocket and handed a ring of keys to me.

"What kind of car do you have?" I asked. "So I'll know which one it is."

He chuckled. "It's an old T-bird, but it's the only car down there." Then he looked at Julie. "It's steep. We'll go slowly."

"This is really nice of you," I said.

He didn't say anything, but he did smile. I slid ahead of them down the hillside. When I saw his car—the T-bird was vintage, beautifully restored from some long-ago era—I smiled, too; it wasn't what I would have expected from a rich boy at a private school. A Mercedes or a Beemer, maybe.

I got it open; Troy guided Julie into the passenger side while Claire, Ida, and Rose climbed into the back. I squished in on top of Rose and she said, "Hey, baby."

The seats smelled like leather. The engine purred as he turned the key. Then he drove us down a winding road.

"This is Route 6 Bypass," he said, "but locals call it Fire Lane. There's an urban legend about a ghost who races down the middle of the road in a white nightgown. She's screaming, and she's on fire."

"Oh my God, that's creepy," Julie said. "This place freaks me out."

"Me, too," Ida said.

"Three," Claire agreed.

"That makes me four," Rose reported in.

The car was close and stuffy. I rolled down the window with the crank handle. Cool, silky air wafted against my forehead.

"Were you here tonight to help Mandy with her prank?" Ida asked him.

"No. I heard about the lake prank from Spider." Troy sounded angry. "Way to nearly get someone killed. I thought I'd better come over and make sure tonight went smoothly."

*A fellow lifeguard*, I thought approvingly.

"You go to Lakewood," Claire said.

"Ever since seventh grade," he answered.

"Have you ever seen a ghost?" Rose asked.

"No." His voice was clipped.

I suddenly had the strangest thought. *He's lying.*

The road seemed to disappear as he turned off his headlights when he reached the Marlwood admin building. He got out, tiptoed around to Julie's side, and quietly popped her door. In silence, we scrambled out of the back, glancing in all directions to make sure no one was watching.

"We'll take it from here," Ida whispered. "If anyone saw us with you . . . " She made a scratching sound and mimicked slicing off her head with her hand.

"Got it." He steadied Julie while I took her arm. Rose popped open the trunk and pulled out the costume.

"Thank you," Julie whispered. "You probably saved us from being expelled."

He grinned at her. "You're too cute to get expelled. Just like Spider told me. Night," he murmured to all of us.

I didn't know if I imagined it, but it seemed that he saved me for last. "Good night," he mouthed, all dimples and that hunky five o'clock shadow.

"Yeah. Thanks again," I managed. He didn't answer, just smiled.

"What?" I asked.

He moved his shoulders. "Just lookin'," he said in a twangy accent. Then he touched my hair. "Springy."

"Wild. Untamed," I replied.

"I like it." His smile made my toes tingle. "So, what dorm—?"

"Guys, later," Rose urged. Plink, our spell was broken.

"Later," he echoed. Then he jumped back in his car, pulled out of the space, and drove away.

"Dang, he's hot," Ida breathed. "And *nice*. And did you check out what he said about Spider and Julie?" She fluttered her lashes at our wounded comrade.

Julie blushed.

"Yeah, but did you see the way he was looking at Lindsay?" Rose smacked her lips. "Yum-yum, freshman hottie."

"Shut up," I said happily.

"And you do not mean that in a trendy way," Rose prompted.

I shook my wild, untamed hair and fluttered my long eyelashes. I felt positively radiant in my skuzzy jeans and tomboy sweatshirt.

It took forever to get to Grose. Ida crawled through the bathroom window we had cleverly left open, then tiptoed down the hall and let us in through the front door. She took the costume from Rose, who trotted off into the darkness.

Ida said, "There was a ghost in the bathtub. She was washing all her bodily cavities."

"You're evil," Claire shot back. They both snickered.

I made Julie go to our room while I snagged the bag of ice from our freezer—practically the only thing in it—put there by Ms. Krige.

I carried the ice down the hall. Julie was sitting on the edge of her bed with Caspian in her lap. She had set the porcelain skull on the windowsill, and it gazed blankly at me as I crossed the threshold.

Our curtains were open; I thought we'd closed them. I saw nothing but the dark expanse of Jessel with its turrets and privet hedge. I wondered if Mandy and the others were back yet, and I marveled that we could do these things without getting busted.

*At least so far. No more for you, Cinderella.*

"Scoot back," I told her. "I need to elevate your foot."

I plucked my pillow off my bed and brought it to her as she obeyed. She sucked in her breath and clung to Caspian. I was seriously worried that her ankle was broken. I lifted up her calf and slid the pillow under it. Then I sat on the bed and carefully laid the ice over her ankle.

"Ow," she said. "Ow, ow, ow."

"Did you stash any painkillers?" I asked her. We were

supposed to give all our medication to Ms. Krige, even our over-the-counter stuff. But who was going to go to all that trouble for cramps and headaches?

She nodded. "Ibuprofen. Little white bottle. In the top drawer of my dresser. My underwear drawer. Don't look at my cup size."

Smiling faintly, I got up and crossed to her dresser. Opened it. "I don't care what your bra size is," I assured her, as I came across a striped camisole and a matching bra beneath it. 32A.

Julie shifted uncomfortably on the bed. "My mom keeps saying I'll fill out, but—"

"Oh, please, you have the adorable ballet dancer look going on." I moved aside some cotton bikini underwear with little clouds and stars on them. Definitely angelic.

A light went on in the second story of Jessel. It was the turret room directly across from us, but no one went in.

I had a clear view; it was furnished similarly to Jessel's downstairs—dark wood antiques, including a big desk and a four-poster bed. I marveled at the kind of wealth that allowed you to redecorate not just your dorm room, but your entire dorm. All I had brought was a picture of my parents.

I saw something on the turret room window and I squinted at it, blinking, making out the shape of a white oval. A face. There were two eyes and a half-opened mouth. It was the same face that I had seen in the window, the same girl whose reflection had appeared in the library.

"That is such a cool effect," I said. I was actually a little creeped out. She—it—seemed to be staring right at me.

"What?" Julie half-turned. "Ow." Stayed as she was.

"There's a face in their window," I said. "Like a reflection."

"Of you?"

I squinted. Definitely a face, but blank. It didn't move as I moved. Didn't blink. The mouth stayed half-open.

"Nope. Just something Mandy whipped up. What was the rest of the house like?" Now I sounded like my dormies.

"Lots of gory fake body parts," she said with a shudder. "They're going to use them for their Halloween haunted house."

The porcelain head sat silhouetted in the moonlight on our windowsill. White face, white brain marked into sections, with big black numbers. Where was the part of the brain that made you want to be with the cool girls even after they ditched your roommate?

*Wait. Did it move?*

I stared at the white head. It stared back at me. I gave myself a stern reminder about my conversation with Lara. I was not a gawker.

But the light glinted off it just then. . . .

"Hey," Julie said, "are you okay?"

"Just really tired," I said. Then I gave her what she needed to kill the pain.

# eleven

**October 31, Halloween!!!!!!!!!!!!**
**possessions: me**
    care package from CJ:
        tons of Dove chocolate, God bless you, Stepmom
        Too Faced makeup (given to Julie)
        wool socks
        some cool pajama pants
        a new parka (her note said it's going to snow. it's very
            sweet of her, but a little too . . . wrong.)
    care package from Jason:
        a Korean horror movie about a haunted girls boarding
            school (thx, Mr. Snark)
        army jacket. i love it!
        OMG, Twizzlers!
        RAWK! his old digital camera!!!!!!!!!!!!
    a best friend ☺

*mood:* moody

*listening to:* "People Are Strange" off *The Lost Boys* ST cuz, well, yeah . . . !

## possessions: them in general

more stuff. it just keeps coming:

clothes

iPhones(no reception, but still...!)

jewelry—their parents send boatloads

more freakin' furniture!

YET more stuff for the haunted house. can you say ENTIRE anamatronic graveyard in their front yard? Light-up witch on the roof? OMG, OMG.

## possessions: Mandy specifically

Lara

Kiyoko, who is acting weird

Alis—in! (and moved into Jessel!)

Sangeeta—in! (ditto!)

and Julie is, like, her total fawning puppy-dog

*mood:* INSANE?

*listening to:* the voices that tell her to be a bitch. ha.

*plus:* HALLOWEEN SCREAMS! TRICK OR TREAT, YEAH!

---

**Julie's foot was sprained.** At the infirmary they iced it and wrapped it. They told her to stay off it, but she was determined to wear her Tinker Bell costume and make the rounds of Halloweentown. Much hopping would be involved. Crutches were out; they clashed with her wings.

And that, pretty much, took care of October 30$^{th}$. During the day, Marlwood was completely transformed. Eerie faces were sprayed on tree trunks with glow-in-the-dark paint. Motion detectors set off hysterical screaming all over campus, and fake bloody fingers writhed on branches and overhanging lamps. Dozens of the horse heads wore witch hats, and all of them disappeared under the obliging blanket of fog that swept over the campus at six-thirty, half an hour before the carnival was scheduled to start.

Grose had a totally lame cakewalk; they had already baked twenty cakes by the time I started school, and I helped frost a few. I made a spider cake and one that looked like a big eye with blood oozing out of it. Ida said I was sick. April offered to buy it then and there for a hundred dollars.

Marica decided we didn't have enough cakes, and had a dozen overnighted from Charm City Cakes—scary Halloween villages, graveyards with little coffins that opened and closed, a big skull with eyes that we could set on fire.

Julie and I ran the cakewalk for the first shift. Since we had eight people in our dorm, and the carnival ran for four hours, we were gone in thirty minutes.

It followed that a girl who wore tattered jeans and sweat-shirts would go minimalist for her Halloween costume, too. An old sheet, two eye holes, and I was a ghost. Ida, who had gone all out as a sexy vampire, told me I was "cunningly retro."

But most of the girls had elaborate, professional-looking

costumes that had been either ordered from Hollywood or
Europe or custom-made. Mandy's costume had been a favor
from someone who used to costume Madonna. Lara's vampire costume was vintage, from an old Vincent Price movie.
Julie's Tinker Bell costume was studded with hundreds of tiny
peridots that she told me were hand-sewn. She wore a crown
of intricate silver and gold leaves, and green and silver ribbons
trailing down her back. Her wings were silvery, delicate, and
heart-shaped.

The carnival swag was amazing. Stewart was giving away
beautiful black enamel earrings as their prizes. Hill House was
handing out a vast assortment of gift cards for high-end stores
like Neiman Marcus. Back home, we made fun of people who
wasted good money at Needless Markup. I could see why Marica
felt the need to compete with some serious cakes. The carnival
prizes were more extravagant than my Christmas presents.

I tried not to do more gawking, even though my mouth
was hanging open. I found out that the parents donated the
prizes and that Claire's costume, which was an authentic rec-
reation of Belle's yellow gown from the Broadway production
of *Beauty and the Beast*, cost sixteen thousand dollars.

And Jessel was the most extreme of all the extremeness. Of
course, the haunted house was the biggest deal, and featured
a graveyard, complete with graves that opened to reveal fake
corpses. Leaves swirled and crunched as spooky laughter rolled
around me on the gusts of autumn wind, rising and falling,
growing louder . . . and stopping.

Strobe lights shattered the blackness of Mandy's turret
room; then Mandy herself appeared in the window dressed

like a really sexy wicked witch—supershort black skirt, bustier, and a black hat with a trailing veil. She slowly raised her arms as she stared down at us. The lights flickered on, off, on-off-on-off, making her arms jerk-jerk-jerk as she raised them above her head. Ooh, she was holding a knife. The strobe glinted off of it. Good effect.

Julie giggled and waved at her.

My breath caught. The ghost-face was in Mandy's window again. The one I'd seen before, through our window and in the haunted house, too. Dark holes for eyes, a wide slit for a mouth. The slit grew, as if someone—Mandy—had carved a jack-o'-lantern mouth into its dead-white skin.

"I have to ask them how they do that," I said aloud, challenging the face to vanish.

"I hope I don't look stupid," Julie murmured, shifting her weight off her wrapped foot as steps sounded on the other side of the door.

"You are cuteness defined," I promised her.

"You have to say that," she fretted. "You're my friend."

"*Wahahaha*," an electronic voice blared from a speaker. "*Come in . . . and die!*"

The door flew open.

Lara stood on the threshold. Vampire teeth jutted from her upper lip. She was wearing a tux and a black velvet cape lined with red satin that looked garish next to her elegant red hair. DracuLara.

"Good evenink." She beamed at Julie and furled her cape. "Come. I invite you, Tinker Julie and ghostling persink."

"Thank you, kind vampire," Julie said, bending her standing leg. I wondered if she'd hoped Mandy would ask her to help with the haunted house, but I figured each dorm had to do their own thing. Julie had been super-extra-nice to Mandy since the prank, hovering around, trying to find a way in that stuck. I'd gone through that, too, when Jane had dangled acceptance in my face.

The open front door was decorated like an enormous bloody mouth; scarlet mist billowed from it, and I thought of that first day, at the hedge. Spiderwebs dangled on either side.

We walked in, or rather, I walked and Julie held onto Lara as she hopped along. It would have been so much easier for her to use crutches.

Rippled black and red veils undulated from the upstairs balcony, allowing for sneak-peeks into the living room. Shadows blossomed behind the sheets; there were screams and rattling chains, laughter and organ music. And they had reupholstered all their furniture in Halloween-themed fabric—actually literally reupholstered it—black roses and skulls against a background of red velvet. A black snack table with jeweled white skulls spiraling down the legs was weighed down with finger sandwiches—thin strips of bread each finished off with half a pimento-olive. The wall by the stairs looked like a torture chamber, with gory fake corpses chained to a blood-encrusted expanse of pitted stone. Whenever anyone went up or down the stairs, the corpses squirmed and groaned. On the way to the downstairs bathroom, a huge stone fountain gushed with red water. Beating hearts floated like lily pads in it.

"Ah, another wictim," Kiyoko said in a fake Romanian accent as she leaned over the balcony. She was dressed like a vampire countess in a black dress with a hoop skirt and a crown.

The place was jammed with Gypsies, witches, princesses, hookers, and belly dancers. "Thriller" started up and a bunch of girls squealed and rushed behind the veils. Through the spaces, I saw an entire forest of artificial dancing black trees decorated with silver skulls and owls. Farther back were a guillotine and a mummy case. In full fortune-teller regalia, Ms. Meyerson sat draped in a shawl and made motions around Houdini's crystal ball.

A girl dressed like Cleopatra walked into the kitchen, and come back out with a bottle of water.

"Want something to drink?" I asked Julie. But she was holding onto the back of a chair and smiling at Mandy as Ye Diva trailed down the stairs in her witch mini-micro. The motorized rubber torture victims on the wall screeched with pain, opening and closing their bloody eyes. "Okay, later," I said. Julie didn't respond.

I eased around a dark fairy and another sexy witch and went into the kitchen. A girl dressed like a Renaissance princess was on the landline. A black metal cauldron filled with dry ice and water bottles bubbled on the breakfast bar. More cauldrons, filled with sodas, sat on little three-legged stools. Mechanized bats flapped their wings overhead. The kitchen was wall-to-wall people; I inched through, snagged a can of diet soda, then made my exit out the side door so I could breathe.

Bolts of fog rolled in off the lake. I wondered what everybody back in San Diego was doing tonight. Last year, I had gone to party at Jane's. Maybe if I had gone all the way with

Riley then, I wouldn't be here now.

"Lindsay? Is that you under there?" It was Kiyoko. She was carrying two glasses of red wine. She handed me one, and we clinked glasses as I pulled my sheet off and wrapped it around my free arm.

"Yes, it's me. In the ectoplasm." She smiled. "How did you guess?"

She gestured to my grubby high-tops. "Only one pair of shoes like that."

"By your shoes shall ye know them," I said.

"You're so funny." She spoke to me over her glass. "We're having a private party at the operating theater." Took another sip. "You should show." She grinned slyly. "There will be guys."

*Don't you ever worry about being expelled?* I asked her silently, but I knew how naïve and bunched up I would sound if I asked her out loud.

"And . . . I think Mandy is going to pull something on Julie there," she added, practically whispering.

I went on alert. "Like?"

Kiyoko hesitated and looked over her shoulder. She'd been all jerky in lit yesterday, and went into this long, involved explanation about why we had to wait to watch *The Crucible*. Short version: we all had to get ready for the carnival, duh. But now . . . I figured she was giving me privileged information.

"I heard Mandy talking to Lara in her bedroom." Kiyoko jerked and rubbed the back of her neck. "Can you check and see if I've got anything on my neck?" she asked me. "It feels weird."

She turned around, and I carefully gathered up her long fine hair and moved it to one side. I touched her skin. Nothing. I remembered that at the Alis-and-Sangeeta prank, *I* had felt something on the back of my neck, too.

"What do you see?" she asked. She was wearing an overpowering amount of luxurious-smelling perfume. "I can feel something."

"A vampire bit you," I informed her as I rearranged her hair. "No, there's nothing, but the other day I felt just like—"

Just then, Julie and Mandy burst through the kitchen door. Laughing hysterically, they were arm in arm, Julie hopping like a pogo stick as Mandy kept her upright. Julie shrieked and covered her mouth, totally OOC as Mandy let go of her. She limp-bounded over to me, glommed onto my shoulder, and grabbed my wine out of my hand. She chugalugged it in three big gulps.

"Whoa there, easy," Mandy said, laughing. "Linz, we're going to the operating theater to party."

"Spider's gonna be there, too," Julie said.

Kiyoko gave me a meaningful look. And I knew there would be no talking Julie out of it, not even if I told her Mandy had a little surprise in store for her.

"No one will miss us for an hour or so," Mandy went on, as if she had to convince me.

But she didn't, not where my best friend was concerned.

# twelve

**Mandy hunted down** her select few and ordered them to come with us. We were a party of seven: Alis, Sangeeta, Kiyoko, Lara, Julie, Mandy, and me. Word spread and more girls tagged along, tentatively, at first, growing bolder when it became clear that Mandy didn't mind. I minded; I thought about all the cool carnival swag I had yet to collect and flared with a bit of resentment. I didn't want to party with Mandy at some operating theater. I didn't even know what an operating theater was. But I didn't want to leave Julie alone with the Joker, either.

We tiptoed into the woods and up a hill. Julie limped along gamely, panting and grabbing onto tree branches, hanging onto my shoulder, swapping over to Mandy and back to me again. We were moving at a pretty fast clip, considering that Julie was an invalid and Kiyoko and Mandy were wearing three-inch heels. Eventually, they took them off, then complained how cold the ground was.

"If Miles was here, he'd carry me," Mandy said. "We were in

Rome, in some hideous catacomb . . . " She trailed off. I really wanted her to keep going . . . all the way to the story of the Lincoln Bedroom.

The trees bobbed in the wind, and the moon shone down, the same moon that was shining down on Jane, Riley, and my old best friend Heather. I felt homesickness, not for what was back home, but for my mom. We had always trick-or-treated together, dressing up, laughing and racing down the streets of our neighborhood like perpetual kindergartners. She died before I got old enough to want to go without her.

The year she got sick and couldn't go, she apologized to me while tears spilled down her face. She clutched her hospital bedsheets until her knuckles turned white and I was afraid her bones would pop through her skin.

But I'd been more afraid that the dam of my own emotions would break, and I would beg her not to die.

Now, as we thundered through the dark woods, I started to feel a little sick. Stress, exhaustion, nerves, no food. Maybe the altitude. Maybe a little breaky-downy-ness.

"The operating theater is from the Victorian era," Mandy explained to me as we hiked along. "Back before cars, this place was so remote they had to perform their own surgeries here at Marlwood. I'm referring to when it was first opened as a girls school, right after the Civil War ended."

I was hazy on Marlwood's glorious past. "But a *theater*—"

"Medical students could watch. Sometimes just regular people, too." Mandy nodded as if to assure me that she was telling me the truth.

"That is gross." I stuck out my tongue.

"Things were different then," she said, with a little smile. "There's a story about some girl who died on the operating table, and it wasn't an accident. It was because she was pregnant and they didn't want the scandal." She moved her hands in a spooky-ooky way. "Now she haunts the operating room."

"Theater," I corrected.

"I heard this wasn't really a boarding school. It was a home for wayward girls," Alis said.

Mandy laughed. "Well, it still is. Right my little ho-babies?"

"Right," Julie chirped. "We are *way* wayward." That snagged her some appreciative chuckles. She glowed.

"And, speaking of ghostly pregnant girls," Mandy said, with a wave of her hand as we pushed our way out of a thick section of pine trees, "I give you . . . the operating theater."

"Yeow," I blurted.

The building was round, like my lit lecture hall—once a height of two stories or more, but now a caved-in heap. The slate-shingled roof had fallen in on itself, and tiny rectangular windows in a row near the top were squashed so that they looked like the narrowed eyes of angry faces rising out of the rubble of bricks and pieces of metal.

Lights glowed beneath the caved-in stairs, through holes in the walls. Shadows of the people inside appeared angular and strange. Pines waved and bowed over the rubble. Music played: cello-based and a little gothy.

"Crap, the boys are already here," Mandy said. "I hope they didn't get into the good stuff."

She sped up, and we watched her go. For a few seconds, Julie and I were a bit apart from the others. She took a deep breath. "Do I look okay?" she asked.

"Yes, Tinker Bell. Spider will die," I said. I dropped my voice even lower. "Listen, I heard that Mandy's going to haze you."

She looked at me long and hard. And then she smiled weakly.

"I know," she replied. "Wait!" she called to Mandy.

Mandy stopped and held out her arm. Julie hopped up to her and held on tight. Then the two disappeared inside the black hole that was the door.

I took a few more steps. Then I smelled smoke. And suddenly, I felt kind of woozy. My stomach clenched and the ground rocked. Kiyoko came up beside me.

"You okay?"

"That smoke smell . . . it's making me kind of nauseated," I said. I drew back slightly. "What exactly is Mandy planning for Julie? Please, just tell me." Maybe if it wasn't anything too bad, I could go back.

"I don't actually know. I'm not even sure it's tonight." She set her teeth together, grimacing for forgiveness.

My mouth dropped open. "But you said—"

"That she *might*." She touched the corner of her mouth and dropped her hand to her side. "I don't smell smoke."

Then she looked hard at me. "You know, Lindsay, Mandy might pull a trick on Julie at any time. If you stay close, you're more likely to be there to pick up the pieces."

"Julie's pretty tough," I declared.

"Julie's a fragile piece of glass," Kiyoko replied, her gaze hard and flinty.

Lara sidled up to us. "Come on, dark-links," she urged. "The boys will drink up all the Grey Goose vodka."

"Do you smell smoke?" Kiyoko asked her.

More girls were catching up to us—so it wasn't going to be just us seven—although I didn't see anyone from our dorm. I spotted Rose. She was wearing raggedy jeans and a curly black wig. When she saw me, she posed, and it took me a second to realize that she had come dressed as *me*.

"You suck," I said with a grin. The sight of Rose perked me up. "Doesn't she suck?" I asked Kiyoko, to show her there were no hard feelings. Suddenly, I saw things with more optimism. Kiyoko had made a valid point—Mandy might decide to haze Julie at any time, and Julie would probably set her own hair on fire if Mandy asked her to. So swag-loss or no, it was good that I had come.

I unwadded my sheet and threw it over my head. "There. Now everyone will be able to tell Rose and me apart."

Rose clasped her hands on either side of her face and drew her skin taught across her cheekbones. "Only now I'm Ehrlenstein."

"Oh, I love it," Alis said, as she came up beside us. "Does Ehrlenbach freak you out? She freaks me out."

"She scares me to death," I admitted.

"Well, that settles it. She's a creepy weirdo." Rose staggered forward with her skin stretched tight. "Let's get this party started."

She led the way into the pitch-black interior, and we followed after. The smoke odor was so strong I coughed. I smelled alcohol—not like drinking, but like in a hospital.

Disinfectant. My stomach seized, and a sour taste rushed into my mouth.

Everyone crowded around me, yelling and shushing each other, then moved past me into the corridor. They were agog to see what mega-bucks Mandy had in store for them next.

I realized I was hanging back. And suddenly, I couldn't go on. It wasn't only that I didn't want to; I couldn't. It was as if someone had grabbed my shoulders or I had walked into an invisible barrier.

Waves and waves of panic crashed over me. I felt so stupid. But as I stared into the nothingness, I swayed. Sweat beaded my forehead. I couldn't breathe.

*It's nothing. Go in. You're making a scene. There is no need for drama.*

*Get out. Danger.* My primitive instincts were taking over. I was afraid I was going to wet my pants. I heard myself whimper, and the weird thing was, I couldn't even retreat. I couldn't do anything except stand there and freak out.

*I'm in trouble*, I thought, standing there in my sheet like an oversized three-year-old. I listened to my fluttering heartbeat and breathed slowly in, out. It felt as if a part of my brain refused to obey me.

A gold circle of light bloomed from behind me, lighting up the darkness just enough for me to see the splintered wood and cobwebs. Just normal, no special effects. Just a little sneak-party, no grand shindig. These people were super-rich, but they were just people. It was just a party.

I turned around.

And there he was, Troy, my knight, dressed in a white

doctor's coat with a stethoscope around his neck. And that jolted me back into normalcy. I was so grateful . . . and so very happy to see him.

I couldn't see the color of his eyes but I knew they were dark blue. His dark hair curled around his ears and I knew it was streaked with blond. Oh God, I couldn't stop staring at him. Lucky thing he couldn't tell since I was wearing my sheet.

He stepped forward and looped his hands around the small of my back, then slid them down to cup my butt. I know I blinked. I probably even gasped.

"Hey," he said, gazing down at me, "you said you were going to be a ghost, but I thought you'd be a little sexier."

I suddenly realized we had a case of mistaken identity, and I wondered who he thought I was. "How do you know what I've got on under the sheet?" I replied tartly.

He let go of me and jumped back. I took pity on him and whipped off my disguise. And to my intense delight, he smiled broadly, obviously happy to see me.

"Whoops," he said, with an evil grin. "No harm, no foul?"

"I'll never wash my ass again," I retorted, and he burst out laughing.

We shared a little amused moment. I was a little deflated, because he obviously had a girlfriend, or some girl he was expecting to meet tonight. But I knew things like that could change. They had changed on me.

"You. Are. Trouble. Casparrrrr." He gestured to the corridor. "You going in?"

I half-turned. Saw the darkness. Smelled the smoke and the disinfectant. And then I was stymied again.

*Not now*, I begged myself. *Act normal.*

"It'll be fun," he said, misreading my fear for shyness. Maybe that was all it really was.

"C'mon." He took my hand—*he took my hand!*—and propelled me forward gently.

"It's downstairs," he said. "In the basement. Vere ve perform zie autopsies."

"Dissect here often?" I asked, concentrating on his hand. Warm. Big. Nice veins. Bulgy muscles. I was okay. Pretty much. I was having a little trouble breathing, but . . .

"Yes, as a matter of fact," he said. "Well, we don't dissect, but we do come over here. We row over. Lakewood bought new rowboats two years ago, and we know where they keep the old ones."

It was intriguing to think of him sneaking around on our side of the lake. "Why don't you drive? And what do you do when you come over?" I asked.

He snorted. "Because we're supposed to be snug in our cubicles, studying. And what do you think we do when we come over?"

"Not going there," I said, feeling my face warm up.

He chuckled. "You crack me up."

"Then my work here is done." After Riley broke my heart, I'd thought I would never flirt again. But it really was like falling off a bicycle.

"Here we go," he said, turning me to the right. His flashlight grazed a dark rectangle, and I stiffened as the stench of cooked meat mingled with the odor of disinfectant and the smoke.

"Oh my God, that stinks," I said.

He looked at me, then raised his chin and sniffed the air. "What? I don't smell anything."

I blinked. "You're kidding." Then I had a terrible thought. What if there was a fire down there? Maybe someone knocked over a candle, and the flames caught on someone's costume; Julie had a hurt leg and . . .

. . . And what if he was pretending not to smell anything because he'd been prepped to help out with a prank and he didn't know the fire was out of control?

"C'mon, be serious, Troy," I ordered him. "You smell it, right?"

He cocked his head. "I really don't."

I exhaled and cradled my forehead in my free hand. Was I losing it? Going crazy?

"Do you have allergies?" he asked me.

"What? No," I snapped at him. I looked past him to the door. Something was wrong. I could feel it. I knew it.

"I smell smoke," I insisted.

"Okay, let's go see." He was humoring me. He walked through the door and started down some stone stairs. The gothy music grew louder; someone hit a sour note and I realized it was live. The hum of conversation grew louder. And the smells became more powerful. Troy looked at me over his shoulder as if to say, "*See? There's nothing to worry about.*"

I could barely make out his features, and I knew he couldn't see mine. He couldn't see that I was sweaty and terrified.

The stairs led to a brick floor. He turned and waited for me, but he didn't take my hand again. He hung a left.

We were staring into low dark room, lit with oil lamps and candles, dotted with antique tables and round-backed chairs that looked too nice to be operating theater relics. I saw Julie standing with Mandy and the others around a high table with a tile center. About twenty feet beyond them, two girls were playing violins and a boy with long blond hair was sawing at a beautiful cello. I looked at the instrument with longing, recalling my five years of lessons and recitals.

Julie was drinking from what looked to be a whiskey bottle, and Mandy the witch-ho and the others were dancing to the music as they clapped and cheered her on. Mandy faced me; Lara and Kiyoko gyrated with their backs to me. Shaking her hips, Alis was feeding Sangeeta what appeared to be a Jell-O shot in a little plastic cup.

I headed straight for them. To my surprise, Troy stayed with me.

Mandy was the first to notice us, and her face broke into a huge smile. I tempered my smile; I wasn't pleased to see her, especially not when she was encouraging my fifteen-year-old roommate to get drunk.

*Like you were so innocent last year,* I reminded myself.

"Well," I said to Troy, but he scooted ahead of me. Mandy struck a pose, thrusting out her hip and placing her right hand on it and her left hand behind her head. Then she let her head fall back as he gathered her up, bending her backward until her hat fell off, and kissed her hard on the lips.

*Oh, crap.*

So that was Troy's girlfriend. Queen Mandy.

I ignored Mandy and Troy as best I could and headed for Julie.

I walked straight up to her. She flushed and started to set her bottle on the table, then picked it up again as if to underscore the fact that I was not the boss of her.

I took that in and moved on to Lara, who was undulating her arms like snakes.

And what I saw . . . I didn't know what I saw. Lara's eyes were black.

And so were Alis's, and Sangeeta's. And Kiyoko's, as they danced. Their beat was off—all of them, out of time with the music . . . as if they were hearing *other* music . . .

Then Lara caught her breath, jerked her head, and stood statue still. She closed her eyes. When she opened them again, they were her usual brilliant green. She began to dance again, this time to the beat.

I ticked my attention to Kiyoko, who was swaying easily, back and forth. Her eyes were normal, too.

"Stop, I can't breathe," Mandy squealed.

"She can't breathe. Call the doctor," Troy yelled. He hadn't seemed to notice the weird eyes, but he was playing along with Mandy's theatricals. He was probably used to it. I wondered briefly how long they'd been together.

As they straightened back up, he lifted up his stethoscope. "Oh, wait, I *am* the doctor." He placed the metal circle at the curving top of her bustier.

"That thing is cold," she told him with a sexy scowl.

"I'll warm it up." He took it back and blew on it, then

rubbed it between his fingers and placed it on her chest again. "There, let's see ... *ach, nein,* you don't gotta heartbeat ... Oh, whoops."

He laughed and stuck the earpieces in his ears. "Wow, Manz, I really can hear your heartbeat. It's *very* fast."

The room was swaying. I felt something closing in on me, the room darkening. I was unbelievably cold.

"Julie, I need to go," I said in a quiet voice. "Would you come with me?"

I moved a bit away. Julie followed. "What's wrong?"

"I'm not feeling good." It was the truth.

She made a face and glanced over her shoulder at the others, who were drinking, laughing, and having a great time. "We just got here. I need to rest my ankle. Besides . . ." She looked around wistfully. "Spider hasn't shown yet."

I gathered up my hair and let it fall. "Listen, Julie, I need to leave. And if Mandy tries to pull a prank . . . " I knew how preachy this was sounding. "I just mean she might not realize how badly hurt you are."

Julie's mouth dropped open. "I don't believe you. Do you think I'm retarded or something? You know, I actually lived through six weeks here without any help from *you.*"

A cork popped; a tall guy wrapped like a mummy held a champagne bottle over his head. Girls gathered toward him and opened their mouths.

Something was creeping closer. I looked over my shoulder, at the faces of the partygoers. A girl began to guzzle champagne as the others squealed and laughed. What was happening?

"Julie, please," I said. "It's ... things are ... "

"Let's check your brainwaves," Troy said in a loud voice to Mandy. He put the end of the stethoscope on her forehead.

Mandy started screaming. The musicians stopped. People whirled around to stare, and Troy grabbed Mandy as she tumbled backward, nearly hitting the floor.

"Manz, what's wrong?" he shouted. "What's the matter?"

And in that moment, Alis, Sangeeta, Kiyoko, and Lara whipped around to face her. Face me. Their eyes were completely black. *All* of them.

Mandy was screaming and people were shouting and I thought, *Julie. I can't leave her there.*

So I turned around and bellowed, "Julie, come on! *Now!*"

Her back was to me, and she, too, was comforting Mandy. She turned around—

—I held my breath—

—but her eyes were normal.

She didn't say anything, but I knew she was going to stay.

"I can't," I whispered. "I just can't."

I bolted and ran, the screaming and laughter bouncing off the walls behind me. I pushed open a door and stepped into . . . ashes. Piles and piles of ashes. It was a mess; I started to turn back around when I saw moonlight pouring into a hole in the roof up ahead. I shuffled through the piles as if they were autumn leaves.

The bricks were black with soot; at the far end, a square of moonlight revealed that a door had once stood there. I walked through and saw I'd been in a tunnel, partly submerged into the ground. I smelled smoke and now there was another smell . . . kerosene, like for camping lanterns . . .

*What's going on?* I wondered as I raced back along the trail through the woods, toward the main campus.

Books on reforming girls with bad behavior. Mandy and her friends with their eyes going all black like that. All the elaborate hazing just to be a part of their little in-crowd. I couldn't understand it. The flashes of cold, the uncertainty I felt whenever I was around Mandy.

I didn't know what all of it meant.

But I was more determined than ever to find out.

# November:
# The Bait

*Worldly wealth is the Devil's bait.*

—Robert Burton

*A dimple on the chin, the devil within.*

—Pope Paul VI

# thirteen

**To my intense relief,** Mandy's freakout killed the party. People started leaving, and Julie, half-carried by Rose caught up with me in the woods. Julie was bummed because she hadn't gotten to see Spider; also because rather than share in the drama of calming Mandy down, Mandy asked her to go back to Jessel and make sure things were going okay—asked Julie, who couldn't even walk on her own. Ms. Psycho wanted to take a minute to compose herself before she and "the girls" resumed their haunted house hostess duties.

It was obvious that Julie wanted to stay with Mandy and the others. Be one of the girls. Not tonight. Not any night, hopefully.

Rose and I somehow managed to get Julie through the forest, a wobbly, pouty Tinker Bell. She swore to me that she would get crutches in the morning; her ankle was throbbing and she was in tears. So once again, I skipped the carnival and got her to our dorm, taking off my filthy high-tops and walking in my stockinged feet down our hall. Julie sniffled as she took off her costume. I knew she was in pain and her feelings were hurt, and she was embarrassed. That kept her attention off me, which was fine with me. Because I was really losing it.

The white head was still on the windowsill of our room. Where else would it be? Across the quad and down the hill, the Jessel haunted house party was still going strong. Julie urged me to go back out, but there was no way. I got in my pajamas and helped Julie; and our big night officially ended.

I crawled into bed. I was trembling. Black eyes. What did that mean? Drugs. Had to be. These girls could hire scientist geniuses to design drugs for them. Mandy had had a bad trip. That must have been it.

I shifted to Troy. *God*, how could he be Mandy's boyfriend? Was there a chip in his brain? Was she that good in bed?

Could I steal him?

*Don't even think that*, I admonished myself. Jane Taylor had stolen my crush, and it had pretty much pushed me over the edge. I could never do that to another girl, not even Mandy Winters.

After a while, I began to drift, going in and out of a heavy doze. My body weighed a thousand pounds; my chest barely rose and fell. The little finger on my left hand twitched.

Drifted, dozed, sank.

Goosebumps rose along my body. I was cold. Had I kicked off my blanket and sheets? I tried to move my hand to gather them up, but I couldn't move.

And I knew, without a doubt, that someone else was in the room.

I fought to open my eyes. A cold breath brushed the crown of my head. I tried to move again . . . and drifted . . .

"*You*," someone whispered in my ear. No, not in my ear; inside my head. And it wasn't a whisper, but an echo, a wisp of a word braiding and unbraiding deep in my dreaming mind.

"*You.*"

I fought hard to wake up; there was a stone on top of my chest and my eyelids were glued shut. The weight on my chest pressed me against the mattress, and I couldn't breathe. I floated, sank; my sheets enfolded me like splashing waves. The bed was a sinking anchor; I was going to drown.

"*You.*"

"*Must.*"

When Julie woke me up at midnight, she said I was sobbing uncontrollably.

"*Stop.*"

# fourteen

**November 2**

"Yes, stress," Julie said, as she and I sat on our beds, facing each other. She had just awakened me from another nightmare. It was my fourth, or fifth. Or maybe sixth.

"You just left home. You're up here in the mountains with a bunch of girls you don't know. And it's getting to you. So, nightmares," she finished.

"So are you," I replied. "New to all this. And those girls . . . Mandy . . . are stress-maniacs." I took a chance. "And Mandy is insane."

Julie pulled her wrapped ankle onto the bed and scooted backwards. "Don't try to change the subject. I don't have to defend them. Or myself." I could see the hurt in her eyes, and the uncertainty—a small victory. She was confused about Mandy. That was a start. I pressed on.

"Okay, not insane. But they were high on Halloween," I insisted. "Their pupils were so dilated I couldn't even see any color."

"*I* didn't see that."

"It only lasted a couple of seconds."

She snorted.

"I'm not trying to BS you, Julie."

Silence filled the chasm. Then she took a breath and cleared her throat.

"You told me they have séances," I said, trying another angle. "Kiyoko's got a bookmark from an occult store in San Francisco."

"Oh, what a horrible thing," Julie mocked, covering her cheeks. "Kiyoko has a bookmark. They do séances. So that makes them crazy."

"I'm not saying I believe that they do anything superweird, but being interested in the occult *is* weird, when you're our age. C'mon, do you know anybody back home who still does stuff like that?"

She ran her fingers along Caspi's eyelashes. "I don't know that many people," she said. "When you're a stable brat, you kind of have a different focus."

She'd had to sell her horse. So did that mean she didn't have any friends, either? Like me? That we were each other's best and only friends?

"You know, if this were a horror movie, it would turn out that I'm right and you're wrong." I tried to make it sound like a joke, but I heard the hurt in my voice. "They would be possessed by Satan, and you would die a hideous death."

"This is definitely the location for it," she volleyed back, with a weak smile. "No cell phones, adults who let us do whatever we want."

"Yeah."

"Anyway, Mandy bluffs," she said. "She would never really do anything to anyone."

I let the sentence hang there. After all, *she* was the one who'd gotten hurt. And Kiyoko had probably been about a minute away from hypothermia last week at the lake.

"Just . . . be careful. Be careful, because you're my friend." I took a deep breath. "My best friend."

"Oh." She was a rosy little cherub. "Same here."

We hugged. Caspian kissed my cheek. I was a bit embarrassed but I made a little kissy noise in his general direction.

"Okay. Next item on the agenda is, I have to pee," I told her.

I trundled down the hall past the bad art and the portrait with the eyes that followed you and . . .

*Come to me . . .*

I flicked on the bathroom light and did my thing, then walked past our five huge bathtubs and turned on the sink. I didn't look at myself in the mirror. I had always thought that fluorescent lights made people look ugly.

*That's why I'm not looking*, I told myself.

I adjusted the hot water. And I forgot I was avoiding the mirror and looked up at myself, and I saw . . .

—Oh God—

"Nothing," I insisted, shuddering as I stared back down at the water. "Nothing is there."

There was no pale reflection staring back at me, with darkened eyes. I hadn't seen that.

The distortion in the mirror was due to the overhead fluorescent lights. Those stupid lights would make anyone look . . .

*. . . Dead.*

I ran-walked out of there as fast as I could. I wasn't even sure that I had turned off the water.

I went back into our room. Julie smiled at me.

Maybe I *had* imagined the whole thing.

No. No, no, no.

"We'll never fight again," she said, but I knew she was asking me, not telling me.

"Agreed." I made myself smile, but my mouth was quivering. "Never."

I padded back to my bed. As I bent over, a coldness pressed against the back of my neck, and I straightened and turned around.

The porcelain head was staring directly at me. It was positioned at an angle, not straight ahead, as Julie kept it. Which meant . . .

*That she moved it when she dusted,* I told myself, turning off the light.

Except we didn't dust.

———

**The First** streaks of sunlight saved me from more nightmares. I woke up panting, and my cheeks were wet with tears.

It was Saturday, which meant free time after roll call and late breakfast at nine. The school put on all kinds of events on weekends to keep us occupied. Some were special electives that parents paid for at the beginning of the semester—extra art and music lessons, for example. There were lots of clubs, too—

French, German, yoga, fencing. I had signed up for yoga, but I
had yet to actually go.

And none of the clubs started at five in the morning.

But I was awake, and restless, so I decided to get dressed
and take a walk. I wasn't alone enough at Marlwood, I decided.
I was constantly surrounded by other people. Most of the
girls on campus had single rooms, except for Rose, who also
shared with someone. And Alis and Sangeeta, when they
moved into Grose so late in the term. Money bought privacy.
Money bought so much. I thought about Julie's pony, and I
decided then and there that if Mandy had been lying about
Julie's chance to reunite with Pippin, or didn't follow through,
I would kill her.

Then I took it back, and creaked open the front door.
Theoretically, five o'clock still dwelled inside the boundaries
of our official curfew, but no one had been busted for curfew
violation yet, and I doubted anyone ever would. These were
kids who drank wine at home and could wake up the chauf-
feur to take them clubbing at three in the morning. The rules
didn't apply, and probably never would for their entire lives. It
would take more trouble than I was worth to treat me differ-
ently, even though I was "different."

I put on my new army jacket because suddenly, with the turn
of the calendar page, it was bitterly, bitingly cold. I could smell
winter in the air, even though, in San Diego, I had never seen
snow on the ground except in Julian, high in the mountains.

I walked past the quad as the sky turned from gray to pink,
hands in my pockets, wondering if I'd been right in the first
place. I didn't belong here, and I never would. But I didn't

want to go home, where I had completely messed up my life. This was my chance to start over.

Soon I was on the blacktop road that led to the lake. I remembered that Troy said there was a little inlet where they tied up their stolen rowboats, and I decided to look for it. The boat of Mandy's Troy.

People were not possessions. They didn't just *belong* to another person.

Birds were chirping by then, and fog coated the lake like whipped cream. I replayed my brief, sweet moments with Troy, and I wondered again why on earth he was with Mandy Winters. And if he ever thought about *not* being with her.

As I walked off the path and onto the granular dirt, I heard a voice. At first, I couldn't register whose voice it was, although I was disappointed that I wasn't alone. But then I realized it was Mandy.

*Oh my God, is she saying goodbye to him? Did Troy spend the night?*

I moved quietly to my right, where a straggly line of large boulders would give me some cover. I was spying on her again. I didn't care. I minced behind the first boulder, then the second, careful not to disturb the little pebbles beneath my hightops. I poked my head out just as a large black bird shot out of the fog with a squawk. I jumped, startled, and whipped my gaze toward Mandy, to see if she had heard me.

Surrounded by rushes, the shoreline curved into a small cul-de-sac—an inlet. Mandy stood beside a white metal sign on a gray pole, which said NO TRESPASSING in chipped black letters. Dressed in a black sweater and black jeans, she had on a black parka, and over that, the beaded shawl Ms. Meyerson had worn in her role as the Gypsy fortune-teller at the Jessel haunted house. She looked old-fashioned, like her house.

There was no rowboat, at least that I could see. Mandy was alone. She was leaning forward with her face tipped down as if she were looking for something among the rushes, or in the water. Her white-blonde hair hung over her shoulders in ripples, very pretty, and nothing I could ever aspire to.

I crept behind the third boulder, which brought me closer to Mandy. I was nervous. I ran through some potential reasons to explain why I was hiding behind a rock at five-thirty in the morning, but really, what was the point? Mandy and I would both know the score.

I craned my neck slightly forward, all the better to eavesdrop. Despite my fluttery anxiety, I had no shame. Mandy was the enemy, and if I could get something on her, that'd be nothing but good.

"Well, I am disappointed, sweet bee," she said, in a slight Southern accent. "You promised me. I thought last night would go better. Here we're already into November, and you don't have enough. Only four."

I frowned. Who was she talking to? Did she have cell phone reception? Was Troy in the lake?

"She's gonna come out sooner or later, and when she does, we need to be ready," she went on, in the same singsong voice.

There was a long pause. I had a crick in my neck and I was cold. Wind blew across the lake, shifting the fog, wrapping around her like fingers. I heard a plop, followed by another one. One or two more. Mandy was dropping something into the lake.

"I'm sorry," Mandy said, in her normal tone of voice. "I'm trying."

"If y'all don't keep up *your* end of the bargain, honey, I'm not sure I can give you what you want," she said, going Southern again.

"Oh, no, you have to. You promised," Mandy pleaded—with herself, it seemed. Whoa. "You promised to get him out of there. It's hell for him. They're the crazy ones. You . . . well, you know what it's like. It's like it was here."

"Not by half," she said in her Southern voice, her tone stony, angry. "You haven't got the first notion what it was like."

"That place is not helping him. It's killing him. If anything ever happened to him . . . I'd die without Miles. I would."

"No man is worth dyin' over, honey," she answered herself. "Not even him."

"You don't know him. Miles is, he's . . . Oh God . . . he looks out for me. Makes sure no one . . . "

Was she *crying*? Over her brother? I was seriously weirded out. If this was a mental breakdown . . . *Talk about stress* . . . I couldn't wait to tell Julie. Who would probably not believe me, because at the moment, I was having trouble believing it myself.

Maybe she was practicing for a prank.

Practicing crying. Hard. In the freezing-ass cold, beside Searle Lake, with me spying on her. The whole thing was so bizarre that I began to wonder if I was dreaming again. I half-expected Julie to shake me gently to wake me up.

"*Please*," Mandy said brokenly. "You said you'd help us."

There was no answer, by which I mean that she didn't

answer herself. *Mandy Winters is schizo*, I thought, trying it out. *She's nuts. Or she went nuts. That's why they sent her here.*

No one had been able to confirm the Lincoln Bedroom story, but after all that netsurfing, I was well acquainted with the Winters' high-powered lifestyle—an endless round of charity bashes and fancy parties. I had gaped at the clothes, the cars, the celebs and VIPs—I was willing to bet her rich, powerful parents could bury any kind of scandal—lock their drug-addict son up and send their crazy daughter out of town. What if she went bonkers again and did something to put us all in danger?

*No way.* I remembered my mom discussing Hillary Clinton. Hillary had held imaginary conversations with Eleanor Roosevelt, to help herself think through important political issues. What was prayer, but talking to someone else about your problems? And Mandy . . . talking to herself in a Southern accent? About having four of something?

More birds rose from the lake, squeeing and cawing. The fog started to boil away. The crick in my neck became a throbbing ache; I was chilled to the bone, and my stomach was in danger of growling. I hoped Mandy was done, but she slid down to her knees and leaned forward on her hands, gazing into the lake. Staring at something.

I was willing to bet it wasn't Eleanor Roosevelt. She had told us there was a ghost in the lake. Maybe she looked exactly like Mandy Winters' reflection.

The silence stretched on. Rushes surrounding the inlet made papery sounds in the wind. My cheeks stung with chill, and my mind was starting to travel down the yellow brick road of what-ifs. The Jessel haunted house was spectacular; she probably had leftover special effects seeded all over campus, like land mines, to scare us and make us do weird stuff because . . . why?

"You're the only one who knows what's going on, sugar. Keep it that way," Southern Mandy ordered Regular Mandy.

"Okay," Regular Mandy replied. "But you'll . . . you'll make it happen, right? You'll get him out?" Her voice was so low I could barely make out the words.

There was no answer. Mandy leaned farther over the lake. *"Right?"*

Her voice echoed off the lake—*right, right, right?* I tipped back my head, not listening to my protesting neck muscles—to see if by chance anyone had climbed down onto the cliff to see what was up with Mandy. There was no one else there.

Then she got to her feet and whirled around so fast I thought she'd seen me. I caught and held my breath, standing as still as I could, clenching my mouth shut so she wouldn't hear my chattering teeth. Her face was blotchy and tear-stained, and she looked younger than I'd ever seen her look. Maybe it was the lack of makeup, or audience. Or maybe it was fear.

Maybe when she and Miles had been busted in the bedroom, she'd lost her mind. Or maybe I was being set up. First, she let it be known that she and her two minions did séances; and then she did pranks about ghosts and haunted houses. And Lara had been working overtime to scare me when we walked back from the lake. And Kiyoko just "happened" to use a bookmark from an occult bookshop to save her place in a story about secret Satan-worshippers. Then, they let me see their black eyes of death and the weird faces. Next, there was that hysterical fit at the party, and now this.

Whatever the case, I was on alert now. I didn't know what I'd do about it, but I sure as hell knew I would make sure my friends—especially Julie—were safe.

# Fifteen

**November 3**

I couldn't believe I had only been at Marlwood for a week. But it was true. And it was time to check in with Dr. Ehrlenbach.

I was terrified. As my long black skirt (my only skirt) flapped against my boots (scuffed, and resistant to polishing), I tugged on the sweater Julie had lent me—it grazed my hips, and not in a fashionable way. I touched my hair. Julie had wrapped it into a chignon and insisted I wear her chandelier jet earrings. And that I put on some lip gloss and, y'know, made an effort.

Then my sweet best friend had kissed me approvingly on the cheek and said, "It'll be fine."

Crunch, crunch, crunch on the gravel; thuddathuddadathudda on the panic-o-meter. My mind raced as I poured over my many infractions: out after curfew, drinking, and I was sure I had screwed up today's test in Spanish. *Mi madre no quiere bailar.* My mother doesn't want to dance. *Mi madre no quiere morir.* My mother doesn't want to die.

At least the project with Kiyoko was on track, even if Kiyoko wasn't. She was a jittery bag of bones. On the upside, working together at Jessel gave me a chance to spy on all of them. Something had shifted; there was tension in the air. Everyone else was usually holed up in Mandy's room.

Mandy looked slightly better than Kiyoko, but not much. Like she wasn't sleeping much, either. Like her drug habit was wearing her down. Or like going crazy really took a lot out of a person. Not that I was one to talk.

I opened the door and saw Ms. Shelley, who nodded at me and said, "Take a seat, please."

And then I saw Rose. She was wearing a plain black jacket, a white shirt, and a short black skirt, tights, and shoes. She looked like a bartender at a catered party. Or a hip inner-city nun. It made me sad to see all her color gone, but I understood why she'd done it. If she'd been summoned to see Ehrlenbach, she must be in trouble.

She was perched on the edge of an L-shaped green leather sofa, beside a table topped with a vase of real fresh flowers. What I at first thought were neat stacks of magazines were actually college catalogs.

"Hey," she said by way of greeting. "Must be that time of the week." I stared at her. "Dude, don't you know I'm the other scholarship student?"

"You *are*?" I hadn't realized there were any other scholarship students. It hadn't even dawned on me to wonder.

"Yes, I are. I have a really high IQ. What's your excuse?"

I actually smiled a little. "Good essay? My dad thinks I'm fulfilling some kind of grant requirement."

Rose recrossed her legs and tugged at her skirt. "Well, then they'll have to keep you. I'm not even a minority or anything. God, I could use a smoke." I nodded, even though smoking was repulsive.

She peered up at the clock hanging above us and let out a slow, shaky breath. "At least I'm missing biology. Today we start on fetal pigs."

"I had it last year," I told her. "I said I had a religious objection to dissecting."

"Oh, shit, why didn't I think of that?" she wailed. The receptionist glared at her and she hunkered forward, grimacing. "I mean golly-gosh-gee-whiz, what a stupid ho I am."

I almost burst out laughing.

"We're probably going to create our own Frankenstein monsters next semester," she went on, pulling back her face in her Ehrlenbach impression. She dropped her voice to a whisper. "Oh my God, could this place be any weirder? Do you know what I did last night? I went to a séance. At Jessel."

I stared at her. "You *did*?"

She nodded. "I was loitering at the door out of the commons, trying to decide if I should go back to get another chocolate chip cookie, y'know, for studying, when Lara and Mandy started to go past me. Then Mandy gave me a long look and asked me what my lucky number is."

"What?"

Rose snickered. "Yeah. So I said, 'Seven.' Even though it's not. I don't have a lucky number. But her eyes widened and the next thing I knew, I was getting invited to Jessel. Lucky me," she added drily.

"I won the lottery, too," I told her. "I'm working on a project with Kiyoko."

"Then you've seen Mandy's weirdatorium."

"No. I've only been downstairs. I haven't even seen Kiyoko's room." I leaned forward, urging her to spill.

"Whoa." She rolled her eyes. "The first thing you see when you walk in is this rotted portrait. She said she found it in that library. *Then*, you see her Ouija board and her books about spirits and hauntings. And that crystal ball from Halloween."

I listened hard. "So . . . what did you guys do?"

"We just hung out," she said.

Ms. Shelley's phone beeped. I was afraid one of us was about to be summoned to Dr. Ehrlenbach's. "Then what?" I pressed.

"It was really stupid. They got out the Ouija board and asked it a bunch of questions, and I could tell that Mandy was moving the little plastic triangle thingy."

"Questions like . . . ?" I prompted.

She waved her hand dismissively but I wanted—needed—details. "You know, like sleepover stuff. 'Are you here, what is your name, how did you die?'"

"And?" Chills ran along my spine.

"It was supposed to be some girl named Gilda who died during an operation." She chuckled at my startled expression. "I know, I heard that ghost story, too. It happened in the operating theater."

"Yeah," I said in a soft voice, shivering as I remembered how I'd felt in that place. The black eyes, Mandy's freakout. Major drugs? Or was there a ghost in there?

She must have mistaken my response as that of a true

believer. "Lindsay, Mandy was *moving* the triangle. She was pranking me and I have to say, I was kind of insulted. It wasn't up to her usual standards. No sound effects, no costumes. I figured it was because I'm a scholarship chick, so she doesn't have to spend a lot of effort on me."

"But why do it at all?" I asked.

"She's bored? She's into numerology? She's crazy?" Rose moved her shoulders. "I'm going with crazy. I think this place is a little beyond her. All these elaborate practical jokes and stuff . . . She always has to be the center of attention, you know? Like when she 'freaked out'"—Rose made air quotes—"at the party in the OT. Then everyone fawns all over her. It's a textbook cry for help. And it's very sad." She smiled at me, not one bit sad herself.

I nodded. "You're right about the crazy part. She's really losing it. I heard her talking to herself."

"Yeah." Rose's eyes widened. "Kiyoko made some comment about that when Mandy went to the bathroom, and I thought Lara was going to hit her. I'm talking serious body-blow."

"Yikes," I said.

"Ms. Cavanaugh, you may go in," Ms. Shelley said.

I nodded and got up, wiping my sweaty palms on my skirt.

"Do you think I should tell . . . you-know-who?" I whispered.

"Debatable," Rose whispered back. "*Mandy* pays tuition. You, not so much."

We shared a look. Rose smiled wanly. Then I walked down the short hall. And there was the statue again. Just like I'd seen on my first day. Edwin Marlwood. He had a very fierce face.

He didn't look like a man who would run a posh girls school. More like a judge for the Salem witch trials.

I knocked. Waited. There was no reply, but Ms. Shelley had told me to go in. So I did.

On an easel inside the office, an architectural sketch of a round building with a canted roof was labeled, WINTERS SPORTS CENTER. Okay, that decision was made. I would not be discussing Mandy Winters with Dr. Ehrlen-stein.

I began to sit down, when I realized that, this time, her desk had something on it . . . a laptop computer and a small, black leather-bound book. Cramped black writing was framed in a yellowed rectangle. I squinted to make out the upside-down words.

*The Science Behind the Lobotomy Procedure*, it read.

*Lobotomy? Yeow.* Darting a glance at the door, I reached forward and flipped the book open, turning it around as I did so.

My heart caught. The first thing I saw was an ink sketch of a skull, the top of its head sectioned into numbers—just like the head that sat on my windowsill. There was a large X across the forehead.

*Separation of the frontal lobes produces a calming effect,* a note read beneath the sketch. *The young women prone to hysteria become biddable.*

"Oh my God," I murmured.

I heard footsteps in the hall. I quickly shut the book and returned it to its original place next to the laptop, and sat down. Dr. Ehrlenbach came in. I looked straight at her, not at the book.

"Lindsay," Dr. Ehrlenbach said, in a professionally cordial way, "how is it going?" Her mouth didn't move. It had to be Botox. I remembered Rose's imitation of her, and nervous giggles threatened to bubble out of me.

"It's going great," I said. "I love . . . I'm enjoying myself."

"I've spoken to some of your professors and you can expect a couple of Bs coming your way. You need to pull those up," she said, and I think she was trying to raise her brows, but they were already quite arched.

I nodded like a bobblehead, sitting there awkwardly in her office, even though I wanted to protest that I had only been there a week. Hardly time to get grades in anything. "Yeah, I mean, yes, I'm doing just that." I smiled too brightly. "Study, study."

"Any concerns? Anything we need to discuss?" She was wearing simple gold earrings and a watch on an expensive leather band. Her nails were buffed. Very elegant and understated. I was mortified by my appearance, even though it was much better than the first time I'd been in there. I shuffled my feet, wondering if I should sit down.

*Yes, yes, yes. We need to discuss the fact that Baby Sports Center is psycho*, I wanted to tell her. *And what's up with that book?*

"Everything's great." I tried to think of intelligent replies, or questions that would illustrate how brilliant and aware I was. The meeting might be some kind of test, a last chance to impress her. But nothing came to mind.

Then I took a breath. I *should* tell her about Mandy. But the architectural drawing was to her immediate left, and I knew that anything I said about Ms. Winters that was negative in the least would seal my fate, not hers. So I pretended to cough.

"Excuse me," I said.

"Marlwood is a very old, very fine school," she said suddenly. "We have a lot to live up to."

"Oh." That surprised me. I felt like I should have known that. "It was a girls school before the Civil War," I said frantically. "I mean, after." I forced myself not to glance at her desk.

"Yes. A fine school." She smiled at me. Maybe. "We have a reputation to maintain."

"Yeah. Yes. Got it," I promised.

She didn't react. Then she pushed back slightly from her desk, indicating I was dismissed.

"Thank you for coming to see me," she said graciously. Ms. Shelley will give you a pass to get you back into class."

I turned to go.

"Lindsay," she said suddenly.

I turned back around.

"I like what you've done with your hair," she said. There was no warmth in her voice, or on her face.

"Thank you," I blurted, and fled.

I came back out just as Rose stood, smoothing her black skirt. I mouthed, *Good luck.*

Then Ms. Shelley gave me my pass, and I had to leave. I didn't know what to think. What was that book doing on her desk? I wished I had had time to check out her laptop . . .

. . . And to read more of that book.

*There's so much more going on here than I can even take in*, I thought. *Secrets and more secrets.*

# sixteen

I spent the rest of the day in knots, rehashing my thirty seconds alone with Dr. Ehrlenbach . . . and wondering about that book . . . and thinking about what Rose had said about Mandy.

"You did fine," Julie kept saying over and over. It was late, and we were both in our pajamas. She sat with her sore leg stretched out on her bed, cradling Caspian, while I paced, ignoring the white head, whose angle had changed again, and the face that might or might not be in Mandy's window. Her drapes were open, and so were ours, but I refused to look in her direction. I just didn't have the nerve. But I needed to have the nerve, if I was going to find out what she was doing. And I needed to know. I knew I wouldn't be able to sleep at night until I figured it out.

Julie continued. "I'm sure she knew how nervous you were."

Julie would be devastated if she knew Rose had been invited to a séance and she hadn't. She'd defend Mandy in a duel to the death if I told her about my—our—suspicions that Mandy was on her way to bonkersville. After all, we were the two scholarship students. What did we know?

*We're outsiders*, I thought. *We're on the outside looking in.*

"Let's go to bed," she said, yawning.

My shoulders sagged dejectedly. "I'm a wreck."

"I have something that will help you sleep. Do you want it?" She was curling Caspian's eyelashes with her fingers.

"It's not anything weird, right? I mean, it's over the counter, or something I could take if I have allergies," I ventured.

She gave me a look. "No, Mandy didn't give it to me."

Mandy, Mandy everywhere. I hadn't even told Julie about the one-sided conversation at the lake. I kept telling myself I didn't know how to go about it, but the truth was, I was afraid she'd tell Mandy. The result being that Mandy would be more careful, and then all future opportunities to find out what was up with her would be lost.

Julie reached into her dresser and rummaged around, then came back with something blue in her hand. "It's mild," she said. "We got them in France. It's very safe. If you want, I'll take one, too."

"You're sure they're the ones you brought with you?"

"Light blue, with a D on them," Julie said, holding it up.

I still hesitated. She popped it into her mouth, dry-swallowing.

"I didn't mean to imply—" But of course I had.

"It's okay," she said.

"So I'd like one," I told her.

She got me another and handed it to me.

"I'm going to get some water," I said.

I went down the hall and flicked on the bathroom light. I looked at the stalls and the row of sinks, the showers and the claw-footed bathtubs. The tubs were so enormous. And there were marks on the rims, as if at one time there had been some kind of fastener or lid that went over each one. Were they the original hot tubs?

The moon glowed on them; I could almost imagine girls lounging in them, chatting.

*Come to me.*

I dropped the pill in a toilet, flushed. I looked at my hands—not at the mirror—and cupped some water. Drank. Left.

Julie was waiting for my return; when I crawled into my bed, she turned off her lamp, throwing the room into moonlit gloom. I thought about getting up to close the curtains, but I could feel myself going soft if not from medication, then exhaustion.

I began to sink into sleep, letting go, floating along as if I were on a river . . . or a lake. Spinning in a slow circle, as the cold water washed over my head . . . as my nightgown weighted me down . . . going deeper . . . down, down . . . and someone was calling my name . . . looking for me . . . if only someone would look down, *look!* into the lake, the black, cold grave of a lake . . .

And I forced myself up from the dregs of the dream, pushing like a drowning woman through the currents and the icy hands that tried to keep me there.

Keep me there.

———

I couldn't sleep after that. I got up and went into our common area and sat in one of the overstuffed nice-hotel-chain chairs, pulling a lap robe around myself, jumping at every creak of the building. The floor moaned and I thought of Julie's ghosts, the ones who walked up and down the halls past all the bad art. Maybe I should have taken Julie's pill after all.

I watched the clock; on school mornings, the early risers got up at seven thirty. I waited, huddled and miserable, checking and rechecking the clock, glancing at the doorway, jerking each time I began to doze off.

The shower went on.

*Finally*, I thought, surprised that I had actually gotten some sleep. I unfolded myself and toddled down the hall back to our room. Quietly, I pressed the latch and pushed it open. Sunlight was beaming into the room, washing away the traces of things that went bump in the shadows.

Julie's arm was thrown across her face, to keep the sun out of her eyes. I walked to her bed, feeling a rush of friend-tenderness, and whispered, "Rise and shine, Jules."

She grunted. "I like Jules. Not yet."

I chuckled and crossed the room to stand at the foot of her bed. I shook the mattress with my knee.

She moaned.

"Come on," I began. "You're going to—"

I stopped when I noticed the pile of thick white material on the side of her bed facing the wall. Frowning, I walked over to it and gathered up a piece. It was thick and there were pieces of a satiny beige fabric mixed in with it.

"Julie," I said.

Something in my voice must have told her I needed her. She pulled back her arm and opened her eyes, looking up at me as I silently showed her what I'd found. She took it from me as I knelt beside her bed. A wad of it hung from beneath the fitted top sheet of her cloud sheets.

I pulled up the sheet.

Four deep gouges ran through the side of her mattress, as if someone had taken some kind of gardening tool and raked it. The stuff I'd found was the innards.

"Look at this," I said.

She leaned over the side of her bed, gasped, and scrabbled off in the opposite direction. Then she limp-hopped around to my side, standing beside me, as together we surveyed the damage.

"Oh God, do we have rats?" She landed hard on my bed and yanked up her feet, groaning as she clutched her injured ankle.

"It's not rats. They did it," I said. "They must have come in here while we were . . . asleep."

"They." She frowned at me.

"Julie. You know it's them. They're hazing you." I gathered up more wadding. "Messing with your head." And possibly escalating the violence, just like Rose said.

Her gaze went from the fluff in my hands to my face and back again. "Are you that desperate to keep me from being friends with her?"

"Julie." I was stunned. "I would never do something like this. Are you kidding? I'm here on scholarship. The last thing I would do is ruin school property for a prank."

She wouldn't look at me.

"Julie, come *on*."

*But you did fall asleep in the common room,* I reminded myself. *Maybe you sleepwalked in here and—did something kind of crazy yourself.*

*I'm not crazy,* I told myself. *I never was. I just had a little breakdown.*

Still, my hands were shaking; and she was scared, too. She stared at the mattress, then glanced at Jessel through our open curtains.

"Okay, maybe she—they did. But it doesn't mean anything. They're just . . . letting me know I'm part of the gang."

"Nice. You could get in trouble for this," I pointed out.

She sniffed. "I have to get ready for breakfast." Looking away, she skirted around me and left the room.

I walked to Julie's window and looked out at Mandy's turret. The curtains were open.

I saw the face. A white oval in the center of the window, with two dark eyes. The mouth was a smaller circle of black.

And it *was* there, right? Or . . . was I losing it? Was I seeing things?

"Hey, Julie," I said, when she came back into the room, toweling her hair. And then I realized I was afraid to ask her. If she didn't see it . . . she might think I'd ripped up her mattress. My best friend. While she was knocked out from her French sleeping pill.

"Yes?" Her voice was clipped, formal.

I looked out the window. "Do you think it's going to rain? Should we take our umbrellas?"

I counted off the seconds before she reacted. She came up beside me. She cocked her head. And then she waved.

I glanced sharply at her. She was looking down. I followed her eyeline. April, our dorm mate, was standing below us in the quad. Dressed in black jogging clothes striped with dark pink, she bounced around in a little circle, then headed toward our front door.

I looked back at the face. *Please, Julie, look*, I pleaded.

"Maybe we'll see what Mandy's going to wear," I said, gesturing to the window. *The face. See the face.*

"You shouldn't spy on her like that," Julie snapped. Then she turned her back and went to her closet, pulling out clothes without another word.

"I didn't do it," I said. "To your mattress, I mean."

"Okay," she replied.

---

**I dressed as fast as I could,** faster than Julie. I stomped to the commons; it was starting to drizzle, and I hadn't brought my umbrella.

I walked in, taking attendance at the various oval tables with dark-green wood chairs. Brass pots spewed green houseplants.

Mandy and the others weren't there yet, but Rose was, getting some coffee. She was wearing brighter colors again—purple, orange, chartreuse.

"Hey," I said. "They . . . *she* . . . is pumping up the volume." I told her what had happened with the mattress. "And Julie thinks *I* did it," I concluded.

"She was knocked out. And you were out of the room." She opened up a little plastic creamer and dumped it in her coffee. There were three such packages on the stainless steel coffee warmer.

"What?" she said when I raised an eyebrow. "I like creamer." She stirred and sipped her coffee, her eyes hooded. "I wonder what they would have done if you'd been in the room."

I made a face. She made one back.

"Plus there was this book on Ehrlenbach's desk," I said. "Did you see it?"

She shook her head. "Wasn't looking."

"It was about lobotomies. And there was a sketch of that head Julie found."

"Lobotomies. Brain surgery. Ehrlen-stein showed it to you?" Rose asked, taking another sip.

"She wasn't in the office when I went in," I replied. "But it was creepy."

"Well, she's creepy," Rose returned. She hesitated. "Are we making more out of this than we should?"

"You should see Julie's mattress," I replied. I thought a minute. "Is there anyone else we can tell?"

"Shayna Maisel, maybe, but she'd probably stomp off to Ehrlenbach. And that would be the end of that." She took another sip. "People like Mandy never get busted. Jeez, if she can have sex with her own brother at the White House . . . "

"We don't know if that's true," I said. "But she *is* really into him. She's freaking out that he's in rehab."

"And she talks to herself like a schizophrenic and destroys school property while girls are sleeping on it." She shivered. "What if she had *hurt* Julie? And blamed you?"

I cared less about the getting-blamed part than the Julie-getting-hurt part.

I sighed. "This sucks."

"Verily." She cocked her head. "You're staying over break, right?"

Of course I was. I had made it clear when I came here that there was no way I was going back to San Diego so soon after escaping.

"I'm staying, too," Rose said. "My parents are so dysfunctional I'd rather stay here."

I knew where she was headed. Rose waited a dramatic beat, and then she grinned and said, "Guess what I have."

"Herpes," I said.

Her face didn't change.

"Shia LaBeouf's phone number."

"Jessel's front door key," she replied slyly.

"No way," I blurted. "How did . . . did you *steal* it?"

She raised her chin with pride. "During the séance. They were so wasted, no one even noticed," she crowed. "I figure once they leave, we can sneak in there and do some investigating. Locate the skeletons. Figure out if Mandy needs to increase her meds."

"They *will* notice," I argued. "Or they'll change the locks or something."

"Nah, there are a bunch of copies. Anyway, I'm willing to

take that chance." She blew on her coffee. "How about you, Lindsay? They snuck into your room and vandalized Julie's mattress. Are you going to stand by and let something else happen?"

My heart pounded. "No, I'm not," I said.

"Good." I reached for her coffee. She let me take it. I raised it in salute, and took a sip. It was mostly creamer.

"We could get in big trouble," she reminded me. Then she smiled grimly. "Expelled, at the very least. Not that I plan on it."

"Still in," I told her.

"Okay, then." She took the coffee back. "Let the countdown begin."

We had seventeen days until Thanksgiving break.

# seventeen

I didn't tell Julie about my nightmare.

Or the one after it.

Or the one after that.

Nearly one every night for the next two weeks. She knew that I wasn't sleeping well, but that was all she knew.

I didn't tell her that I still saw the face—sometimes in the window, sometimes in the bathroom mirror. I didn't tell anyone. I pretended not to see it more often than not.

Mandy invited her over to Jessel nearly every day. The first couple of times, Julie would come back and try to be cool and restrained about what she'd seen over there. From what I could tell, it seemed all Mandy had to do was snap her fingers (via the internet or the landline) and fabulous things made their way up our mountain—such as chocolate madeleines from Knipschildt Chocolatier for $250 apiece.

But it was all vicarious, and precarious—Mandy could cut Julie off at any point. Maybe she knew that; or that was why she stopped talking about it, and got quiet and vague when I asked her what she'd done over there—they'd hung out; they'd watched TV. I tried to look at her eyes without being obvious, to see if she'd taken anything. I felt like her mother.

Then, she told me that Mandy had taken her to the operating theater a few times to see Spider. He and Troy rowed over together and hung out. I was sorry that she hadn't told me right away. That was the kind of thing you told your best friend. Unless there was something you didn't want your best friend to know. I wondered if she had done the deed with Spider. Did I need to give her the birth control lecture? The "he could be using you" lecture? Or would she stuff my mouth full of mattress guts?

No one came forward about the ripped mattress. Julie collected all the stuffing and put it in a plastic bag, which she kept in her underwear drawer.

I wondered if Troy and Mandy did the deed . . . and tried not to wonder. I certainly didn't ask Julie. He had fallen off the radar; no one seemed to remember the way hunky chainsaw guy had batted his lashes at me. No matter. I hadn't seen him since the operating theater, and I doubted I ever would.

Meanwhile, I snuck down to the lake whenever I could. On occasion, Mandy would show, and I could hear her talking to herself in her two voices. But bad weather was rolling in, and most days I couldn't make out the conversation over the rumbling of thunder and heavy wind. The birds were agitated, dipping toward the lake, then swooping back up as if they were afraid to land on it.

Rose and I checked in numerous times. She hadn't been invited back to Jessel since the night of the séance.

"Maybe they figured out I stole their key," she said. But no one had confronted her.

I went over, but I never got to see Mandy's room. I finally did see Kiyoko's palace of wicked-modern Asian sleekness, shiny lacquer and old brass. Not a thing was out of place; she even hung her clothes in the closet according to length, color, and function. And what clothes—made just for her, all of them, by famous designers all over the world.

It sleeted on the seventh day before break. Then it rained for five days in a row after that, and though I braved the downpour every morning to creep down to the lake, Mandy didn't come. Maybe she was done; maybe it was too cold.

The rain came down so heavily that I could no longer see the windows in Jessel. Maybe that was why the face moved into the shower stalls when they were misty with steam. In the cold, blue fluorescent light, bouncing off the tiles and the stainless steel sinks, two black eyes, one O of a mouth . . . that no one else seemed to see. I did ask, cautiously, and the others accused me of trying to scare them.

I remembered what it had felt like back in San Diego, right before I broke down. When I kept asking my "friends" if Riley still liked me. And how they kept telling me that he did. So I told my dorm mates that, yes, I was trying to scare them by asking them about the face in the shower . . . and I stopped looking through the steam as best I could.

Another weird thing happened before Thanksgiving break—our cell phones started working. But only in a few places, and of course, one of them was Jessel. You could stand on Jessel's porch or go inside for a signal. But walk across the quad toward Grose, and you couldn't get through.

Rose was as intrigued as I was by this change in cell phone fortune, even if she laughed so hard she almost wet her pants when Ida put forth the theory that maybe cell phones worked near ghosts. Since Jessel was so haunted and all.

———

**Finally,** it was the day before break, and Jessel invited Grose over for tea. Wisps of snow powdered the waning sunlight, landing on the foreheads of the white horse heads lining the walk. The tea was a formal girly event, so I had broken down and let Julie fix me up. I had on my black wool skirt and one of her tops. She added a wide black beaded belt. Then she dusted my cheekbones and collarbones with gold body glitter; and I gathered my hair into a messy bun that she held in place with beautiful gold enameled barrettes.

She was glammed up, too, in pale pink and white. Sweet, non-threatening.

All eight of us Grose-ites knocked on Jessel's red door, as if we were Christmas caroling—Ida, Claire, April, Leslie, Elvis, Marica, Julie, and me—and it opened to the scent of ginger-bread and the amplified celestial tune of a music box version of "Hark the Herald Angels Sing." Pine swags laden with matte gold balls and cherubs adorned the balcony and the stair rail.

"Ladies," Mandy said. She was wearing a rust-colored satin bubble dress trimmed in gold. Her eyes were swollen, and beneath her expertly-applied makeup, her face had broken out. Stress and more stress.

"Hi," Julie said for all of us. And we all trailed in.

As I passed, Mandy gave me a look. *Oh my God, she knows we're going to break into her house*, I thought. But of course she didn't. There was no way she could know, unless she'd planted bugs on Rose and me. Or she was psychic. Or her Ouija board told her.

I cleared my throat. "Hi,' I said.

Alis, Lara, Sangeeta, and Kiyoko were dressed up, too. I saw some other non-Mandy girls as well. Susi Mateland and Gretchen Cabot. Gretchen smiled at me, then said something to Sienna Thibodaux, who gave me a once-over. I felt myself go chilly. I was embarrassed that I'd even tried to change my image. Then I saw Charlotte Davidson, determinedly goth in an upscale way—black on black on red—and I felt a little better.

"Let me take your jackets," Mandy said, like an actual polite person. There were so many more layers of clothes in Northern California than I was used to.

I heard a ringtone, something vaguely Euro-pop. Mandy caught her breath. Her eyes lit up. With a squeal, she said, "My brother. Excuse me," and yanked a wafer-thin phone out of a pocket in her dress. She popped it open, scanned, and laughed. Color rose up her neck and fanned across her cheeks. Before I realized what she was doing, she swept beside me and took a picture of us together.

A second ringtone indicated an actual incoming call. Mandy connected, listened, and said, "You're a pig." Then she laughed and held the phone out to me. There was something odd in her expression, more strain around her eyes. She looked bad.

"My brother wants to talk to you," she informed me. "His name is Miles. Be very nice to him."

*Oh my God*, I thought. I was actually going to speak to her infamous brother.

"Miles," I said, into the phone.

"Wow," he replied. His voice was very deep and husky. Sexy. "You wore black to my sister's frou-frou tea party. You are very, very bad. Be glad I'm locked up."

"Why, what would you do?" I asked, and he chuckled.

There was a pause, then a puff of air. He was smoking. "Let's just say I'm protective of my little sis."

"Uh," I said, at a loss for words. Was he threatening me?

"So . . . I like people to be nice to her. I don't like it when they're . . . not nice. Are you being naughty or nice?"

"Say bye," Mandy told me, with an edge to her voice.

"I have to go," I said into the phone.

"Parting is such sweet sorrow," he replied. "And . . . " He lowered his voice. "My bet's on *naughty*."

I didn't answer. I didn't know what to say. Shaken, I handed Mandy the phone, and she broke into a grin as she put the phone to her ear, half-turning.

"No," she said, sliding a glance at me. "No, no, no, you are a thing of evil." She laughed and put her hand to her hair. "All right. Love you too."

She snapped the phone shut. Smiled. At me. Then she said, "Miles would just *kill* anyone who was mean to me, you know."

A chill skittered up my spine. I had the distinct feeling that she wasn't kidding. Maybe he wasn't in rehab at all. Maybe he was in jail . . . for murder.

*Stop it*, I chided myself. *Don't fall into drama mode.*

Julie glided over to me with an extra brownie on a rust-colored cloth napkin that matched Mandy's dress. I took it.

"That was Miles," I said, fishing for a reaction. Maybe Mandy had discussed the exact nature of their relationship with her.

"He's so funny," Julie said.

My alarm bells went off. "You've met him?"

"Only talked to him. But Mandy says I'll meet him someday."

"Oh." I smiled weakly at her, but I didn't like the idea of her getting anywhere near Miles Winters. And I felt bad, not telling her what I was up to. "Let's get tea."

"Spider and I are texting," she said, showing me her cell phone. Sure enough, Spider had plastered emoticons all over the faceplate. She was all blushy and giggly. "I think he's going to come see me during break."

"That's nice," I said, and I meant it. Though I was a little sad, too. Julie's relationship with Spider was happening so fast, and I was missing it all.

Kiyoko and Sangeeta were standing like proper hostesses behind a table that had been set perpendicular to the fireplace. Kiyoko's face was shrunken, gaunt. There were hollows under her eyes, and her cheeks were cavernous. The table was stocked with teacups and little finger sandwiches, but I sincerely doubted Kiyoko would be eating any of them.

The fire was low and pleasant, and the mantelpiece had been decorated for the holidays. Two white porcelain pots of trailing ivy bookended a cluster of ornate wooden picture frames.

I stepped closer to the mantel and looked at the brown-and-white photographs, three of the same girl, and one of a trio of girls dressed in black high-necked gowns and light pinafores, like maids.

The three were seated on a settee holding hands with each other. The one who sat in the middle had long, flowing hair crowned with wildflowers, and she was smiling at the camera, her head tilted to the left. Flirting. She reminded me of Mandy. To her left, a chubby girl had two braids looped around her ears, then twisted into a little crown on top of her head. The other one a long braid, like Julie sometimes wore her hair, held in place by an oversized bow.

I gazed into the steely eyes of the lone girl, who looked more grown-up than the others in a dark, high-collared dress of lace over a sheeny, solid fabric. The long sleeves encased her arms, and the outfit looked tight and uncomfortable. Her light hair was slicked back in a bun. The skin on her face looked stretched, and her ears stuck out. She was wearing jet bead earrings. A large cameo was pinned to the high collar. It was so big it would have made it difficult for her to lower her chin.

I couldn't imagine having to wear anything like that; she was probably imprisoned inside a lace-up corset, too. Her gloved hands were clenched at her sides. She looked like she wanted to scream in each of the three pictures, each one so similar to the others that at first I thought they were duplicates. But in one she held a single rose in her fist, and in another, she had a death grip on a Bible.

"Are these relatives of someone?" I asked Kiyoko.

"We think they lived here," Sangeeta replied. "We found a lot of old pictures in the attic. There was an old trunk. The workmen must have found it and left it there."

Lara took over. "Actually, there is no 'we.' Mandy found the trunk. Before your time, Sangeeta." She shot laser beams at Sangeeta, who swallowed, crestfallen.

"Well, they're very interesting," Julie chirruped. "They tie in with your decorating." She smiled at Sangeeta. "Are you going anywhere special for the break?"

"Mumbai, maybe," Sangeeta said, regaining her composure. "We'll see."

"I'd love to go to India," Julie said.

We moved on. Ms. Meyerson leaned out of the kitchen and waved at us.

Once we were out of earshot, I said to Julie, "That was fun."

"Lara is a bitch," she murmured under her breath. "I think she's in love with Mandy in a gay way. She hates Troy."

Then I felt someone watching me, and turned my head. It was Kiyoko. She walked to the panorama window and looked at me again. She wanted me to go outside?

Just then, Elvis came up to Julie and said, "We need you to settle a bet." She glanced at me apologetically and added, "It's a horse thing."

"Go, go," I urged Julie.

Kiyoko was walking into the kitchen. I sauntered after her.

Kiyoko took the side door; I did, too; and we walked out of the kitchen, into falling snow. I halted, admiring it, snow in November. Then she hurried me through the gate to the other side of the privet hedge. We didn't have on jackets, and she was so incredibly thin I half-expected her bones to snap when she began to shiver.

"I need to talk to you," she said, glancing at the house. She moved us farther away, so that I could see the empty window above the kitchen. Her teeth were chattering and she rubbed her hands.

I looked at those hands. Her once-perfect French manicure was a thing of the past. Her nails were ragged, the cuticles bleeding.

"Do you want to go on a walk?" I asked her. "Or over to Grose?"

"No." She stuffed her hands into her armpits and hunched. Then she looked at me, hard. "Something is going on. Something's not right."

"Something . . ." I said slowly. "Something like . . . ?"

"I heard noises in our attic last night. And I went up there . . ." She licked her lips. "It was scary. I don't know how to describe it, except that I didn't want to stay in there. I had to leave."

*Where Mandy found a trunk.* I nodded and opened my mouth to say something, but she rushed on.

"When I came back from the attic, I heard Mandy talking in her room. I thought she was talking to Lara or Alis, but she was talking to *herself.* Only, in another voice. And she was laughing. And she said something about her luck changing. That things were going to start moving fast."

*Oh my God. Wait until I tell Rose*, I thought.

"Do you know what she's talking about?" I asked.

Kiyoko shook her head. Her face was pale. Her eyes darted left, right, and she leaned toward me. "Have *you* ever heard her say anything like that?"

I leaned toward her and said, "As a matter of fact . . . "

She crooked her neck, as if to catch every syllable I was about to share. And something stopped me. I looked into her ashen, hungry face and it was almost like an actual voice inside my head warning me, *Don't trust her.*

"As a matter of fact," I said, "I haven't." It was clumsy. But I stuck to it, clamping my mouth shut.

Her forehead creased. Then she looked me straight in the eye and pulled up the corners of her mouth, as if she really did want to smile, but couldn't quite force herself to. I was fascinated, trying to figure out where she was going emotionally—and what part of it was real.

"It's okay to tell me," she said, in a low, confidential tone of voice. "It'll stay between us."

Uh-huh. I had almost forgotten that Kiyoko was a Mandy-minion first, and my project partner second. We'd worked well together, and we'd gotten a great grade. Maybe at another school, we could have become real friends.

"What did Mandy say?" I asked her, throwing her loyalty back in her face. "I assume you asked her about talking to herself?"

Kiyoko gave her head a little shake. "She said she was on the phone to her brother." She took a breath. "And then she asked me why I was spying on her."

I waited. Kiyoko's eyes welled. "Lindsay, everyone says Jessel is haunted. And then this morning, when Mandy decorated our mantel for the party, I think I heard her *talking to the pictures.* And she called one of them Gilda."

She shivered harder. I could practically hear her bones cracking. "We contacted Gilda the other night using our Ouija board. When Rose was over here. Maybe Rose mentioned it?"

*Oh my God, I'm getting the low-rent prank treatment, too, just like Rose,* I thought. Or maybe this was just the warm up. Kiyoko knew I was staying here over break. Everyone did. I was ripe for terror and humiliation. Maybe if I played along, Kiyoko would throw out some hints—planted or accidental— about what I could expect. If anything. Maybe Kiyoko was truly scared—an unknowing pawn.

"Kiyoko," I said kindly, "maybe she was pranking *you.*"

"I thought of that." She took a deep breath. "I . . . sometimes I blank out, and it's like I'm almost awake, or . . . or aware, or . . . " She looked down. "Plus, I had a horrible nightmare last night."

That pricked my interest. "You did? What about?"

She stared down at her fancy matte bronze high heels. In the snow. "I don't remember."

I hesitated. "Do you guys do drugs?"

"No!" She looked horrified.

"Do you ever slip things into our drinks?"

"No way, Lindsay. That would be so horrible." She licked her lips. "But we . . . "

She blanched, and whatever she said was lost as I glanced

back up at the window over the kitchen and saw Mandy framed in the dying light. She was watching us. Kiyoko saw her, too.

"You what?" I pushed.

"We should go in," she said.

"Kiyoko . . ."

"Forget it." She lifted her thumb to her mouth, realized what she was doing, and covered her hand with her other hand. Then she turned on her heel and practically ran from me.

"Kiyoko," I called after her. She stopped, but didn't face me.

"At least . . . try to calm down and eat something," I said. "Please." It wasn't at all what I had planned to say. It sounded stupid.

But she bobbed her head once before she went into the house. I looked up at the window where Mandy had been standing. She was gone. But the white face with the black eyes was there in her place.

"You're a trick," I said, as I looked down, and away. Glanced back up, and the hair on the back of my neck stood straight up. Its lips were moving, and it was staring down at me.

*Special effects,* I told myself. *Nothing real.*

But as I headed for the kitchen door, I felt that awful coldness on the back of my neck again. I clapped my hand down and . . .

*Did I feel someone's hand beneath mine?*

I whimpered and whirled around. There was nothing there.

"Of course. There never is," I said aloud. "But it's still a trick."

And just like in the operating theater, I was frozen. I couldn't move. I was so afraid. Something washed over me, cold and terrifying, and suddenly I wanted more than anything to go home and stay home and never come back here.

# eighteen

**November 20**

Rain was washing away the snow when Julie's parents pulled into the lot and her strapping older brother hoisted her suitcases and boxes into the gigantic trunk of their Mercedes station wagon. The Statins were very nice people. Beneath umbrellas, they thanked me for taking care of their girl during her first semester at a boarding school.

"She's told us so much about you," Julie's mother said, beaming.

"I'm a keeper," I joshed, and then Julie darted forward on her crutches and hugged me. In the wake of parting, she had forgotten her anger toward me.

"I'll miss you this week," she said. "Hang around Jessel and I'll text you."

"Okay, I will," I promised. I would be hanging around Jessel a lot. Then whispering, I added, "Keep me posted on Spider."

She giggled, then bounded over to the car like a happy-go-lucky, beloved little girl. Her father took her crutches as she slid in and her brother put them in the trunk. All the Statins waved at me as I stood beneath my umbrella, and they joined the departing parade of luxury vehicles as the rainy sky grew darker, and darker, and darker.

The lights winked on in the admin building as I turned and headed back toward Grose. Through the drizzle the horse heads stared blankly at me, holding their chains in their mouths.

*Did one clank?*

*Clank like the chain of a ghost?*

I chuckled aloud at my jumpiness to show that I wasn't really scared, and concentrated on other things, like the pungent aroma of dinner: in the commons, to be served in less than an hour. Rose would be there. If I trotted onto Jessel's porch, I could text her. But as I walked along, the rain turned into hail, pelting me with painful stones of ice, and I ducked into Grose, which was closer.

I shut the door and leaned against it, listening to the *tick-tick-tick* on the roof two stories above me and the *snick-snick-snick* against the windows. The howl of a gust of wind rattled the door as if someone were trying to get in.

"At least she took that stupid head with her," I said aloud. I had watched her pack it myself, in a cardboard box we scrounged from the commons recyclables. She'd surrounded it with socks and underwear.

Ms. Krige was in the kitchen. Christmas carols played on the music system in the common room. I listened for a few seconds, reminding myself that I wasn't alone.

*We weren't alone when someone tore up Julie's mattress, either.*

She still hadn't told Ms. Krige about it, and I thought that was a mistake. If anything happened to *my* mattress, I was going to raise holy hell. I was not a victim, not a wimp. I had never been either of those things, and I wasn't going to start now.

*Tick-tick-tick, snick-snick-snick.*

And the wind blew against the door again.

Snorting, I walked through the gloom of our hallway and opened the door to our room.

The white head sat on Julie's windowsill, hollow-eyed and blank, and staring at me.

# nineteen

I blasted out of Grose and raced through the wet to Jessel's front porch, punching in Julie's cell phone number as I went.

"Hello?" Julie said.

"The. Head," I managed. I was panting.

"Oh, you're so sweet," she said, and I didn't even register her explanation of what it was doing in our room until after she had said it: she was worried that her mom would make her throw it out or that one of her brothers would take it, so she had left it with me for safekeeping. Of course, she had no idea how afraid of it I was. "So I left it."

*God, God, God, God,* I thought, shutting my eyes.

She fuzzed out; I figured they were hitting a dead spot and I waited for about a minute. Then I gave up and disconnected.

Sheltered from the hail, I stood on the porch and looked down at Jessel's doorknob. I wasn't sure who was still in Jessel. Girls had been leaving in a steady stream all day. The coast was not yet clear for sneaking in.

I moved off the porch and lifted up my sweatshirt hood because I hadn't brought my umbrella. Then I stared out over the blackened rooftop silhouettes of Marlwood. The rain had turned to snow and it made me feel claustrophobic; I had the thought that it would fall and fall until it filled up our bowl of a campus and smothered us all.

I had the landline for Rose's dorm, and I punched it in. Rose was my ally, my fellow lifeguard. Hearing her voice would help me stay afloat.

"Stewart." That was Kim, another girl who lived there.

"Is Rose there?"

"She's in her room. There's a Do Not Disturb sign on her door," Kim said.

"Oh." I hadn't expected that. "Thanks. This is Lindsay," I added.

"We're going to watch a movie after dinner. You can come over if you want."

"Thanks." I was already racing through the snow.

---

**I went** to Stewart and knocked on Rose's door. I opened it slightly. We didn't have locks on our doors at Marlwood.

"Rose?" I whispered.

"Lindsay, I'm sick," she grunted.

I crept into her room. It smelled like incense. A nightlight was on and Rose was a big lump in her bed. There was a poster from Cirque du Soleil in a wooden red frame over her bed. There were a lot of signatures on it.

"Sick like how?" I asked, bending over her. It frightened me that I couldn't see her face. I half-expected her to pull her coverlet back and I would see . . .

She threw back her covers. It was Rose. Her eyes were normal, but her face was swollen. "I think I'm having an allergic reaction."

"To what?"

"I don't know."

"Or Mandy put the whammy on you."

She chuckled wanly. "I thought of that. But get this: it's most likely because they just changed the brand of creamer they use in the commons."

"*What?*"

She actually laughed. "I went to the infirmary and that's what Dr. Steinberg said. Can you believe it? So I took some allergy stuff and it's making me sleepy."

"Oh."

"But I won't be sleepy tomorrow, I promise."

A beat. "So you think we should do it that soon?"

She hesitated, too. "Let's see how it plays."

"Okay."

"No offense, but I want to go back to sleep."

"Got it," I said.

I went back out to watch the movie with the other Stewart girls, but I realized I would have to walk back to Grose in the dark if I finished it, so I left. The wind blew snow in my face. The horse heads stared and rattled their chains.

I was cold, and tired, and scared.

---

*See on the model.*
*The center of the forehead.*
*Section number seven.*
*Try it on Number One.*
*Tomorrow.*
*Skip the back of the neck.*
*It causes too much damage.*

---

**I bolted upright.** I was panting and covered in sweat in the grayish darkness of my room. I avoided the head as I looked over at Julie's empty bed. She had taken Caspian with her. Taken him and left me the head.

The room was freezing. I stepped onto the floor in thick wool socks and fished for my bathrobe from my wadded covers. The head was a blur of white in my peripheral vision; before I knew what I was doing, I looked at it straight on. The forehead was not one of the numbered sections. There was no big X on it, like there was in Dr. Ehrlenbach's little black notebook.

A pain shot across my own forehead. I started to pant again. Oh God, oh God, I was losing it. I was having a panic attack. I had to stop it.

*Give yourself some air.* That was what Dr. Yaeger had taught me. If you filled your lungs with air, you would cut down the adrenaline.

I dropped my bathrobe and stripped off my pajamas, threw on a jog bra and sweats. Slipped on my athletic shoes and grabbed my army jacket. My cell phone was in the pocket. I had stashed the digital camera Jason had given me in the same pocket, and I unwrapped a stick of sugarless cinnamon gum and popped into my mouth.

I scribbled, "Running" on the little whiteboard beneath the statue of our saint in the lobby and blasted outside, into a frigid, dark morning. Clouds smothered the sky, almost as dark as the lake. They billowed and moved, became shapes, rolled into new shapes.

I didn't look at Jessel as I ran down the hill, then past it, unsure where I was going. I smelled breakfast cooking and wondered how Rose was feeling.

I ran. I had to calm down. God, what a nightmare. That I didn't remember.

I took the nearest hiking trail, which was on an incline, running past more horse heads and drifts of snow frosting brown grass and bushes. I saw my breath, and kept going past walls of pine trees. Their branches hung over the trail; someone needed to cut them back.

I heard the rumble of thunder, and was surprised. Could it rain while it was snowing? The weather here was very different from the weather at home. The birds were cawing like crazy. Maybe the thunder bothered them, too.

My path forked to the right, and I took it. I had a hitch in my side; I was out of shape. I hadn't gone running much while I'd been at Marlwood, and it showed. If I had had to run away from . . . *something* . . .

"Stop it," I whispered to myself. The thunder rumbled again, more faintly, and I listened to the rhythm of my footfalls.

Then I realized that the birds had gone silent. I cocked my head. Not a sound. The world was still, hushed. Holding its breath.

About ten feet ahead, something white and misty drifted across my path, like a wisp of smoke. Chills washed over me as I stopped, tripping over my own feet. Had I just seen a ghost?

"Oh my God," I said aloud. My voice sounded unnaturally loud.

I didn't know what to do. I was afraid to turn around . . .

*Turn my back.*

So I ran kind of sideways, wild to get away, unsure where to go. I crashed through the trees; if I had wanted to hide, I was definitely out of luck.

Then I finally burst through, to find myself on a cliff, looking down on Searle Lake. Black on black on black; but farther out—*was something moving beneath the surface?*

"Boo," said a voice behind me, and I screamed.

# twenty

**My scream** echoed off the mountains as I almost leaped off the cliff, but two strong arms grabbed me around the waist and pulled me backward, against a hard chest.

"God, I'm sorry," Troy said, as I whirled around. "I didn't mean to scare you."

I couldn't speak. I didn't know if I was angry or relieved, or both. I covered my eyes for a second so he wouldn't see my tears, then lowered my shoulders and dropped my hands to my sides.

Troy's hands were still around my waist. He was wearing his Lakewood sweatshirt with the sleeves pushed up to his elbows. It was unzipped; beneath, an oatmeal-colored T-shirt clung to his body, damp with sweat. He was wearing a pair of dark breakaway running pants. A navy blue parka was wrapped around his waist. A dusting of snow frosted his dark brown hair.

"I'm okay, hi," I said. I looked up at him. His blue eyes were focused like lasers on me. His face was broad across the cheekbones, then tapered to an angular chin, where a third dimple created a cleft. It struck me all over again that he was really handsome, like movie-star handsome, and he was still touching me although he really didn't need to.

My adrenaline was spiking again, but in a good way. I could hear the background chatter in my mind convincing me that what I had seen was some mist. Because Troy was here, and there was no such thing as ghosts. Suddenly all of it, from the faces to Mandy, seemed like a bad dream . . . or an equally bad movie.

*Down, Lindsay, down.*

"So . . . do you just *happen* to be stalking me or something?" I asked him.

He grinned mischievously. "I told you, I like to explore around here. To find new and exciting places to hide the bodies." He rubbed his nose. "And . . . Julie told Spider that you were staying over the break."

*What?* I gaped at him.

"I hope you don't mind, but she gave Spider your cell phone number for me. I called you but the reception over here is really bad."

My mind rocketed into fantasyland, punctuated by mini-reminders that he was spoken for. Or not. Maybe they had had a fight. Maybe they had broken up.

*My hair is wet with sweat. I didn't even shower. Oh God.*

I was horrified and exhilarated.

I pulled out my cell phone. I had no bars, so I couldn't tell if I had any messages. It was eight thirty in the morning. Breakfast would be served from nine until ten. It wasn't mandatory.

"So you're just wandering about?" I asked.

"I signed out for the day. Upperclassman. We have more privileges. You will too, I'm betting."

"Cool." I nodded. And then I realized he was looking over my shoulder. I turned.

From where we stood, he had a clear view of the back of Jessel. I saw the forbidden fourth turret, casting a long shadow that reached for the lake.

Then he was looking at me, at me only.

I didn't ask about Mandy. He didn't say anything.

We hiked beside the lake for a while, not talking much. He knew where there were trails, and a couple of times, he walked in front of me to hold back branches. I couldn't take my eyes off his wide shoulders, his double-rock butt. My hormones gyrated out of control. He was incredible, adorable. I hadn't realized how much I'd missed having a boyfriend. Losing Riley had hurt, deeply, in a different way than losing my mom; but where I thought I'd formed a scar, it was still an open wound.

As my euphoria ebbed, I wondered if he knew about Mandy and Miles. Then I wondered if *I* knew about Mandy and Miles.

"I have some trail mix," he said. "And a water bottle."

He wiped off a flat rock with the edge of his parka and spread it out, inviting me to sit. He plopped down beside me and opened his bag of nuts and raisins. Opened his bottle and offered the first sip to me.

I was about to swoon; it was so romantic. Our fingers brushed when he handed me the bag of trail mix, and I worked over-time to keep from reacting. I nibbled, grateful for something to do. He stretched his back and rolled his shoulders. I could smell his cotton-and-sweat scent. His thigh rested so close to mine that I could feel his body heat.

"So, how's the first day of break?" he asked.

"Pretty good," I allowed. "You?"

He grinned at me. "No complaints so far. We have a reading list, though. Homework."

"That sucks."

"That's Lakewood. I'm sure Yale is worse."

"That's your legacy?"

"My father's bribes—I mean donations—are substantial," he drawled. "I thought maybe I'd go overseas instead. But everyone else says, why fight it?"

It boggled me that he had an easy entry to one of the most prestigious universities in the world, and was thinking of not playing that card. It made me like him more.

But why did he like me? He barely knew me.

"My whole life has been pretty much mapped out for me. I'm the rich kid cliché," he continued. "Mandy's father and my father do a lot of business. We've known each other since before we were born."

That would be a hard act to follow.

He looked from the lake to me. "She's under pressure, too. She used to be so happy. Her parents expect a lot. And that brother of hers . . . " He trailed off.

"Not a big fan?" I ventured.

"He's insane," Troy said.

"He's in rehab," I ventured.

He stared at me. "Is *that* what they're calling it this time?"

I waited. He didn't say anything more.

"So . . . it's hard on her. Anyway." He dropped his gaze to the sprinkling of cashews and peanuts in the center of his palm. A well-bred guy like him must have known it wasn't very attractive to discuss Mandy Winters during a . . . whatever this was. Encounter in the woods.

"It's so beautiful here," he said. His chest expanded. "I wish I'd brought my camera."

*Into photography,* my Troy-radar fed into my database.

"I have mine," I remembered suddenly. I fished it out of my pocket and offered it to him.

"Thanks." He examined it. I wondered what he thought—that it was a cheap camera, and he was used to so much better. "Stand there," he directed, gesturing to the cliff. "But don't go too far," he added, smiling that electric smile of his.

"I'm a mess," I protested, remembering how Jane used to drill her followers—including me—on proper "woman etiquette." *Never apologize to boys; never point out your own flaws.*

I smiled. He aimed, depressed the button, and the camera whirred. He studied the picture, and grinned. "Nice," he said.

"Let me see."

"Another one," he insisted. He took it.

I came around and stared into the viewfinder. I was standing with the vast lake behind me. Gack. My crazy hair . . .

"I want to take one of you," I told him.

He hesitated for the merest second, and I wondered if he was afraid he would get busted by Mandy if there were a picture of him on my camera. Maybe this little interlude wasn't so romantic after all. Maybe it was kind of skanky.

Then he seemed to make some kind of decision, and smiled at me as he handed back my camera.

I raised the camera and snapped a quick picture. We looked at it together. Oh, yeah. Very nice.

We walked on, exploring, and I heard myself talking to him. I told him a little bit about my mother, and then, somehow, I was telling him private things I had never shared with anyone, not even Dr. Yaeger.

"My mom and I used to read aloud together. She loved poetry, adored Robert Frost. *'Whose woods these are, I think I know.'* Sometimes she would be overcome, and me, too, and our eyes would well with tears because we were just . . . I don't know. Moved."

Troy listened.

"After my dad married CJ, I was playing the melody line of *Ode to Joy* on my cello and it was so beautiful. My chest was tight. I couldn't remember if Beethoven had gone deaf by the time he wrote it. But I was hearing it. I was alive to hear it. And I started to cry."

He took my hand.

"My stepmom came into the room and saw me crying, and asked me if I was missing my mom. And it wasn't really that. I told her, 'It's just so beautiful it makes me cry.'"

He gave me a squeeze.

"And CJ said, 'Then why do you play it?'"

Troy was silent for a moment. I glanced at him, mortified that I had revealed so much. "TMI," I blurted.

"No. That's why." He ticked his blue eyes my way.

"Why what?" I asked quietly.

"Why I like you. You're... you're real." He stopped walking. "There's so much phoniness in the world. *My* world, anyway." He smiled sadly. Then he shook his head, as if *he* had said too much.

I stared out at the lake, and I saw my past in the inky reflection. I saw myself standing in the hall of my parents' house. I was having a party for Jane; it was her birthday, and people I didn't know were spilling guacamole on our rug and breaking our glasses. I had cleaned up three shattered glasses so far; I'd refused to buy paper cups because Jane thought they were tacky.

I was looking for Riley; Aimee, one of the cheerleaders, said he had a surprise for me. I *knew* he was going to ask me to go to Homecoming with him. As I walked down the hall, I rehearsed my *yes*.

And then I heard...

I heard two people, moaning and giggling and...

They were in my parents' room.

I heard them.

Aimee had come up beside me, making a face. "Oh my God," she'd whispered.

"Who is that? My dad is going to be home any second," I had whispered back.

"Oh." Aimee blanched. "Hey, guys?"

There was a lot of fumbling and whispering and the door had opened...

I shook my head, snapping out of the uncomfortable memory. I reminded myself that Troy had a girlfriend.

Suddenly thunder echoed across the lake; bluish-white lightning crackled directly overhead and the sky cracked open. Ice-cold rain poured down on us like a waterfall. I yelped, and Troy unwrapped his parka and threw it over my head. We raced back into the cover of the trees. A wind rushed by so hard I felt as though I had been slapped. It caught at my hair, my crazy hair.

"Come on," he said, moving to the left, more deeply into the trees. I remembered the mist. *Mist, not a ghost.*

We found shelter beneath a thick tree and stood close together, panting. Troy pulled me close so we could share the parka—it was waterproof, I realized—and as we huddled, I felt his warmth and smelled his skin.

"Stay close," he urged me.

The ground was turning into mud and slippery mats of pine needles. I wondered if Ms. Krige would send the cavalry out for me. I was with a boy. That could not be good. On impulse, I whipped open my phone. I had programmed in the Grose landline number before I'd left San Diego.

To my amazement, I had good reception, and she answered on the second ring.

"Hi, it's Lindsay. I wanted to tell you I'm okay. I'm going to stay put until it stops raining."

"Tell her you're at some dorm," Troy whispered, as I stood in the crook of his arm.

I grimaced. All she had to do was call that dorm's house-mother, and I would be busted.

"I'm at—" I began, and then I froze, as a cold, sick dread clutched at my throat. I recognized the path we were standing on.

I turned my head. The black hulk of the operating theater

peered through the pines as if it were crouched, waiting for us to get closer before it sprang, ripping itself off its foundations and crushing us to death.

"I'm with some girls," I said, and hung up.

"We can go in there," he said, gesturing to the OT. "Wait it out."

The operating theater, where Julie and Mandy hooked up with Spider and him.

Mandy's screams and laughter still echoed in my head from that night. I smelled smoke. And burning meat. I smelled them as surely as I smelled the wet cotton of Troy's sweatshirt.

And he didn't.

*He didn't.*

Or he was pretending he didn't.

Then *his* cell phone rang, and he looked startled. He pulled the phone out of the front pocket of his parka and stared down at it. Then he put it back in his pocket without answering it.

I knew it was Mandy.

And my suspicious mind started connecting dots—I go jogging; Troy jumps out from behind a tree; he leads me to the operating theater; Mandy checks in.

Prank.

I said, "I want to go back to Grose."

His face fell.

"I'm going," I said. My voice shook. I wouldn't let him see me cry, wouldn't admit how devastated I was.

"Okay."

The rain fell, and we half-ran the distance back to Grose. We didn't speak; we were too cold and wet, running too fast.

When we neared Grose, I saw Ms. Krige standing beside the open door in a red-and-black-plaid parka over a pair of black pants, her kind face wrinkled in concern. I turned to Troy, who saw her, too, and we moved out of her line of vision.

"I have to go," I said, searching his face, his blue eyes, for some sense of how things stood between us. I wanted to be wrong.

His eyebrows and lashes were dusted with white crystals. "Lindsay, why . . . ?" But he didn't press. He probably knew why. He licked his lips. "I wasn't taking you there, y'know, for a *quickie* or anything."

I blushed awkwardly.

"I'll text. Or call," he said.

I didn't know what to say. So I didn't say anything. I opened the door and flew into Grose. I was trembling. Nearly weeping.

I smelled hot chocolate, and I knew Ms. Krige was nearby. I didn't want her to ask me what was wrong. "Oh my God," I called, still breathless from our dash across campus, or from what had passed between Troy and me—I wasn't sure. "I am sopping wet."

I listened to my shoes squeaking and squishing on the hardwood floor. I wrenched them off, and my socks, too. Gathering them up, I trotted down the hall, past the kitchen, and into my room.

Swathed in black cashmere lined with white fur, Mandy Winters was sitting on my bed. She smiled pleasantly as I ground to a halt.

"Get caught?" she asked me.

# twenty-one

"Caught. In the rain," she said. She clicked shut her cell phone and leaned back on her hands.

"I thought you'd left," I replied, which bordered on rude and awkward. I set down my shoes, pulled off my socks, and stepped into my slippers. "I have to squeeze these out," I added, as a drop narrowly missed our tapestry rug.

"I'll leave you to that," she said. "I just dropped by on my way to the car." She tilted her chin. "So I passed the time, talking to Miles. He thinks he'll be able to come home soon. For Christmas." There was a small smile on her face.

I glanced around the room, saw nothing out of place. Wondered how long she'd been in here, waiting to pounce. I wished she would take that stupid white head with her.

She saw me looking at it, and smiled. "Do you know what that's for?" She went over and touched her finger to its forehead.

No snarky comeback occurred to me. I shook my head.

"I don't, either," she said.

I knew she was lying. A chill rippled up my spine. Why would she lie?

She got up. I almost took a step back, but I caught myself in time. She gazed hard at me. I held my breath. Something was going to happen. I was about to find out what was going on. I was. Right now.

Then Ms. Krige said from the doorway, "The cocoa's ready, Mandy. Why don't you ask your driver to wait a few more minutes?"

"No. I really need to get going," Mandy said. She brushed past me and went out of my room. "Have a nice break . . . *down*," Mandy whispered as she passed me.

*She knows.* I was speechless. How could she know? No one—

Did Dr. Ehrlenbach know? Had my parents told her?

Oh no. I closed my eyes.

"Lindsay? Cocoa?" Ms. Krige asked sweetly.

---

**My heart was pounding.** My face felt numb.

I was outed. Not even Julie knew about my breakdown.

*So what?* I asked myself. It was practically required to have some kind of issue at Marlwood. Look at Kiyoko. Look at Mandy. And Alis, Sangeeta, and Lara. All of them. The girls with the black eyes.

*Has she been setting me up, all this time? Doing things to scare me so I'd snap?*

That was stupid. Why would she bother? I was nobody.

Then why had Troy come looking for me? Did Mandy know we'd been together in the woods just then? Would she tell Miles? Mandy had said Miles would kill anyone who ever tried to hurt her. So what would he do to Troy if he found out Mandy's hot boyfriend had spent all morning sharing his trail mix with *me*?

"Lindsay, phone," Ms. Krige said, holding the landline portable out to me. I hadn't heard the phone ring, hadn't noticed her go into the kitchen to answer it.

*Troy*, I thought.

"It's Rose," Rose announced. "And I'm feelin' groovy. You want to break into Jessel after dinner?"

*Wait*, I thought. *She conveniently has a key. She's rushing headlong into going in there.*

Was she part of a prank? Or was I totally losing it?

"Oh God," I blurted aloud. Did I actually think there was a giant conspiracy to drive me insane?

"Yes? God here," Rose chirped.

"Nothing. I'll see God at dinner."

"God knows," Rose said cryptically.

We hung up, and I looked across the quad toward Jessel. The drapes in Mandy's room were shut...but I saw a dark oval on the glass. I knew I saw it.

And I trembled as if I had tumbled head-first into the icy blackness of Searle Lake.

---

**We decided** that the first night of break was too soon. I half-expected Mandy to reappear, and bust us flat for breaking and entering, and we agreed we had to be careful. So the next day, we began our recon, sitting in my room and studying Jessel. I made the observation that there might be security cameras we didn't know about. Maybe they had something to do with the improved cell phone reception around the building.

Next we went on a long walk, circling Jessel, then heading down to the lake where we called each other on our cells until we figured out where our signals went weak. Lots of bars along a wide swath of shore, but the best reception was on the grounds of Jessel itself.

Jessel, which was located lower than Grose. I would have expected the opposite effect. Which worried me about going in there.

We watched TV with Ms. Krige that night; then after she went to bed, we sat in the dark, studying Jessel's many windows. The shades were drawn. There was no porch light. Rose had brought a flashlight and some extra clothes with her; she dressed in black, including a black ski mask, which she pulled over her face as soon as we left my dorm. I had on my army jacket and some jeans, my boots. My only concession to stealth was my black knitted cap, pulled tightly over my hair. And my gloves. We both wore those.

We scurried through the slushy wet and made our way silently onto the porch. We both took off our shoes and tied the laces together, and slung them over our shoulders. She unlocked the door. It swung open, no melodramatic creak, no ghostly laughter. No faces. I gazed into the darkened room, seeing nothing but black on black, hearing nothing but our breathing. Jessel was a building. It was bricks and wood and glass.

I walked over the threshold in my stocking feet. Rose shut the door and turned on her flashlight. The hardwood floor was highly waxed and I saw . . . I saw . . . *It's just me*, I thought, flinching at the blurred face in the wood, captured in the filmy glare.

A floorboard creaked. I gasped, and Rose elbowed my side.

"That was me. Jeez. Chill." She cupped her hand over the beam so that only a thin, watery film of light played over the floor. The dimmest outlines of furniture swam in the shadows; it was like being in a shipwreck.

Rose headed for the stairs. I looked up at the balcony, seeing nothing but Christmas decorations—of course—and followed close behind her. Her body heat reassured me.

I looked back over my shoulder once, twice; I thought I saw a sliver of light around the jamb of the front door and tried to remember if I had heard it click shut.

We reached the top of the stairs, our backs to the balcony. Mandy's door was to our right. I had never been in her room, ever.

"It's probably locked," I said.

"No locks at Marlwood," she reminded me.

"But it's *Mandy's* room."

Rose turned the knob and we were in, shoulder to shoulder in the pitch-black. The drapes were closed.

"You're so pessimistic," Rose chided me.

Wordlessly, she swept a low yellow arc. Mandy's incredible room was revealed in blurs and smears of light: the canopy bed, the gilded nightstands, the ornate desk cluttered with gold frames of photographs. Her drapes were damask; I'd never seen them from this side before. She had ropes of necklaces draped one over another like pirate treasure; she'd just left them out. Half-open drawers revealed sweaters and scarves, gloves, knitted hats, a digital camera, another digital camera, an autographed picture of Prince Harry that said *Thank you, Amanda!*

Then Rose's flashlight hit a three-foot-tall portrait of a girl with a deformed face; half her flesh was eaten away. My throat clamped down over a scream. *Picture*, I told my panicking brain. *Damaged picture.*

It was a photograph, tea-colored like the ones on the mantel, and half-covered with mold. The frame it rested in looked like shellacked shredded wheat. The girl's hair was black, and she was wearing a wide-brimmed hat adorned with large feathers and roses. Her eyes were dark and wide, and her chin was tucked in slightly, as if she were gazing at something that frightened her.

As if she had seen a ghost.

I jumped back and Rose snorted.

"That's pretty much what I did. The picture's rotted. It's from the *attic*." She said the word with undisguised eagerness.

The beam hit a faded rectangular cardboard box with OUIJA! COMMUNICATE WITH THE SPIRITS! in faded letters on the top. A cartoon drawing of a scary-looking man with intense, dark eyes glared up at us. He reminded me of the white face with the dark eyes, and I looked away.

"He looks like that Munch painting called *The Scream*," Rose said. "That's the very Ouija board we used to contact Gilda, the spirit Mandy was trying to call up."

The flashlight washed over a tall bookcase. "Let's see . . . *Haunted Houses of Northern California. Demonic Possession. Beyond the Grave.* She's got hobbies, our Mandy." She clicked her teeth. "We could be here all night, you know?"

She was right. And I was beginning to wonder why we were here. What had we hoped to accomplish? To find out "the truth" about Mandy. But what could we find? A bottle of pills marked ILLEGAL DESIGNER DRUG, DILATES PUPILS? MASTER PLAN TO SCARE LINDSAY? Her rocket launcher?

Rose walked toward the center of the room. I followed; her flashlight washed over my stockinged feet like a searchlight.

"Oh ho," she said. She came up to me and dropped to her knees, reaching beneath the satin coverlet over the bed.

She pulled out a dark wood trunk with shiny brass fittings. It made a sliding noise against the wood floor, and I worried about telltale scratches.

*Is it the trunk from the attic?* I wondered.

"Come here," Rose urged, patting the floor. I was afraid to sit; I felt more vulnerable. "No one's here," she insisted.

Remaining standing, I took a breath as she handed me the flashlight and ran her gloved hands along the trunk. She handed me her shoes, too. Then she pushed her finger under the brass lock in the center, and grunted.

"Okay, well," I said. "That's that."

"Hold on." She grinned at me and reached into her pocket, bringing out a small plastic case and flipping it open to reveal several five-or-six-inch-long pieces of black metal that looked like screwdrivers. As I watched, she selected two and crammed one of them into the keyhole.

"What are you doing?" I whispered. But I knew. She was picking the lock.

"I had a boyfriend once," she muttered, by way of explaining how she knew what she was doing.

"You can't. She'll know," I protested.

But it was too late. There was a click.

"Did you break it?" I asked her.

She didn't answer. Instead she lifted the lid. She put the tools back in her plastic case and handed that to me, too. I didn't want to take them.

*Julie*, I reminded myself. *I'm doing this for her. And, maybe, for Kiyoko, too.*

The first thing on top was a piece of silky white material, and then another one . . . I realized they were underwear . . . and then Rose whistled, and when I saw what else was in the trunk, my mouth dropped open in shock.

# twenty-two

**Inside was a photograph** of Mandy and a guy who looked almost exactly like her, only older—white-blond hair, dark blue eyes, and the same slightly cruel smile. He had to be Miles. She had on a fire engine-red bikini, and he was wearing slim boardshorts that left very little to the imagination. Their arms were coiled around each other, and her boobs were pressed against his chest.

"Houston, we have liftoff." Rose handed me another photograph. This one was of the guy only, lounging in a pair of baggy pajama bottoms, smiling seductively at the camera. "Holy moly, who took these?"

Another picture: Miles standing behind Mandy, with his arms around her.

And then *another* one of them . . . kissing, eyes closed, in ecstasy. Mandy and Miles were kissing each other in a rumpled four-poster bed. There were handcuffs on the poster above her head.

*Oh my God, what if it's the Lincoln Bedroom?*

"Maybe it's an automatic," she said. "Camera, I mean." Then she started laughing. I just stared. She went through the rest as I watched. "The rest are more of the same," she muttered, disappointed. Then she put them back, in the order in which we'd taken them out, and laid the underwear back on top. She clicked the lock shut. Did something. Tested it. Smiled at me.

"It's not broken?" I asked.

She pushed the trunk back under the bed. "She'll never know," she promised me.

She turned to me with glittering eyes. "You mentioned something about the attic. Several times."

"But—"

"Come on."

We left Mandy's room. The air felt thick as mud as we tip-toed to the balcony in the darkness. I scanned for the front door, detecting a matte grayishness that I guessed might be the leaded window in the door. Then we turned around and faced the hall, where Kiyoko's and Lara's rooms were located. Sangeeta and Alis shared on the other side of the hall.

We went down the hall. The doors were closed, and Rose slowed down, gazing at me with an impish grin.

"I wonder what we would find in Lara's room," she said. "Or Kiyoko's."

I was beginning to move from nervous to panicky. Ms. Krige might check on us. Rose's housemother might give her a call.

"Let's go," I said. "Let's come back later."

"Don't be such a wuss. We have to at least check the attic," she insisted.

"Then let's do it fast."

Rose charged noisily down the hall. I wanted to hit her. She stopped at the last door on the right, and turned to me.

"This is the turret room no one can go into," she said, rattling the door. "And, hoohoowahaha, it *is* locked."

She put the flashlight under her chin. "Good evening, mortals. Beyond this door, we have . . . vampires, dreaming of succulent virgins. Such sad dreams. Because there aren't any virgins at Marlwood."

*Speak for yourself*, I wanted to say.

I thought about the books I'd seen back during that prank in the old library. The rumors that Marlwood had never been a girl's prep school in the past, but an asylum, a reformatory for "wayward" girls. What did "wayward" even mean? And why was that book on Dr. Ehrlenbach's desk?

"So...we'll pick it," Rose said. She reached into her pocket and pulled out her tools. Then she bent over and examined the door. "Huh. Let's see..." She traced the keyhole with her fingers and glanced back at her kit. "This stuff won't work on that."

I felt unaccountably relieved. I didn't know why. Of course I was curious to see what was in there. Just...not tonight.

"Well, poop," she groused. Then she shrugged and guided me to the left, and we sailed around a corner to a narrow set of wooden stairs beneath a low, angular ceiling.

"I'm betting these were for servants," she said, as she headed up. "Or mad scientists, wahaha."

"Anorexic mad scientists," I said, trying to bolster my courage with my usual snarky jokes. My shoulders brushed the walls and my feet hit the hollow, uncarpeted stairs, creating echoes. I was glad we had taken off our boots. The sloping ceiling overhead made me feel claustrophobic.

"Third floor, coming up," Rose sang as we looped around and continued up. She was enjoying every moment of this. I was terrified.

The flight of stairs ended at a plain wooden door. There were scratches down one side of it that reminded me of the cuts in Julie's mattress. I tried to swallow, but my throat was too tight.

"Here we go. The door at the top of the stairs," Rose said, smiling evilly at me as she put her hand on the knob.

*Let it be locked*, I thought, but as with Mandy's room, it opened on the first try.

I had a moment where I thought about turning back, but Rose entered and fanned her flashlight beam. All I saw were bright white plaster walls, brick floors, and an assortment of cardboard boxes. Very mundane. Very normal.

"Okay, let's see what there is to see," Rose said.

I walked inside. Then I felt the familiar sharp iciness inside my skull, as if someone had replaced my brain with a block of ice. It hurt; I staggered over to the far wall with the intention of leaning against it. But my knees gave way and I fell forward, hands outstretched, and slammed against a pile of boxes, which hit the wall.

"Lindsay!" Rose cried.

The plaster gave way; the flimsy board beneath cracked, and I fell face first into a space behind the original wall. I landed hard on my palms—I heard myself shout as the bottom section of the wall remained intact, catching me in the ribs.

Rose dropped to her knees beside me, gathering up my hair and going nose to nose with me. "Jesus, are you all right?"

"What is *that*?" I asked, grunting.

A little bit of light streamed in; I saw a hulking shape deeper in the crawl space or secret room or whatever it was. It was narrow in there, like a hallway, as narrow as the stairs had been. It took me a moment to realize that the shape within it was the silhouette of an old-fashioned wheelchair—a regular wood chair with a slatted headrest attached, and two long planks for someone's legs. Two shorter planks were angled to create footrests. The wheels wore a sheen of rust, and it was swaddled in cobwebs.

"Holy crap," Rose said.

She helped me to my feet, and threw down my boots. I stepped into them without lacing them; she did the same, and we both stepped over the jagged lip of the wall and minced toward the wheelchair. Sections of yellow-tinged wood peeked beneath streaks of dust—streaks that looked as if someone had recently tried to clean the chair with a sweep of the hand. But how? It had been on the other side of a *wall*.

"I'm seriously freaking," Rose reported.

I reached out a hand against the wall as a spasm of pain rolled through my stomach. Sweat broke out across my forehead, and my lips and fingertips tingled.

"Rose, I'm sick," I whispered.

"Here, sit down." Rose plopped me into the wheelchair. "Let's check it out."

"No," I protested, but I needed to sit down. I felt dizzy, and gripped my hands in my lap as Rose began to move the wheelchair forward, into the depths of the space behind the false wall. Where was she taking me? I tried to stand up but felt weak, disoriented, the room spinning.

She angled the flashlight down over my head. The floor was filthy, littered with mouse droppings and dust bunnies. Cobwebs draped from one side of the tunnel to the other, like party bunting. It was getting colder. I wanted to tell her to let me out of the chair, or use the flashlight to clear away the cobwebs, but I couldn't speak. Suddenly, my head bobbed forward, brushing my chest.

"This is so freaky," she whispered.

I didn't hear another word she said. My stomach clenched so badly that I moaned; I tried to lift my hands out of my lap to wipe the sweat off my forehead but I was paralyzed.

Words echoed off the filthy walls: *Strap down Number One. Get the ice pick.* It was a man's voice.

I thought I knew that voice.

"No," I murmured. "We didn't do anything."

"What?" Rose said.

My eyes slowly opened. Rose was bending over me; she'd pulled me backward in the chair, and we were back where we'd started.

"Hey, Lindsay?" She shook me gently. "Are you okay?"

I leaned my head back and my eyelids fluttered.

*We should hide*, I thought. *We should get out of here.*

Two opposing thoughts.

She stepped around me and headed back into the tunnel.

"Rose, no. We have to leave," I said.

She looked at me. "Why?"

"*Rose.*"

"Lindsay, this is incredible," she said, going deeper into the blackness. "This is a hidden tunnel!"

"We're so busted," I said. "They'll find it."

"Maybe not. We can push all those boxes in front of it. Maybe we can make it look like they fell over and caused it."

I was clammy. "Rose, I have to get out of here. *Now.*"

She looked at me. Really looked. "Are you going to, like, faint?"

I shut my eyes as a wave of nausea hit me. "Help me up. Please."

"You're shaking. You're really scared."

"Aren't you?" I asked her, dumbfounded.

"Heck no. This is *cool.*"

I flipped up the wooden slats for my feet, and she wrapped her hands around my wrists. I planted my feet on the floor; as she tried to raise me up, the chair rolled forward. I shuddered, hard; I couldn't stand being in it. I practically threw myself out of it, and she staggered backward from the momentum.

"Except that you're sick," she said. "That is not cool."

I backed away from the chair. But Rose shone her flashlight over it, examining it, then took a step forward. "What does it feel like—?"

"Don't," I begged her. "Rose, let's go."

Rose took off her jacket and took a few swipes at the floor to conceal our footprints. Descending the stairs, I kept my arm on Rose's shoulder. We tiptoed out of the attic, down the stairs, hurried down the hall to the balcony, and then we were on the ground floor, and out the door. Rose made sure she still had the key and then we flew across the quad. My heartbeat roared in my ears; I couldn't help but look over my shoulder, up at Mandy's window.

There was no one there. Of course.

We crept into Grose, still panting as the saint on the table by the door waved hello; then we got past Ms. Krige's door, and into my room. By mutual consent, we didn't turn on the light, only flopped onto my bed side by side in the dark, heaving.

Rose said airily, "That was so weird. What happened to you?"

"I don't know." I shivered. I couldn't stand to think about it.

"I'm thinking black mold. My aunt had a reaction like that. Just muttered to herself and passed out cold. She was flat on her back for *months* until they tore out a wall in the bathroom and, oh my God, it was all over the place."

I rubbed my head. "I heard voices. Something about an ice pick."

"No way," she said. "You know what this means."

"That Mandy planted that wheelchair?" I asked, rather desperately. "That she made Kiyoko tell me about the attic and then let you steal that key? And this is all one big stupid practical joke?"

"Maybe," Rose said. "But what I was going for, was that we have to go back again tomorrow night." She smiled and waggled her eyebrows. "And take pictures. Of ze pictures. And ze wheelchair."

"Why, so we can make sure there's evidence to confirm that we broke in?" I was bewildered by her reaction. "Are you, like, a psychopath or something?"

"Lindsay, we went in there to find out why Mandy's acting so crazy. Maybe she's crazy because she's having sex with her brother *and* the black mold is doing a job on everybody who lives in Jessel. Like in Salem. Historians now think the girls who accused all those people of being witches were having hallucinations." She held up a finger. "Which they got from eating moldy rye bread. *Mold.*"

"Why do you know all this stuff?"

"I read a lot," she said simply. "I have a high IQ, remember?" She folded her arms. "Okay, so, what's your theory?"

"Maybe . . . maybe it's a haunted house," I said. There. I had said it out loud. My face burned and I felt stupid. But I didn't take it back.

"*Oh.*" Rose swung her head toward mine. She blinked at me. "You believe that. You really do. That it's haunted."

"I just *told* you that I heard voices." *And I've had nightmares. And I've seen faces.*

*And Mandy knows I had a nervous breakdown. And it's probably drugs that make their eyes go black; and maybe they've slipped me some, too.*

She shrugged. "You're impressionable."

"Are you saying that you think I'm crazy?" I heard the edge to my voice. "Or that Mandy's crazy?"

She crossed her legs. Then she got up and rested her hand on top of the white head. "It's just like Lara said that night they practically drowned Kiyoko. Stare into the lake long enough, and you see things."

She patted the head. "Sometimes I think this thing moves," she admitted. "It totally creeps me out."

"But you're touching it."

"I know it's just my imagination." She looked so superior. If Mandy had told her about my breakdown . . .

"So . . . we'll go back and investigate some more," she said. "Don't you want to go down that tunnel?"

I shook my head. "No."

"Where's your sense of adventure? Oh, never mind. I'll go by myself," Rose said.

"Rose, don't," I pleaded. "We've done enough as it is."

"And we can undo it." She cracked her knuckles. "We can fix the wall and no one will ever know we were there."

"Fix it? How?"

She thought a moment. "Maybe we could get a ride into San Covino and buy stuff. Whatever we need. Boards, paint." She grinned at me. "Know anybody with a car? Say, a T-bird?"

"I think Troy went home," I said, trying to sound ignorant.

"Let's find out," she replied.

# twenty-three

**November 21**

The next morning, I stood on Jessel's porch and called Troy. His number was listed in my messages. Standing in the frosty air, I listened to his cell phone ringing and crossed my fingers. I couldn't decide if I wanted him to answer or not. Rose was on a mission. She was already talking about other ways to get to San Covino if Troy didn't work out—such as asking to be taken to a movie by a driver, then making a side trip to a store to buy some materials for "a project."

*This is a very bad idea,* I thought. Both versions.

Rose had gone around to the kitchen door of Jessel and let herself in, though with the key or her lock-picking tools, I had no idea. She was upstairs in the attic, assessing the damage and making a list of things we would need to buy in San Covino.

"Hey," Troy said. He sounded surprised and pleased to hear from me. Also, kind of muzzy, as if I had awakened him. I tried not to picture him in bed. Did he wear pajamas? Did he go commando?

"Lindsay?"

"Yeah. Hi, uh. About yesterday . . . " What was I doing?

"It's all good," he said quickly. "I know things are, well, complicated. . . . " He trailed off. Then he said, "I'll row over."

*No*, I thought, but before I knew what I was doing, I was saying yes.

"Okay, then," he said. "I'll come over in about an hour."

And that was that. I flipped the phone shut and waited for Rose. And waited. I sat down on the porch and sighed. I called Julie, but I got her voicemail. I called my dad. The same.

I thought for a moment about calling Heather, my old best friend. My finger hovered over the buttons. I'd left without telling her. But by then, we weren't speaking anyway. I couldn't exactly call her in the middle of a crisis and expect her to be there for me.

Ms. Krige opened our front door; I quickly put my phone to my ear and pretended to be talking to someone in case she noticed me on Jessel's porch. She'd pointed out, quite reasonably, that we could use the landline to call out. When I'd told her I'd rather use my cell because I had unlimited minutes, that made sense to her.

The sun had risen over the top of Grose by the time Rose appeared inside the privet hedge, looking rather pleased with herself. She joined me on the porch and we moved quickly away from Jessel, as if we both were eager to put some distance between it and us.

"He's coming over here, but I am not okay with asking him to take us to San Covino," I said. "He's Mandy's boyfriend.

You don't think he might mention to her that he took us to Home Depot to buy some lumber and paint?"

"No worries," she declared, posing as if to say *ta-da!* "Did you know they kept tons of props from the haunted house? Props and building supplies? They're stashed in an empty bedroom and I mean stashed, girlfriend. I used all their stuff. I got a couple boards and a staple gun and some tape and I actually painted over it."

"You put the wheelchair back in the tunnel, right?"

She shook her head. "No, I left it out in the middle of the room for them to notice." She leaned in and waved at me. "Hello? Do I look like a moron? Of course I put it back."

"And . . . so . . . "

"And so it looks . . . bad, but then I pushed all those boxes in front of it. By the time anyone notices it, they won't be able to connect it to us."

"So you hope," I murmured, but I had to admit, this was good news.

She gave the back of my head a playful bat. "There you go again with the pessimism, Lindsay. What am I going to do with you?"

---

**Troy came over,** and this time I met him at the lake. He rowed to the little inlet he had mentioned by the No Trespassing sign, and I watched him move like an athlete. I thought about all the things I had told him yesterday and I was sorry I had. He must have thought I was a whiny loser. Boys liked winners.

He looked over his shoulder at Jessel, as if he, too, was worried that Mandy was there, watching us. Then he shrugged and smiled at me, just me.

I didn't like walking along the same stretch of lake where Mandy had done her *Exorcist* routine but I kept it to myself. We climbed over some wet rocks and I nearly slipped; Troy caught my hand and kept holding it, like the day before.

I wanted to say, *What's your deal? Are you cheating on Mandy with me?* But I didn't. He brought his camera this time and took pictures of me, and the sky, and the lake. He had a good eye.

"I heard from Julie," I told him. "She and Spider went riding with, um, Mandy." I had forgotten that I would have to mention her in the telling of the story. "They had a great time." Although I would have rather bitten off my own tongue, I added, "That was nice of Mandy."

"Yeah, I wonder what she wants," he muttered. Then he shook himself and cleared his throat, as if he hadn't meant to speak aloud. "Anyway." He took my hand again. I let him again.

Was I a boyfriend thief?

Maybe I'd wonder about that tomorrow.

---

## Or maybe not.

Because that night I was certain I saw the face in the

bathroom mirror, and I ran out of the bathroom without dry-ing my face. Water streamed down my face like tears.

Mandy came back the very next day. I didn't know why. Maybe someone had told her Troy's loyalty was in jeopardy. She swept back into our lives like a viral infection, and Troy must have gotten the memo, because he didn't make any badly timed voyages across the lake to see me.

I don't know if he came to see her, because Mandy didn't hang out with us. Dr. Ehrlenbach let her stay in Jessel alone, without her housemother. Rose and I were silently freaking out but we kept it together. We wondered what she was doing.

So one morning, I followed her down to the beach, and I so wished I hadn't. Troy was rowing across the lake to see *her*. I stayed crouched behind the boulders, my face burning as they greeted each other as if they both had been gone for a year. I was humiliated. It was Riley times two. And even though it should have hurt less—Troy and I were not a couple—it didn't hurt less; it hurt more.

She tied up the rowboat like an old hand and took his gray backpack in a single, easy motion. Then they disappeared for hours.

It was dumb to cry, but I couldn't help it.

And I stayed up until dawn, keeping the nightmares at bay.

---

**Then the break was over,** and everyone else came back. Julie rushed into my arms and told me she'd brought me some presents—another skirt, this one dark purple shot with silver threads, and a pair of jet earrings. She said she'd done hardly anything except talk to Spider and/or text him.

"What about riding?" I asked, sounding disingenuous even to myself.

"Oh, except for riding. It was sick! I saw Pippin *five times*," she said, her eyes shining. "Mandy is the *best*."

"Oh." I wasn't totally petty; I could be happy for her even if Mandy was the one who made her happy. Could I get there with Troy?

No.

# twenty-four

**December 2**

Mandy's birthday. She invited all of Grose to her party. Midnight, off-campus, and nowhere near the operating theater.

"At an old lake house." Julie lifted her hair up and turned her face left and right as she checked herself out in the bathroom mirror—the same one I had stopped being friends with. "Spider's going. We've *got* to show."

And Troy, too, I figured. I didn't want to go—

—who was I kidding? Of course I wanted to go. I had no shame. Maybe when he saw me again, the magic would happen. He would realize she was a psychobitch and dump her. On her birthday.

The eight of us Grosians kept the whole thing under the radar, drumming our nails waiting for Ms. Krige to go to bed.

Julie and I went to bed fully dressed, me in my new purple skirt, and a black sweater, with a couple of streaks of purple eye shadow, lip gloss, and ballerina flats in a bag. I wore my hiking boots for the mucky trip through the woods. Julie was all grown up in a light blue-and-gray cashmere sweater and matching wool trousers. She carried a pair of heels in a little Neiman Marcus bag. Julie put the birthday card and wrapped journal that we had bought for Mandy in the student store in her purse, plus a brush and her lip gloss. I took my cell phone. It probably wouldn't work, but no harm in trying.

Then we climbed out the bathroom window and took the blacktop path down to the shore behind Jessel. The other six of us swarmed from behind trees and hopped silently over the horse-head chain link. My heart tugged as we passed the No Trespassing sign. He would be there. He would see me semi–dressed up.

The moon hung low, full, and strangely red. The lake rippled. Frogs croaked, then fell eerily silent as we passed.

"Are you sure this is the right way?" Ida asked Julie.

"Hey." Julie stopped and stared. "Did you see that?"

"What?" April, Marica, and I spoke at once.

"There was something . . . " She gestured with her hand toward a thick stand of pines. "I thought I saw something white moving through the trees."

I squinted, aware of how far away from the campus proper we had gone.

"I think we should go back," I said. "This doesn't feel right."

"No," everyone else said in a chorus, followed by a lot of shushing.

"Mandy wants you there," Julie whispered as she picked up her pace, like a toddler zooming away from her mother so as not to be denied her fun. "She asked me about six times if you were coming."

That did nothing to make me feel better.

"Serious, Julie," I said. "I'm getting a bad vibe."

"Well, guess what, we're here," Julie announced.

Julie shined her flashlight on a dilapidated structure hanging over the lake. It was a tumbled-down foursquare wooden house with gables on each of the sides of what remained of the slanted roof. Tarps covered up holes and rock music played over the water. It was a slow dirge, something very metal-goth, like the music from the party at the operating theater.

"I don't see any lights," I grumbled.

"They're in the basement. Once we go inside, we'll see the stairs. Come on."

Julie hurried on ahead. Her ankle was definitely healed. The others zoomed after her.

The ground was damp, then soggy; my boots sank into mud, creating suction, and I grimaced as I lifted my feet. Julie trotted through the muck like a little Pippin mare.

Julie reached one of three rotted steps leading to an angular rectangle of planks—what was left of a porch. She climbed up and extended her hand to Ida.

"It's safe," she said.

*Famous last words,* I thought.

———

I tested the shredded planks of the lake-house porch before I followed Julie and the others onto the porch. The wood was spongy and stinky. A heavy beat pulsed through it from the music inside.

There was no door, only a rectangle of black; when Julie's flashlight played over it, roaches skittered away. *Gross.* Something squeaked, and Julie pulled her shoulders in tight as she stepped across the threshold.

I was right behind her.

Julie paused and ran her flashlight around bulges and shapes in the room—furniture, some of it covered with rotted sheets. There was a skeletal sofa coated with slimy bits of stuffing. A disintegrating carpet stretched in tatters against the floor.

There were pictures on the wall in cracked frames—faded photographs of girls in lacy white dresses, their hair twisted into little topknots or hidden in bonnets. A blackened mirror threw our reflections back at us.

"Oh my God," Ida whispered. "*More* weird stuff."

"Yeah, no kidding," I said. I wondered just how many dilapidated buildings weren't mentioned in the Marlwood Brochure, and what Ehrlenbach was smoking, promising parents that this campus was safe.

"Look. The way down." Julie aimed the yellow beam of light at a square hole in the floor. She began to cross the room, and I caught my breath, afraid that she'd crash through it and really hurt herself. I caught up with her, and she looked at me so sweetly and with so much excitement that I gave her a quick hug.

We peered down into the square. Stairs led downward, but there was no railing. In two lines at the bottom, oil lamps like the ones on the Jessel mantel flickered a welcome. Someone had hand-lettered a sign on a piece of copy paper that read

PRIVATE PARTY HAPPY BDAY MANZ!

"Here goes nothing," Julie said. She smiled at me, and then the rest of the group, and opened her Neiman Marcus bag, dropping three-inch shimmery heels to the floor and unlacing her boots. "We are gonna have a blast!"

It became a group ritual as we all sat down and changed our shoes. Then we got up and clattered down the stairs. As we reached the bottom, the lamps flickered; a door opened, and Troy appeared. The light played over his face and put highlights in his tousled hair. He was wearing tight jeans and a dark sweater that clung to his chest. The sleeves were pushed up to his forearms and he was wearing a silver ID bracelet with big links that gleamed against his hand. He had a five o'clock shadow, and he was so sexy that my heart broke a little.

*No. Don't even go there,* I told myself.

He saw Julie first and smiled pleasantly at her; but when he caught sight of me, his smile disappeared.

*Nice,* I thought, humiliated. So there was no hope after all. I wanted to run back up and leave.

"Hi, Troy," Julie said. "We're here."

"Go on in," he told her, keeping his gaze fixed on me. "Spider's been moping, afraid you wouldn't show."

"Really?" She turned to me, making no attempt to hide her joy. "Meet you inside?"

I nodded. The other girls crowded her, eager to go in, and Troy smiled at them as they walked passed him, showing all his teeth, as if he were a golf pro or a politician. A fresh crack ran through my heart, because I knew I had misread our times together so completely. He thought we were just friends, nothing more. I could tell.

"Hey," he said.

"Yeah." Whatever.

"Lindsay," he began, but I walked steadily into party central: a low, semi-dark room flickering with light and crammed with girls and guys, presumably from Lakewood. Fluttery white Happy Birthday streamers swagged the ceiling. The low room was furnished with small tables covered with lacy white tablecloths and wooden folding chairs. There were black and white vases of white roses on the tables. I found the gift table and some cards that had been opened and set out for display. There was a very large, ornate card bordered with black lace.

*To my sweet Amandy,*
*Love always,*
*Miles*

There were Lara and Alis, holding beer bottles; Kiyoko clutched a wineglass in both her bony hands, so wraith-thin it probably took all her strength. She looked even worse than before break—dark shadows haunted her usually golden skin. Kiyoko was the real ghost of Marlwood.

I marveled briefly that they'd managed to cart real wineglasses and so many other supplies from campus. And people. The room was bursting with beautiful Marlwood girls and hot Lakewood guys. I hadn't seen this many boys at once in over a month, not since I'd left San Diego.

The birthday girl was seated on a white stuffed pillow on the floor, bitchy-sexy in tight black leather pants and clean, unmuddied Catwoman boots. Julie balanced on another white pillow across from her, with Spider looking indulgently on with a Jell-O shot in each fist. Julie and Mandy's fingers rested on a triangle of plastic on a game board covered with letters laid across Mandy's lap. Her Ouija board.

And then I heard a blood-curdling scream, and leaped backward, crashing into a tall redheaded guy I didn't know.

Rose barreled through the doorway, sopping wet in a black wool dress and coat, chased by a guy in a hockey mask waving a chainsaw—not on—over his head.

"You suck!" she shouted at Mandy, and then she burst out laughing.

Mandy and all those around her started laughing and hooting. All those except for Julie, who was looking at Mandy as if she were wondering why she hadn't been in on the joke.

The guy whipped off his hockey mask and turned in a little circle to hoots and claps. Then he bowed to Rose.

"You're evil," she informed him, making as if to grab the chainsaw from him. "He chased me half the way here."

"Someone give that girl a drink," Mandy ordered. "She totally deserves it."

Sangeeta handed her a lime Jell-O shot, and Rose flashed me a you-know-I-love-you look as she slurped it down.

Mandy and Julie smiled up at me as I walked over.

"Linz. Wonderful of you for showing," Mandy said over the music. Troy, get her something. The best we have." I hadn't realized he was still right behind me.

"On it." He wasn't smiling. He looked . . . wary. Afraid. Did he think I was going to blow his cover? Tell Mandy I wanted her boyfriend? Then she'd sic her crazy brother on him?

That was crazy. Too much even for Mandy.

"Hi, Mandy," I said. "Happy birthday."

"We bought you a present," Julie said.

"You're both wonderful," she cooed. "Oh! It's moving!"

Mandy and Julie dropped their gazes to the plastic triangle. It whirled and slid under their fingertips, then shot across the board and pointed to the number seven. I felt strange, as if I should know what that meant.

"Hmm." Mandy cocked her head. "Number seven." She lifted her chin and narrowed her eyes at Julie, as if waiting for a response. Julie jerked slightly, looking puzzled. Then both of them stared up at me.

Troy returned with two shot glasses filled to the brim with clear liquid. Kiyoko was with him.

He handed me a shot. "Vodka. My contribution. Grey Goose." His smile was detached, pleasant, as if he were speaking to someone he didn't know very well.

Which was true.

"Because it's my favorite," Mandy announced. "It's moving again. M-E-M-M."

I jerked. Tried to remember if I had told Julie about my mom's nickname. No, I hadn't. I hadn't shared it with anyone here.

"Wow, I can feel it," Julie said. "It's going crazy! M-E-M-M-Y-M-E-M-M-Y. Memmy-Meemy? Eenie meenie?"

I sucked in my breath as the room fuzzed out.

"Memmy Memmy," Mandy corrected. "Does that name mean something to you?" She sounded truly innocent as she looked up at me.

"Are you okay?" Julie asked me. "Lindsay?" She kept her fingertips on the triangle, obviously torn about whether to continue their "game."

"Sure," I said, reaching for Troy's vodka shot. He gave it up and I threw it back. Beside him, Kiyoko's skeletal face was bone-white, her forehead wrinkled.

I pushed my way past a couple of jocks talking to Ida and Claire. Claire smiled and handed me a lime-green Jell-O shot as I passed her, as if we were in a relay race. I slurped it down.

"Go, woman," said one of the jocks, handing me another. I took it.

By the time I was halfway up the stairs, I realized I was massively wasted. I staggered outside onto the porch, trying to catch my breath.

Tears welled; I felt myself shaking and eased myself off the porch, stepping into the mud just as I remembered that it was there . . . and that I was wearing my flats.

If they were using her nickname to tease me, prank me . . . it was underhanded. It was . . .

"I miss you," I whispered to the darkness. "I need you. I don't know how to do any of this." My throat burned, trying to keep fresh tears at bay.

I heard someone coming up behind me and slid in the mud for the shelter of the trees. Just as when I had eavesdropped on Mandy behind boulders, I slunk behind two pines growing closely together. I slid down until I was sitting in mud, my whole body trembling, the tears finally forcing their way out.

# twenty-five

I don't know how long I sat in the darkness, out of it, crying.

"It's just another trick, a mean trick," I whispered. But I knew I had never, ever spoken that name aloud.

*But in my dreams, during my nightmares . . . maybe Julie heard me.* They'd spent the break together, riding. Mandy had charisma. All queen bees did. She could be mean as hell to someone, then turn around and convince them she was their best friend. I'd even caught myself responding to her artificial sunshine.

So if she asked a few questions, now and then . . . collecting ammunition in the form of personal information and secrets . . . Julie might not have even realized it . . .

I hiccupped with tears. I felt stupid for hiding, but I cowered behind the tree trunks, embarrassed and angry and out of control.

Then someone called my name from the porch of the lake house. "Lindsay?" It was Kiyoko. "Lindsay, are you here?"

I peered around the tree. Kiyoko was alone. She was staring into the darkness, obviously unable to see me, as she navigated down the stairs and started heading toward the water.

I was just about to step into her field of vision when a wave of dizziness hit me and I closed my eyes. When I opened them again, I couldn't see her.

I scanned the shadows, the shimmering blackness of the water. An owl hooted; the lake rippled. But I didn't see Kiyoko anywhere.

After a few seconds, Mandy appeared in the doorway, the moon bleaching her face skull-white. Her eyes were black.

Alis and Lara sauntered from behind her, slipping their arms around her waist. And their eyes were black, too.

"Sweet bees," she cooed in that schizo Southern accent I'd heard before, leaning over and kissing each one on the cheek.

"Is anyone here?" Mandy sang out in her Southern accent.

"*Dios*, we were so wrong about Kiyoko." Alis's accent was Hispanic. "She's just fine."

"Then where *is* she? We don't have much time," Lara said. Her accent sounded vaguely New-Yorkish, not normal for her.

I rested my chin against the tree, dizzy, sick, and bewildered. Was it a game? Were they on something?

*Like whatever drug I must have been on in the attic?*

"Don't you fret. She won't get away. We'll find her," Mandy said.

"That's impossible," Lara said. "There are too many of them."

"Don't be silly, sugar." Mandy chucked her under the chin. "We're doing very well. After all, *we're* all here. That sweet little girl has my undying gratitude."

*Are they talking about Kiyoko?* I couldn't make sense of it.

"Oh my Lord, it's been so long," Alis said.

Then Mandy turned. "Child," she said, "you are a sight for sore eyes."

"It took forever, didn't it?" said a familiar voice. "This one was very strong-headed."

And then Rose stepped from the doorway. The moonlight bleached her face . . . and cast her eye sockets into shadow.

I shivered in the cold night.

I had a terrible feeling.

*Not Rose*, I begged.

Then she took another step forward. No color, just ebony.

"I am so blessed," Mandy said, as she wrapped her arms around Rose and kissed her cheek. "Here you are, sweet as ever. All of you."

"We weren't sweet. We were wicked," Lara said, grinning.

"We never were, honey. Ever," Mandy retorted.

"I was." Rose's voice was low and sad.

"Ssh, don't you talk like that." Mandy trailed her fingertips along Rose's cheek. Rose pressed her face against her hand and smiled.

They turned and walked back into the lake house. I watched it spin and tilt and blur as I sank to the ground, sick, shivering, and about to pass out. I leaned my forehead against the tree and sank, deep. . . .

"Lindsay."

The sound of my name woke me up. Troy gazed down on me, his eyes a little bloodshot, his face pinched. "I saw you leave. You looked upset," he said. He was slurring.

*And you care because? Oh, please do not say that Mandy ordered you to look for me.*

"Uh huh," I replied, enunciating each word. "Mandy was trying to be funny with her Ouija board thingy. And it wasn't funny." *There, that came out well.* "She was out here. I think she's crazy."

"She's drunk. Mandy also made her Jell-O-shots about five time stronger than usual," he added, sounding angry. "My friends didn't realize it, and they're getting totally wasted. I could strangle her."

*Then Miles would kill you*, I thought.

"How's Julie doing?" I asked, turning my head to the lake house.

"Spider's cool. He'll take care of her." He bent down and touched my cheek. "But I think I should get you home."

Then he did the most amazing thing. He picked me up, mud-covered skirt and all. I inhaled his smell, and felt the softness of his sweater in the cold, dark night. And I was so happy to see him, so very happy.

He carried me down to the lake. One arm was around my back, and the other one was under my knees. I laid my head on his chest and shut my eyes, willing away all the weirdness and the questions. Just breathing him in—the comfort of being taken care of.

There were three rowboats pulled up on the shore, each with

LAKEWOOD painted on the side. They had to be the rowboats he and the other guys "borrowed" to come to our side of the lake. He gently set me down in the nearest one. He pushed off, sloshing into the water—his feet must have been frozen—and then he slid in and picked up a paddle.

*Mandy's going to be so pissed,* I thought, but I couldn't help my sheer joy. Troy had picked me. Me.

I stared at his bulging arms as he pulled the oar deep into the cold, dark water. In that moment, I had no idea if he wanted to help me or harm me. He could be dangerous, after all. And here I was alone with him, on a tiny boat in the middle of a vast, icy lake.

I shivered.

"They were talking so strangely," I told him.

"Who?"

"Mandy and her friends."

"That'd be a first." He huffed. "She really used to be nice, Lindsay. Something happened to her. Something bad."

"What was it?" I asked.

There was a beat. "I don't know."

*Liar*, I thought, as the boat glided on the black water. Oh God, I was so drunk. So dizzy. It had to have been the extrastrong Jell-O shots; a little bit of vodka had never felled this party girl in the past.

"I keep thinking she'll get over it," he went on. "And be the way she was." He sighed. "She was so sweet. So smart. Like you."

I didn't want to listen to him brooding about Mandy, even

if I came out looking better than her. He was drunk, too. He might not even know what he was saying.

I drifted and laid my head on the slippery, cold edge of the boat. The water lapped against the hull. The moon shimmered like silver. And I knew, somehow, that if I gazed into the water, the face that looked back at me would not be my own.

I heard a splash and somewhere beyond our brave little boat on the wine-dark lake, an owl yodeled. Music wafted toward us, a slow song—a song that sounded kind of old-fashioned . . . someone was singing:

*"My love is like a red, red rose . . . "*

"Troy, do you hear that?" I asked.

But before he could answer, I drifted again. I heard myself calling for Memmy; I felt her kiss my cheek. Someone was making a promise to me, or a bargain: if I was good, if I helped . . .

If I helped?

*"Get Number Three ready. We'll do them all tonight."*

"Lindsay, can you help me a little?" Troy murmured. I jerked awake. He was trying to keep the boat stable and pick me up at the same time. The boat was tied up to the No Trespassing sign in the inlet below Jessel.

I stifled a giggle, because he was rocking back and forth like a circus clown; it just struck me as so funny; and I eased myself up, all boneless and goosey. I was drunk, and I let everything just wash over me, wash away, the hell with all of them.

"God, you're sexy," I blurted. Then my eyes bugged out and I said, "Whoops!" as Troy put one foot on shore and grabbed hold of the sign while he supported my forearm with the other.

He laughed, low in his chest like a rumble; then harder, almost silently. I smelled the alcohol on his breath and saw his white, white teeth.

I had no idea how he managed to drag me onto the bank; by then we were both laughing hysterically, our arms around each other like two drunken sailors. We started to hoot; then we shushed each other. I fell against his chest and he wrapped his arms around me, pulling me against him.

"Oh," I gasped, and he bent his head down toward me. And then he kissed me. His lips were incredibly soft and warm. My head exploded as I kissed him back, moaning softly, as if my soul were flying out of my body toward him. He eased his tongue into my mouth, gripping his arms as he pushed up against me, just a little. I could taste the alcohol, feel it tumbling through my veins and igniting me; my inhibitions evaporated and I pressed my body against his.

"Lindsay," he whispered, "Oh God."

The comet blazed until I had to catch my breath; then it was over, our first kiss, as we gazed at each other as if we'd just realized who we really were.

"That was. So nice," he whispered, running his hand through my hair, trailing his fingertips down the side of my face.

But then a cold wind passed between us, and I thought of the days Troy had spent with Mandy after she'd come back. He had been her date tonight, but he'd left with me. He was her *boyfriend*, for God's sake. And now he was making out with me. Was *this* the kind of person I had become?

A spot prickled between my shoulder blades and skittered

toward the small of my back. Coldness wrapped around my chest and squeezed. Someone was watching us. I was sure of it, and I jumped away from him. With a puzzled frown, he reached for me, and I shook my head, crossing my arms over my chest.

"I don't think we're alone," I said under my breath.

"It's okay. Everybody's at the party," he said.

But I knew it wasn't okay, deep in my bones. As I studied Troy, so handsome and so Mandy's, who kissed me so easily, that was all I knew.

# twenty-six

**I went to my room,** undressed, and passed out. The next thing I knew, Julie was shaking my shoulder.

"Wake up, Linz. We have to leave."

"What?" I sat up slowly, still dizzy, as she pointed to our window. I heard people muttering in the hallway. I reached for the light on our nightstand. It didn't go on. Then I realized how cold it was in our room. It was *freezing*. It must have been around 3 a.m.

"There's a blizzard, and we've lost power," she said. "We're going to stay in Jessel."

Jessel. Mandy's turf. And I had just kissed her boyfriend.

I was shaking with cold. It was icy. "How did you get back? Is everyone okay?"

"The weather was turning bad. We all left. No one knew where you went." She gave me a look. Or did I imagine it? "Troy was gone too."

She was supposed to be my best friend, but I couldn't tell

her. I knew that as she looked suspiciously at me. Had Rose said something? Rose had thought to call Troy to get us to San Covino, and left it to me to do it.

I still didn't know if Rose had seen us on our walks.

"Is he okay?" I asked, trying to sound as innocent as possible.

"I don't know. I don't know if Spider's okay, either." She pulled out her cell phone. Her face was pinched; her hand was shaking. "I can't get through."

*Oh God.* I thought about the black, cold lake. A rowboat in a blizzard. My stomach clenched; my chest tightened. I had to force myself to breathe.

"Maybe Mandy got hold of them," I said.

"Hurry, girls," Ms. Krige said, poking her head into our room. She was holding a blindingly bright lantern.

Snow and wind blasted over the mountains and down into our valley, filling it to the brim, suffocating our buildings. Sideways squalls transformed into a whiteout blizzard, dropping tons of snow on the gables and roofs all over campus. The horse heads were buried; two Marlwood custodians dug the snow from our front door so we could get out.

We dressed in our warmest clothes; each of us brought a backpack filled with our toiletries and tramped down the hill to Jessel. Rose was there, having already secured permission to spend the night before she'd left for the party. She had a gift for staying out of trouble.

And Kiyoko was there, looking frightened and alone in the crowded living room as we refugees put down our things and

Ms. Meyerson and Ms. Krige passed out hot tea and cocoa. She stood beside their beautiful white Christmas tree, decorated with white and silver ornaments. A menorah of eight rabbis-a-leaping sat on a chased silver table beside it.

Julie and Mandy hustled away into a corner, hustled back. Julie nodded at me. Troy was safe, then. I sagged with relief.

Ms. Meyerson put our names in a coffee cup and distributed us. I would be rooming with Alis and Sangeeta, who already shared a room because they moved so late that Ms. Ehrlenbach didn't want to furnish two. At least, that's what we'd heard. Claire and Ida were paired up in Kiyoko's room. April and Marica with Lara, who was none too pleased; she pointed out that there were *two* empty bedrooms and asked why they couldn't stay in one of them. Ms. Meyerson told her the heat was out in one of them and Elvis and Leslie had the other empty bedroom, which was unfurnished. There were air mattresses and sleeping bags for us, and couch cushions. Ms. Krige would sleep in Ms. Meyerson's room.

That left Rose and Julie, who would stay with Mandy. Rose looked at me cross-eyed when no one else was looking. I didn't smile back. I didn't want Julie in Mandy's room at all, ever, but as I watched the shining excitement on my friend's face, I knew I wouldn't be able to make a decent case for why she shouldn't. I couldn't tell her that while I was totally drunk, I had watched Mandy, Alis, Lara, and Rose act like the witches in *Macbeth*. I couldn't say I was afraid of Mandy Winters. Julie already knew that. But she wasn't scared; she was charmed. Enthralled. Impressed.

As the housemothers busied themselves with our

arrangements, I felt someone staring hard at me, and I turned. It was Mandy. I felt myself go cold inside.

*Oh God, she knows,* I thought. *Maybe he confessed. Maybe he broke up with her.* My surge of hope was inappropriate, given my situation. But it was there nonetheless.

I was on an air mattress in Alis and Sangeeta's room. Alis's furnishings were antique, like most of the rest of the house. Sangeeta had gone Indian, with dark blue brocade bedclothes, mosaic-and-brass furniture, and an amazing gold jewelry box glittering on her dresser.

I wanted to call Troy, make sure he was all right. Ask him if he'd said anything. I pulled out my phone. One bar. Maybe the snow was affecting my reception. I'd try later.

It was then that I realized I'd left my charger back in Grose. I'd have to be careful not to use up the battery.

The snow pressed against Jessel's windows until we couldn't see out of them at all. I didn't see any faces in the glass, not even our reflections. All I saw were piles of white.

"It's like living on a glacier," Rose said, as we gathered in Kiyoko's room, waiting to use one of the bathrooms, clutching toothbrushes and toothpaste, some of us in borrowed robes.

"Or underneath an iceberg," Kiyoko said quietly, standing as far away from me as possible.

Sounds came from Mandy's room: laughter, her voice rising and falling. Mandy was alone in her own room, making more space for Julie. Hiding the trunk, probably.

"She's talking to herself again," Ida whispered to me. "Wacko."

"Psycho," Claire corrected.

Rose grinned wryly at me.

I glanced over at Julie, whose cheeks were turning pink. She'd obviously heard. She cleared her throat and walked out, heading, I knew, for Mandy's. I darted after her.

"Julie," I said, catching her in the hall. She turned and looked at me, her expression a cross between impatience and maybe a hint of fear. "Julie, something is seriously wrong. With her."

Julie looked coldly at me.

"I think it would be best . . . to maybe sleep in the room with me," I insisted. "Please."

"Oh God, you're still jealous of her," Julie cried. At my stricken reaction, her features softened and she laid a hand on my arm. She whispered, "You're still my best friend, sweet bee."

*Sweet bee.*

I swayed as she smiled at me, all of fifteen, and rapped softly on Mandy's door. She went inside, as if she belonged there. And I felt a sharp terror grip my insides and shake them hard.

*Breathe in.*

*Become one of us.*

I walked to Mandy's door and raised my fist. Lowered it. Turned, and saw Kiyoko in the hall. She was watching me with huge eyes, and as I took a step toward her, she bolted.

"Please," I said, catching up to her. "I know something's up. What did you want to tell me?"

By then she was blinking back tears. "Nothing."

"You were looking for me last night."

She stiffened. "How do you know that?"

"*Kiyoko.*" I touched her shoulder. So bony. She was wasting away in front of me. "You've come to me twice. Just tell me what's going on."

She took a deep breath and gazed past me, at Mandy's closed door. "Not here," she whispered.

*Thank you.* "Where?"

"I'll—I'll let you know. Nothing can happen while . . . while we're stuck . . . " She bit her lower lip, which was chapped and bleeding.

"Nothing like what?" I insisted, but I could sense her detaching from me.

She half-turned, turned back to me. "When it stops snowing, we . . . we'll go for a walk. Or something."

"Just tell me *now*," I said. "This is stupid."

She shook her head and walked away. It had been the wrong thing to say. But I didn't know the right thing. I thought about checking in with Rose about it, but I couldn't trust her anymore.

We all settled in. I tried one more time to call Troy, holding my phone like a Geiger counter as I walked down the hall. I walked beneath the balcony past the pretty Christmas tree to the panorama window. Still one bar.

*Maybe I have to go higher. Maybe . . . to the attic*, I thought. My heart stuttered. I had to know how he was.

I backtracked, not wanting to so much as think of those dark, claustrophobic stairs, the door at the very top of them . . . the wheelchair behind the boxes.

I headed past the door of the forbidden turret room.

My cell phone registered three bars. I stopped and smiled. I started to dial, then realized I might get Troy in trouble with a voice call, and that I might be overheard, so I texted him instead. Simply asked, "U OK?" and pushed send.

CALL NOT COMPLETED, my cell phone screen reported.

My reception wasn't good enough. *Darn*, I thought. I started to walk to the back stairs . . .

. . . And the bars went down to one.

"Huh," I said aloud. I took a few steps backward. Three again.

And then *four*.

If I stood directly in front of the turret room door . . .

I tried again. Surely, with four, I was in business.

CALL NOT COMPLETED.

I looked at the door. At the doorknob. I reminded myself that no one was allowed in, although no one had told us why.

*Maybe it's unsafe*, I thought. *These buildings are so old. Look at the wall in the attic. Maybe they knew about the tunnel. Maybe there's something even worse in here.*

I looked left, right. The hall was empty, except for me. I put my hand on the knob and tried to turn it. It was locked.

*I'm not going to the attic*, I thought, as my heart raced. I moved away from the door and licked my lips.

"Lindsay?"

I jerked, whirled around. "Hey."

It was Alis, standing in the doorway of her room. She yawned.

"You okay?" she asked me.

"Yeah." I nodded. Waited. She stood there. I had the feeling she was going to stay there, waiting for me. Alis, whose eyes had gone black. Alis, who had talked with a Hispanic accent at the party.

"I just . . . I had to go to the bathroom," I said.

I walked up to her, and her smile didn't reach her eyes. Then she stepped back, ushering me back into her room.

Sangeeta was sitting up in her bed. She looked at me.

"We were worried about you," she said. "Julie says you sleepwalk."

"I . . . " I was stunned. Were they *guarding* me?

"Thanks," I said, and lay back down on my mattress. I didn't think I would sleep.

But I did.

---

*Number Seven . . . I think she might be a problem . . .*
*Smoke.*
*Everywhere.*
*The door . . .*

---

I woke myself up. Gloomy, thin sunlight washed the walls. I was sobbing gently.

I forced myself to stop and wobbled to my feet. Alis and

Sangeeta were both in bed, Sangeeta on her side, her face to the wall. I bent down to get my toiletry bag when a hand shot out and grabbed my elbow.

"Boo," Alis said, with a grin.

"Boo," Sangeeta added, rolling over and grinning at me.

# twenty-seven

**"Ha ha, guys,"** I said weakly. Alis and Sangeeta both started to get out of bed, and I hurried into the hall, wanting to put some distance between us. Ida was pounding on the one-stall upstairs bathroom door, yelling, "I am dying! Hurry up!"

I headed past the bathroom. Ida saw me, wagged a finger, and said, "It's just as crowded downstairs."

*Downstairs.* I saw a mental image of the kitchen. *This building has a landline*, I realized. Could I call him from there?

"Coffee," I mock-croaked.

"There's probably a line there, too," said Rose, as she wandered out of Mandy's room. I studied her face; she cocked her head and frowned at me. "What?"

I shook my head. "I just thought you'd be at the head of that line, Little Miss Addict."

"Ouch. Wounded." Rose grinned at me. "I'm cutting back."

"Not me." I breezed past her and went down the stairs, heading for the kitchen. Ms. Meyerson and Ms. Krige were there, already dressed, discussing what to serve for breakfast.

"Can I use the phone?" I blurted. I didn't have to say whom I was calling. Our parents had probably heard about the blizzard. They would be worried.

"The phone service is out," Ms. Meyerson said, with a shake of her head. "But don't worry. Dr. Ehrlenbach has notified all your parents that you're safe."

"Oh." I forced myself to smile. "And everyone is okay?"

"Yes." Ms. Krige looked at Ms. Meyerson, and then at me. She got up and gave me a quick little hug. "Everything is just fine." Her voice was singsong. "There's no need to worry about a thing."

*Oh my God. She knows about my breakdown, too,* I thought, mortified, pissed. Had I just been stupid thinking it would stay my secret? Now no one would believe me if I tried to tell them about any of the weird things I had seen. About black-eyed Mandy and her black-eyed minions. I was alone in this.

And I still didn't know if Troy was all right.

---

**We ate breakfast** in shifts; there were no classes. Some of us did homework; others watched movies on the big screen or their laptops. I roamed the house, searching for cell phone coverage and saving my battery by borrowing other girls'. The best place was still in front of the turret room, but despite the four bars, my call wouldn't go through. If the phone service was out, did that mean cell phones, too? I didn't think so.

*The attic*, I thought. But nothing in me wanted to go up there.

So I sat and fretted, hanging out in the living room with Rose, Claire, Ida, Sangeeta, and Alis—my two new best friends. A movie was on, but I didn't even know what it was.

It was almost noon, and Julie, Mandy, Lara, and Kiyoko had not yet shown. They hadn't come down for breakfast. I listened to every muffled bit of conversation, every laugh, and wondered what they were doing.

As swelling music played over the movie credits, Mandy stomped down the stairs with a hairbrush in her hand. She was wearing blue-and-white plaid pajama bottoms, Uggs, and a soft blue cashmere sweater. She walked up to the couch, glaring down at me, and held out her brush. Long, curly black hairs were tangled in the bristles.

"Not cool," she said.

I shrugged. "That's not mine."

"No one else around here has frizzy, slagged-out hair," she said, narrowing her eyes. "I'm willing to bet that where you come from, people use each other's toothbrushes, too."

"Whoa," Ida said. "PMS much, Mandy?"

"Stay out of it." Mandy tossed the hairbrush to me, and it hit me in the chest, hard. "You may as well keep it. *I* won't be using it again."

Freaking, I looked at the brush, which had fallen to the floor.

*She knows about Troy and me.* I was sure of it.

That afternoon, I didn't see Mandy and the other three—Kiyoko, Lara, and Julie—until they sat down at the table while Ms. Meyerson and Ms. Krige, Ida, Alis, Sangeeta, and I put out some cold cuts, bread, and condiments that had been delivered by the dining commons staff. They swooped in like hawks, Mandy first; she stared hard at me.

Julie scooted in after, all smiles and hugs for me, but there were deep circles under her eyes. It was the first time I'd seen her all day.

Behind her, Kiyoko gave me a stricken look. I tried to read her expression, but she looked away.

After dinner, some of us did the dishes. All those rich girls, cleaning up their own mess. Mandy didn't participate, of course. After she made herself a plate, she left. I was hoping Kiyoko would stay behind, but she, Lara, and Julie did the same.

"I wonder if we'll still have Midwinter," Alis said, as she loaded a coffee cup in the dishwasher. "It sounds cool."

"We'd freeze to death," Rose retorted.

"Maybe it'll warm up before then," Ida said.

Midwinter had been scheduled to be held in a week and a half, on the last day of school before holiday break: a nice dinner in our commons, and then a bonfire "to burn the winter cold away." Lakewood was invited for the bonfire.

"I hope the boys are okay," I blurted, as I dried a platter. "The ones who came to the party."

Rose smiled lazily at me. I looked away and put the platter on the counter.

*Enough of this,* I thought. I practically slammed the platter down. *Enough.*

# twenty-eight

I fought to stay awake that night, waiting until Alis and Sangeeta were out. They fell asleep, and I got up, in my pajama bottoms and my mom's sweatshirt. I was going to try again.

I was nearly out of the room when I stumbled over something by the door. My boots. As I picked them up to move them, I heard a sigh. Clutching them to my chest, I tiptoed out.

If I just stood in front of the door and—

The hair on the back of my head stood straight up.

The door to the fourth turret—the one that was forbidden—hung open.

I stared at it. It seemed to stare back, with one big black eye. I stood completely still, seeing nothing beyond the threshold except blackness.

Looking over my shoulder, I pushed on my phone light. The thin light cast a hazy, gauzy sheen about three feet in front of me. The floor looked . . . clean. Freshly swept. I stepped inside the room.

And suddenly, I had five bars.

*Yes, yes, Yes,* I exulted. *I'll just stand right here,* I told myself. *Just inside the door. If someone sees me, so what? I'll just say I wanted some privacy. And, hey, I can use my phone. I can text people. It's all good.*

Or as good as it could be, snowbound inside Jessel with Mandy and the others.

I texted Troy: "hey how ru?"

I held my breath. It was after midnight. He was probably asleep.

I waited. Looked over my shoulder again. Looked at my battery charge. It was on low.

"C'mon, c'mon," I whispered, not even aware I was talking out loud until I heard myself. I debated turning off the phone to save what little charge I had left.

Nothing.

I sagged. I was being dramatic. Of course he was all right. Spider would have told Julie if he wasn't. Something like that would have been all over Jessel.

I turned to leave the room.

And my phone vibrated. I stared at the faceplate. It was Troy. Not texting back, but calling. And then I saw that I had three messages.

I connected.

"Lindsay," he said. "*Finally.*"

"Oh," I said. *He'd* been calling *me.* "I'm sorry, I—"

"I can't hear you. Can you speak up?"

*Not really.* But I reminded myself that I wasn't a prisoner in the house. I was allowed to call people. No one else had to know it was Troy.

"This snow . . . we're locked down tight over here. It's insane."

"I was worried about you," I said.

"We're good." He paused. "Lindsay, I . . . I can't stop thinking about what happened. Between us."

I closed my eyes. Here it came. I knew what he was going to say: He was sorry it had happened. He was Mandy's boyfriend. It was wrong, blah blah blah . . .

"And I want you to know—"

*Hide!*

I blinked. What was happening?

*Hide!*

I felt something moving me—moving *inside* me, forcing me to shut the door, sealing myself inside. Something almost dragged me through the blackness into deeper blackness. Frost swallowed me up; my hands hit something solid.

"Lindsay?" Troy said.

Voices ballooned in the hall. Footsteps. And the door opened.

I cut the call as light flared to my right. I was standing near a wooden wardrobe and leapt in, hidden from view.

"Careful with that candle." It was Mandy, in her Southern-belle voice. "We don't want to burn the place down."

Grim laughter greeted her. "That's *her* job, after all." That was Lara, sounding New York.

"And we've got her, sweet bees," Mandy drawled. "Number Seven is ours."

"Are you sure?" That was Sangeeta . . . *minus* her cultured British accent.

"As sure as I'm starin' at that little stuffed horsie with the pointed horn," Mandy replied.

*What?* My eyes widened. They were talking about Julie.

"I can't wait until this is over. I can't stand this girl. So coarse. No manners. And her *clothing*. Shameful," Rose muttered. *Rose?* I'd been right not to trust her.

"Wayward." Sangeeta again.

"They'd all be locked up in here," Mandy drawled. "Starting with *my* girl."

"They'd be dead," Alis chimed in. "Like us." Her voice was hard. "*Muchacha,* you're wrong about this. You've been wrong all along. I think it's true. I think you're truly out of your mind."

There was a slap. "How dare you, after everything I have done. Everything I've gone through."

Alis sniffled. "I only meant—"

"Either you trust me, or you don't. I know who she is, and I'll take care of her. And we'll be free. I guarantee it. In fact, I bet my soul on it." She laughed.

*Help me.*

I heard the voice in my head. The closet walls seemed to blur, and melt; the stench of kerosene made my eyes water. I felt a horrible jumble of images: a tiny room, a long hall—*the* long hall. Bars.

Dark water.

The lake, above me.

A blurry white face with dark eyes staring at me . . .

An ice pick.

*My love is like a red, red rose . . .*

And as something inside me forced me to shuffle to the

right and peer out, I saw shadows thrown against the cob-webbed brick of the room.

Five shadows, female shapes.

And I saw Mandy and Alis standing with one of the lanterns from the mantel—

—and my legs wobbled.

Gauzy white images floated over their bodies and faces—the bodies of young girls, like them, but wearing shapeless long white gowns. Hospital gowns. And their faces . . .

. . . *Oh God* . . . I began to pant, silently.

Their faces were bone white, gouged with dark circles for eyes, and black holes for their mouths. But they were shadows. I didn't understand what I was seeing. My heart shot into my throat; I couldn't move, couldn't breathe. There was nothing in their eye sockets, they had no teeth, and their noses were two tear-shaped holes. Skeletonlike, in white gowns . . . burial shrouds . . .

I was going to scream. I was going to open my mouth and—

"We'll get her," said Mandy, or the skeletal shadow that hovered above her. I couldn't tell. It flared like a flashbulb, shooting up toward the ceiling—I saw wooden beams and a brick wall. I heard screams. Someone pleading.

*Help me!*

The Mandy-ghost shrank back down to its original size and said, "Now, tell me that you believe me. It's no good if you harbor doubts."

The other glowing thing reached out hands—no, they were Alis's hands. No, I couldn't tell. . . .

"I'm sorry," she whispered. "I believe you, Belle."

*Belle?* She called Mandy *Belle.* Why?

Something inside me quivered with terror at the name. I swayed, fighting not to drop my boots or my cell phone. I was trembling, hard. I was terrified I was going to lose consciousness, the way I had in the attic.

*This house is haunted. I was right.*

"Then we're agreed. We'll have to move fast," Mandy-Belle said. "I'll make sure Li'l Ol' Three has the plan." Light flared around her silhouette. "Those two gals stick to her like glue."

Two gals . . . My mind raced. Which two gals? Who was "Li'l Ol—?"

Kiyoko. Kiyoko was Three. And she didn't want to have any part of this. She'd been trying to tell me. No wonder she'd been so terrified.

"And that'll be it? Finally? You promise?" Lara said.

"That'll be it. We'll be free of this place. I swear it."

The two—the five—embraced. Light blazed and shifted. It was too bright; I couldn't see.

"And we'll go to a better place . . . " the Alis-thing said.

"Seven's our lucky number," Mandy-Belle said.

"We'll make her scream first," Lara hissed.

"We'll roast her alive," Mandy-Belle said. The light flared, blazed. It was as brilliant as . . . fire. "Number Seven must die."

There were five in the room. Six was missing. That was Kiyoko.

Seven. The stuffed horsie.

Julie. They were going to kill Julie. Right?

*Oh my God, now I really am going to scream*, I thought. I wasn't going to be able to stop myself. My mouth was opening; my lungs were filling—

—and then I was outside the turret room, in the hall. I blinked, hard, and caught my breath.

*What? How?*

Lara was standing at the other end of the hall, just inches from her bedroom door. She was wearing a bathrobe over her pajama bottoms.

"Do you mind? I have to go really badly," she said, rushing to the bathroom. I shrank back; maybe she didn't notice. She opened the door to the bathroom and shut it behind herself. I heard her peeing.

I shook hard, afraid I was going to throw up or fall over. I looked down to see that I was wearing my boots. *When had I put them on?*

*What did I just see? Am I crazy? Am I hallucinating?*

I seized the moment and turned to the turret room door.

The toilet flushed.

I grabbed the knob.

I heard a creak behind me and dropped my hand to my side as I whirled around.

No one was there.

The bathroom door opened and I turned and faced it just in time. Lara gestured to the bathroom and glided back into her room.

I waited until her door shut and tried the knob again. The door was locked. I pressed my ear to the door and listened. I heard nothing. *Had I even been in there? Was I dreaming?*

I couldn't feel my feet on the floor; I couldn't tell where my body ended and the rest of the world touched it. *Oh God, oh my God,* I thought. *They are going to kill someone. I don't know who, but it could be Julie. I have to do something. I have to tell someone.*

*Troy.*

I looked at the phone. I was back to four bars. I could only get five inside the room. *The attic.* The words came unbidden. I didn't even want to think them.

*You have to*, I thought. *They might be going after her right now.*

*Then just scream. Raise holy hell.*

And who would believe me? Mandy and the others would put their plans on hold. Wait until I was carted off to the asylum, and the coast would be clear.

"No," I whispered. A tear welled in the corner of my eye.

And then I hurried to the back stairs.

To the attic.

# twenty-nine

I tiptoed halfway up the dark, narrow stairway and looked down at my phone. I had no idea how much time had passed since I'd been inside the turret room. My battery indicator was blinking. I was almost out of juice, and I only had three bars. I kept going.

The fourth bar began to shade in, fluctuating, as I took the last few stairs. It started coming in stronger as I reached the top.

The door to the attic hung open.

I pressed the flashlight function on my cell phone, and stepped into the room. I gasped. The boxes had been moved, and Rose's crappy repair job must have broken apart, because I could see into the tunnel. Who had done it? Rose herself? Because she was one of them now?

*Where's the wheelchair?* I thought. But it didn't matter. I didn't care. I just wanted to call for help and get out of there.

*And go where? Back downstairs?*

I aimed the weak light down the secret passage. There were

cobwebs and piles of trash and mouse poop, but the wheelchair wasn't there. I straightened, turned . . .

. . . And inhaled sharply.

The wheelchair stood before me.

Between the door and me.

I backed up, covering my mouth with both hands; my flashlight beam grazed the wall, the ceiling, as I stared at the wheelchair. My mind hurtled down pathways of possible reasons: *I just didn't notice it; tilted floor; sure, the doors open by themselves here . . . they tricked me to get me up here . . .*

*It's something they rigged; there's a wire on the door; it's remote-controlled, ohmyGod it moved—this is all a terrible practical joke; oh, please, let it be a prank.*

I studied the worn slats of wood, the rusted wheels.

"Ha ha, you guys," I said in a low voice. "Very funny. You got me."

My phone vibrated; at that moment, the chair rolled toward me, one revolution, and then it stopped.

A chill ran through me. I couldn't move. Correction: I couldn't remember how to move.

The wheelchair rolled forward. The wheels squealed.

I whimpered.

*Answer the phone. Answer the phone. It's Troy. Get help.*

It rolled again.

My eyes darted left, right. I tried to judge the distance on either side of the chair, to see if I could get around it and out the door. But what if it turned? What if it came after me?

*It only moved because the floor is warped,* I told myself.

It inched forward.

I lost it, completely. I didn't think I was going to, but I did. Mindlessly, I staggered backwards; my heels hit the broken section of wall and I stepped in—

*What are you doing?*

The wheelchair squealed and rolled another inch. And I saw something on the floor, a weathered piece of newspaper in all the trash and mouse droppings. There were faces . . . faces I recognized, from the mantel downstairs. The headlines swam before me as I shined the light of my phone toward it to read:

## DECEMBER 20, 1889
## MARLWOOD REFORMATORY FIRE
## SEVEN GIRLS DECLARED DEAD

*Belle Johnson, an inmate at Marlwood Reformatory for Young Women, and six others were the victims of a terrible accident on the grounds of the reformatory owned by Edwin Marlwood. . . .*

A fire.

*We'll roast her alive. Number Seven. Belle Johnson and six others. Who was Number Seven? It was Julie, right?*

As I stared at the clipping, trying to make sense of it all, the wheelchair began to roll. I tried to scream; I couldn't. I couldn't do anything but mindlessly run.

Down the passageway.

*It wants you to go into the tunnel; it wants to trap you and run you down—*

"Help," I whispered, but my voice was bone-dry. I fled,

through cobwebs and fragments of rusted metal dangling from the ceiling. There were hooks along the walls, sticking outward in the dark—

My foot connected with an object on the floor and I kicked it out of my way. I bounced to the left and thrust out my arm to keep my balance. Pain sheared through me like a poker as one of the hooks sliced my palm.

I ran; the floor canted down sharply and I nearly fell over my own feet as I ran. I kept going, registering that the phone was vibrating. I put it to my ear and yelled, "Help!" but no one answered. No one was there.

The passageway wound down, down, like an exit in a parking structure. I was so scared I couldn't stop, and my feet went faster than my body; I couldn't slow down and I didn't know where I was going.

Like Alice in the rabbit hole I went down, down . . .

. . . And my cell phone went flying. It rolled away like a fireworks pinwheel and hit the wall, the faceplate casting a beam . . .

. . . Over an image that hovered in my way. It was completely white, the figure of a girl shorter than me, in a long buttoned-up nightgown, with black hair trailing over her shoulders. Her eyes were black; her mouth was a black hole. *It was the face.*

She looked like she was reflected on the wall, in the light cast by my phone. But she was moving. And I was still tumbling forward. She held out her arms as I tried to stop from colliding with her, tried to scream, but it came out as a cross between a grunt and a sob; I was about to make impact.

From head to toe, I gasped as ice water engulfed me, knocking the breath out of me, making me go blind. The shock paralyzed me, and I began to flail. Where was I? What was happening—?

Then I was on my hands and knees, gasping, panting, weeping.

I smelled smoke, thick and acrid; my skin prickled. My face was on fire.

"*Tie her down*," said a voice in my head. A voice I didn't understand.

Wedged between my palm and the filthy brick floor, my phone vibrated. Whirling around on my knees, I grabbed it with shaking hands.

It was Troy.

"Hello?" I sobbed, putting the phone to my ear. "Troy! Help me!" But I had missed the call. I pressed redial and willed the phone to ring.

Cold hands rested on my shoulders, burning like dry ice. As I panted, they moved to my upper arms and helped me up. I whimpered again; then my head fell back and I almost fainted as something *slid* into me through my back, centering inside my body, as if I were a cocoon.

"Oh my God," I said, weeping. "Please."

And a voice inside my head . . . *inside my head* . . . echoed, *Please. Help me, please.*

Cold air wafted against my face. Something moved my feet as if I were a doll, a puppet . . . moving stick-legged, I staggered through the frosty air . . . and out into the night. The night: the cold, whispering sky, the hard, black surface of the lake. Trees huddling together, making their plans.

And me, tears freezing on my cheeks. My lips were chapped and my head ached as if I had eaten half a gallon of ice cream by pushing it up my nose.

I lost time.

———

When I came back to myself, I was staggering along the lake. My boots were covered with mud and my pajama bottoms were sopping. My hands stung; they were covered with tiny cuts. I shambled past the boulders and saw the No Trespassing sign, and a Lakewood rowboat tied up to it. I blinked rapidly, trying to remember how I'd gotten out there. The wind caught my hair and ruffled it.

I was crying, and panting; why was I—?

I saw the white shape bobbing half in the lake, half on shore, about twenty feet past the sign. I saw a shadow stretch across the shape, and I began screaming because I knew it wasn't a *shape*. I knew exactly what it was. And I knew the shadow was Troy.

He turned and focused his flashlight on the shape in the lake as I screamed and screamed and ran toward him. He caught me, hard, and I kept screaming.

"Lindsay," he cried. "Oh my God."

We both stared at Kiyoko.

Washed up from the icy lake.

Dead.

# December:
# The Trap

*"The evil that men do lives after them; the good is oft interred with their bones."*

—William Shakespeare,
*Julius Caesar*

*"For among my people are found wicked men: they lay wait, as he that setteth snares; they set a trap, they catch men."*

— Jeremiah 5:26

# thirty

**possessions: me**
> nothing. i feel like i've lost everything, including my
> mind.
> nothing
> nothing
> memories
> nightmares
> something has hold of me; something is so wrong; i'm so
> scared.

> *haunted by:* the sight of Kiyoko's body. her eyes. her hair
> was *frozen.*
> *mood:* terrified
> *listening to:* lies. Mandy said, "i would give everything
> i have in this world if it would bring Kiyoko back
> again."

**possessions: them**
> oh.
> my.
> God.

> *haunted by:* her death? will they stop now? do they see now
> what a horrible game they're playing?
> *mood:* crazed
> *listening to:* things I cannot hear

**possessions: Mandy**
> all the answers

> *haunted by:* she is doing the haunting.
> *mood:* every mood; she's like a shattered mirror.
> *listening to:* demons?

---

**They life-flighted** Kiyoko's body out of Marlwood.
She was still fully dressed in warm clothing, carrying her purse.
Her cell phone was missing. I heard that blocks of ice chipped
off as they loaded her into the stretcher. She had fallen into the
lake, and possibly frozen to death before she actually drowned.
We were unclear on the details. All we knew for sure was that
she was dead. I remembered with pain what a terrible swimmer she'd been. Why would she have gone anywhere near the
lake, let alone in it?

*She knew what was happening. She was trying to escape.*

All through that horrible night, Mandy sobbed and played some weird Eurotrash music that never let up with the pounding beat. Ms. Meyerson didn't say a word, didn't tell her to turn it down. Between songs, I heard her in the bathroom, throwing up. The other Jessel girls cried, too, and their tears seemed so real I began to doubt myself. I had lost time. I came to wandering along the lake.

Had I dreamed what I thought I'd seen in the turret room? It was locked. It was always locked.

---

**December 4**

Dawn came. Phone calls. Ms. Meyerson announced that Dr. Ehrlenbach was coming to see us with some police officials and Dr. Melton, our school counselor. She told us not to talk to the media if anyone got through on the phone.

"Are you . . . *okay?*" Ida asked me. Claire, Leslie, and April gathered behind her, looking afraid of me. Their eyes were wide, their smiles . . . careful. It was obvious to me that Mandy had told everyone about my breakdown. Unless Julie had. But everyone knew, and they were treating me like someone who might explode into babbling hysterics at any moment.

"You found her," Claire said. She trailed off, as if she wanted me to give them details. Tell them what Kiyoko had looked like. I would never do that, ever.

"It must have been a nightmare." Sangeeta added, drifting

past me, as we gathered in the living room for our meeting with Dr. Ehrlenbach.

"We're all shaken," Ms. Krige said, passing out tea and hot chocolate, offering some to the police captain of San Covino—we were under their jurisdiction—and Dr. Melton, who kept looking at me.

"It was a terrible, unfortunate accident," Dr. Ehrlenbach agreed. I had the feeling she was teaching us the official school explanation that we were to recite whenever possible, to keep from getting sued or losing students.

"Dr. Ehrlenbach," I said.

Heads swiveled toward me. Mandy gave me a long, measured look. Dr. Melton looked alert.

I wanted to shout, "Why didn't you take better care of her? You saw her every day. You saw how skinny and scared she was." But I knew I couldn't look crazy. Or sound crazy. I hadn't had any sleep and I was a mess.

"Yes, Lindsay?" she asked with chilly calm.

I shook my head. "Nothing, sorry."

Mandy kept staring at me.

*I didn't make it up. I didn't imagine it.*

*But I lost time. What if I had something to do with her death?*

Dr. Melton sipped his tea.

———

**By midafternoon,** the Jessel landline service was restored, and I used it to call Troy. The power had been restored at Grose and everyone was busily packing to go back. For a few minutes, I had the kitchen to myself.

"Lindsay, what's going on over there?" he asked. "I was so worried about you I rowed over. And then I found . . . " His voice trailed off. "For a second, I thought it was *you*."

I started to cry. I wanted him. Needed him. What could I tell him? What *should* I tell him?

"We need to meet. We need to talk. I have to *see* you."

"Me . . . me, too," I said.

"I'll row over as soon as I can."

"Okay."

I hung up. Walked out of the kitchen.

My heart turned to ice. Mandy was halfway down the stairs, glaring at me. I should have told Troy not to come.

"They're going to let Miles come home," she said. "Our family should be together . . . now . . . now that I'm . . . she . . . " Her face broke, and she threw her head back; she began to wail like an animal. "Oh, God, Kiyoko, Oh, God!"

I licked my lips and went out the front door. I sagged against the porch and cried.

---

**It was Freezing** on the porch. After a while, I went back inside. Mandy was nowhere to be seen . . . or heard. The coast was clear.

I hurried into Alis and Sangeeta's room and put my few things back in my overnight bag. Rose poked her head in, saw that I was alone, and bustled in. I tried not to show my fear.

"Oh, my God, this is horrible," she said, wiping her eyes. "I can't wait to get out of here."

"Rose," I began. I wanted to make her talk to me, tell me what was going on. She looked at me, her face blotchy from weeping. "I went up to check the attic. To see how my camouflage job is holding up. The door's locked."

My mouth dropped open. "I . . . I . . . " I couldn't speak. Did she remember what had happened? Had she really been in the turret room with them?

She sniffled. "No one's going to care about that now," she said, sobbing.

"Rose," I said. "Mandy—"

"We were wrong about her," Rose cut in. "Okay, she's crazy in love with her own brother, but she's not big D dangerous. Her heart is broken. Poor Mandy."

I knew then that I really couldn't trust her. I had no one to talk to.

Except Troy.

The Jessel girls lined up to wave goodbye to us. I studied each one in turn: Alis, Sangeeta, Lara, Mandy. Rose, too, although she was going back to her own dorm. Mandy, as she made Caspi kiss Julie's cheek, then placed him in Julie's arms.

No skulls, no eye sockets.

No evil secrets, no plots?

**The snow poured down** on us. I called Troy on our landline. No more worrying about cell phone coverage. I was past that. He hadn't been able to leave Lakewood—the windy road between Lakewood and Marlwood was shut down, and the lake was too dangerous.

"I'm going to break up with her," he promised. "I'll do it as soon as I can, Lindsay, but I should do it face-to-face."

"Please, wait." I held on tightly to the phone. "Wait for the break." I couldn't tell him why. I was so very afraid. What would she do to him if he dumped her? What would she do to me?

Or to Number Seven?

"But . . . "

"Please."

"Okay." He took a breath. "But I'll try to get there soon. If I can't drive over, I'll get a boat as soon as I can."

"Don't row," I begged him. "Please, Troy." And then I cried some more.

"It's okay, Lindsay. It's going to be okay," he promised.

But I didn't see him. He didn't come. I waited, watched. Some mornings, I woke up panting, dreaming that he had rowed out on the lake, and the wind had pushed his boat over on its side; he tumbled out and sank.

*Down.*

*Down.*

*Down.*

"God," I would whisper, jerking awake. I would stare at the head, and Julie, sleeping. I would wonder what Troy would think, if he knew what I knew. If he knew about my break-down. Mandy must have told him. I hoped she had; because if she had, it must not matter to him. And if she hadn't, I would have to.

# thirty-one

**The days went by** in an awful blur of grief counseling and study sessions. Most teachers had given their students permission to take finals at the beginning of next semester, after a mourning period. Some classes were held; some were cancelled. Some people attended; some stayed in their rooms, staring out the window at the bleak weather, the dancing firs in the cold wind.

I told Julie what had happened—or rather, what I *thought* might have happened. She would have none of it. None. She didn't want to hear it, much less discuss it. As the days froze together, one after the other, and nothing more happened, the lack of drama seemed to confirm her suspicions that my reality was not the same as hers.

"They've just been waiting for a good time," I said. But over a week had gone by, and nothing else bad had happened. Kiyoko was gone. Everyone was in shock. But there had been no further plots. Maybe Kiyoko had been Number Seven. Or maybe I really had lost it completely.

And the face? I stopped looking in windows and mirrors. I couldn't have told anyone if it was there or not.

Dr. Ehrlenbach had decreed that we would indeed follow through with our Midwinter celebration. She said the dinner and bonfire would be a way to lift the school's spirits. *Ha, spirits.* I wondered what Ehrlen-stein *wouldn't* do to bury the nasty secrets of this place, to make it seem like everything was normal, when it was anything but.

———

### December 16

It was the last day of term and we were preparing for our formal dinner. Julie said to me, "Well, time is up. We're going home for break." She gave me a look and picked up Caspi. Her long red plaid skirt reached the tips of her black boots. Her white ruffled blouse completed her outfit for our formal dinner—Midwinter. It was the last meal we would share as a school before the end of the term. A lot of girls were leaving tonight, since another possible snowstorm was predicted. Julie was one of those. Others would skip breakfast, and eat on the road with their parents.

All our things were packed. I had put out some jeans for the bonfire tonight and some sweats and my mom's sweatshirt for the trip back. I was wearing my long black skirt, a black turtleneck sweater, with my wild hair wound up in a knot. I had on some eye shadow and earrings, too. Tonight I was going to see Troy.

"Promise me you'll see your therapist back home," she continued.

I was pacing. "Julie, I know what I saw. What I heard. They wanted to . . . kill someone. I'm sure of it. What if it was Kiyoko? What if you're next? They said they were looking for Number Seven. There used to be seven of you in the clique, until Kiyoko died. Is that just a coincidence?"

"No," she said, "because none of that happened. It was a dream. Or . . . or you're . . . " She looked down.

"Julie, there are things about the history of this school that you and I don't fully understand. Frightening things that happened years ago, and bad things are happening now, too. Don't you see?"

"You mean like, evil spirits possessing Mandy and my friends?" She raised a single brow. "And they want to kill someone named Number Seven because then they will go to heaven?"

*My friends.*

I stopped walking. "I don't know about the heaven part. They'll be able to move on. I know it sounds crazy—"

"It sounds *insane*." Julie snapped. Then she softened, blowing her bangs out of her face as she cradled Caspi against her chest. "I didn't think you would be so . . . " She played with the unicorn's eyelashes. "It's like a bad movie, Linz, you trying so hard to make me stay your best friend. It's scary."

"You should be scared," I blurted. "But not of me. Julie, please." I welled up.

And then she looked at me very hard. I saw tears in her eyes, too. She said, "Mandy's nice. And so are the other girls. But I thought that you . . . you and I . . . " She licked her lips. "You get it. How hard it is to be at boarding school. Everything is so easy for them."

"Julie," I said, moving toward her.

She stiffened and turned away, as if she had said way too much—shown her vulnerable side to the wrong person. Me.

"I still think of you as my best friend," I told her. "Please, Julie, please, listen to me."

"Lindsay-girl, phone," Ida said, poking her head in.

I wondered if it was my dad. The snow was coming down, and more parents were hastily readjusting their already-changed pickup plans.

I hurried to the kitchen and picked up. It was Troy. I had asked him not to call on the landline, since I didn't want anyone to know about us.

"Lindsay, I'm doing it tonight, at the bonfire. Breaking up with her," he said. "Meet me where I tie up my boat."

"You can't row," I pleaded. I was a mash of emotions—joy, terror, dread. Hope. Fear. For him.

"Meet me at the tie-up," he repeated. "I have to go." The phone went dead.

"Troy?" I whispered. "Hello?"

I waited in case he called back. I dialed him.

No service.

I went back to our room to grab my cell. Julie was gone.

I raced out of Grose and caught up with her. I wanted to make a detour to Jessel's porch to call Troy back, but I didn't want to leave Julie again. I was afraid. I needed her, and I needed to keep track of her. Tonight was the last night anything could happen.

"Hey," I said.

"Ida told me that was Troy on the line. Are you seeing her

boyfriend behind her back?" she asked me. Her face was set with intense disapproval. "So you made up all this stuff about her?"

"Julie, no," I said. "No, it's not like that at all."

She didn't speak to me again as we walked to the dining commons with the rest of the school—a walking fashion magazine of yuletide glamour. The horse heads stared. Mandy and her girls were up ahead and I watched Julie watching them. Her eyes narrowed. Oh God, was she going to tell Mandy?

The commons were breathtaking, with silver and gold tablecloths and ice sculptures of reindeer illuminated by floodlights. The tables were set with silver plates decorated with little gold stars around the borders. Our napkins were folded into stars. Silvery confetti trailed down embroidered runners with ornate Ms entwined with more stars.

Julie stayed with our Grose table for dinner. But her attention was on Mandy's table, and she was very quiet. When we cleared out to go back to our rooms to change for the bonfire, I lost track of her.

Nor could I find Mandy and the others.

I panicked, working my way through the moving mob, calling her name. Girls were staring at me; teachers were frowning. I was causing a scene. I didn't care.

I ran up the hill to our dorm. Julie was in our room, already changed into a pair of jeans and boots. She was pulling on a dark green sweater over a long-underwear top; she jerked when I slammed open the door and fell against the wall, gasping for breath.

"Thank God," I heaved, leaning forward.

"Oh my God, you *are* insane," she said.

"Julie," I said, "I'm *not*. I—"

And then my attention ticked to the white head. It was sitting on my bed, gazing blankly at me.

"Why did you move that?" I heard the tremor in my voice.

"What?" She looked at the head, frowned, shrugged. "I didn't. Maybe I did. I don't remember."

"Julie," I began. "Please, let me talk to you."

She grabbed her coat and walked in front of me. "Excuse me," she gritted her teeth, and made a point of keeping her distance as she circled around me and went into the hall. But I could hear her slow footsteps; she was waiting for me even if she didn't want to admit it.

"I'm coming," I said softly. I stared at the head. It stared at me.

I left the room and hurried after her. She gave me a once-over and frowned, gesturing to my clothes, my army jacket layered over my skirt.

"You can't wear that to the bonfire." She was practically running away from me. "Just . . . leave me alone."

"Julie, please, *please* listen." We were outside, and I saw the bonfire, burning at the entrance of Academy Quad. Above us, on a hill, the administration building was ablaze with lights.

The bonfire was ringed with huge logs and sawhorses with caution tape—not as quaint and picturesque as I had imagined it—and it rose at least fifteen feet in the air, yellow and crackling. Girls in jeans were gathering around it—girls with silk mistletoe pinned to their hair; or wearing silver garlands around their necks. Charlotte the goth wore black bat deely boppers. I saw Sangeeta in a puffy Indian-style embroidered jacket and gathered black wool pants.

Mandy stood beside her, dressed in black, like me, with a heavy parka. The fire played over her face, smudging her eyes and cheeks with deep hollows. She looked very tired. Thin.

Kiyoko had started out looking like that. Maybe the stress of channeling some Ouija board nightmare was too much for her.

I met her gaze, held it. I would not back down. I would not—

But when Mandy smiled, she looked so evil that I missed my footing, and stumbled.

Julie shot on ahead without looking back at me, and headed straight for Mandy. Mandy held out her arms like our Catholic saint, and Rose and Lara greeted Julie like a long-lost relative—like the missing sister of the girls in the photographs. Alis was there, too, wearing a backpack. I thought of Kiyoko's backpack, filled with rope and alcohol, back on the night of her prank almost two whole months ago now.

One-two-three-four-five, not counting Julie. Maybe they couldn't do anything with only five. Maybe Kiyoko had known that. Maybe she had meant to drown in the lake, break the curse and save Julie.

*Kiyoko, I'm sorry I didn't listen to you when I had the chance. Oh God, they're going to do something.*

I started to head toward them, just as Ehrlenbach appeared in a long black wool coat and black pants, a black knitted cap like a rotten mushroom accentuating her bony, tight face. A cheer rose up and dozens of boys in jeans and jackets loped from the direction of the parking lot by the admin building.

Lakewood had arrived. The girls' side did not greet them with the usual giddiness. Our faces were grim. Everyone was quiet, shuffling around the fire to get warm. Trying not to think of Kiyoko, lost out there, swallowed and then spit out by that awful lake.

I saw Troy in a black leather jacket and jeans, the blazing flames surrounding him like an aura. Then he turned and saw me, and his intense blue eyes startled me. I wanted to run to him and tell him what was going on. He trotted over to Mandy and brushed a casual kiss on her lips.

Julie looked around, and for a minute I thought she was looking for me. I raised my arms and waved.

"Get away," I shouted, but my voice was lost in the roar of the bonfire. She rolled her eyes and her gaze moved over and past me; I realized she was scanning for Spider.

"Excuse me," I said, working my way through the mob as stapled song sheets began to make the rounds. The snow fell heavily, and I saw Dr. Ehrlenbach glance up anxiously, then turn to Ms. Shelley, the receptionist, who checked her watch.

A tall guy moved in front of me, blocking my view. By the time I got around him, Julie, Troy, and the others were gone.

"Oh no," I whispered. "No." I fought to stay calm. They wouldn't do anything around Troy. Julie was safe—

Unless Troy was in on it.

"Oh God, oh my God," I gasped.

"Hey, Linz," said a voice behind me. It was Elvis. She was holding Caspi out to me.

I blinked.

"She said to give this to you."

"Julie?" I blurted.

Elvis shook her head. "Mandy."

I looked down at the unicorn. A white rope was tied around his neck, with a little folded slip of paper attached to it. As Elvis walked away, I unfolded it. The handwriting was ornate, old-fashioned.

> *Now. You know where.*
>
> > *B. J.*

B.J. What? I *didn't* know where.

*Help me.*

Yes, yes I did know.

"Belle Johnson" wanted to see me.

In the operating theater.

# thirty-two

**Snow fell like dirt clods** and the bonfire blazed as I ran into the forest. No flashlight, in a skirt. I could hear the singing—"We Wish You a Merry Christmas." My mind was hyper-alert, keeping track of every detail around me—the distant singing, the snowflakes, the wind. My breath.

And the ghosts of details: the odor of burning wood, and . . . other things on fire; wisping curls of vapor that looked exactly like smoke.

*They're Devil worshippers. Phantoms. Demons. Let it be a prank. Let it be a big fakeout. They'll laugh their heads off like they always do. Except when Kiyoko died. Oh God.*

"Help me," I said aloud.

My skirt tore on the undergrowth, I fell over a tree root, got up, and stumbled over a rock. My hands were cold and bleeding. Every once in a while, my mind would explode with an image of Julie, dead, and I would start crying. I couldn't cry. I had to get to her. I held onto Caspian as if that would keep Julie safe.

The snow was falling, tapping my head and shoulders like bony fingers. Branches yanked my hair; the icy bluster smacked my cheeks. Finally, I stopped, winded, scared, and hopeless. I didn't know where I was.

"I'm here!" I shouted, but the noisy forest swallowed up my words. "Damn it, Mandy!"

I panted, trying to catch my breath; mixed with the smoke, I smelled blood on my face. My left ankle throbbed. Something skittered across the tip of my boot and I was too exhausted and scared even to react.

I sank to the ground and sobbed.

"Help me. Mem," I whispered; because I hoped that whatever had been guiding me really was the one whose nickname was M-E-M-M-Y.

An owl hooted, and something inside me moved. It told me to get up. It *helped* me get up. I took one weak, staggering step forward. Another. I couldn't see where I was going. I didn't know what I was doing.

But something did.

"Memmy?" Was she there?

In the forest, I remembered something I had buried a long time ago: a memory of my mom, when she was in the hospital. We were going to visit her. My father had brought a bouquet of flowers. I got scared and told my dad I had to go the bathroom. He said to go ahead; he'd meet me in her room.

I stood paralyzed in the hall; then, ashamed, I hurried to catch up. I was concealed by the pale green curtain that stretched across the room, for privacy.

I heard my mother start to sob; she said, "Help me, Evan. I'm so scared."

I'd reeled. If she was scared, then things were bad. Then she must have sensed I was there, because she sniffed one more time, then said in a cheerful voice, "Oh, what beautiful flowers."

"Mem, things are so bad," I pleaded. "If you can help me now, please, please do it."

I let myself be moved, imagining she was holding my hand and guiding me through the darkness. If that was a lie, like the flowers, I would use it anyway.

The smoke smell grew stronger. I didn't want to go there; I didn't want to see the dark hulk of the operating theater. But as I staggered out of the dense stand of pines, I saw lights flickering through the holes in the walls, and I knew that they were waiting there. For me. I took a deep ragged breath.

*Okay,* I thought. *Bring it on.*

Then I remembered the other entrance, the tunnel half-buried in the ground, filled with ashes and blackened bricks. I crept around, searching for it. I saw the empty square where a door had once stood, and walked through it.

*No,* something protested inside me. *For the love of God, no.*

It wasn't my mother. But I didn't know what it was. I wanted to listen. I wanted to leave. But they had Julie. Whoever they were.

So I crept through the ashes, wishing I'd listened to Julie and changed into jeans. Wishing that I had never come to Marlwood. I was shaking, and I could feel myself beginning to unravel, the way I had back in San Diego. But I couldn't; there was too much at stake.

The ashes seemed to thicken around my shoes like quicksand, or hands. I remembered the article about the fire. Were these . . . those girls who had died . . .

I thought I heard groans, and the memories of screams. *Roast her alive* . . . oh God, I should have made Julie believe me. Or at least tried to tell Dr. Ehrlenbach what was going on.

Seven girls died in a fire in 1889. Somehow beyond what I could fathom, it was happening all over again. Another seven girls, another fire. I knew it—the truth rang out from inside me. But why? Why was this happening? I stumbled onward.

The door to the basement was ajar. I pushed quietly. It made no noise as I entered the basement. It was pitch-black. I stood in silence, listening, hearing my own panting, short breaths. They weren't there. I hadn't been to many other parts of the building. I didn't know my way.

Above me, I heard noises. And then a shout, cut off. My hair stood on end.

*Julie*, I thought. *Hold on. I'm coming.*

I held my hands out in front of myself and took a step forward. I couldn't see anything. There was no light anywhere. I took another step, stopped, tried to catch my breath as I trembled and my teeth chattered.

One more step. My foot touched something. I drew back with a gasp and moved to my right. Were they in the room, waiting to jump out?

Another step. Footsteps, overhead. They grew fainter.

I shuffled forward, the hair on the back of my neck prickling. Suddenly, I was certain that I wasn't alone in the dark room. I could feel that coldness against the back of my neck and I had to bite down hard on my lower lip to keep from crying out. I hunched my shoulders together; the coldness remained, like a frozen hand.

*Kiyoko?* I thought. *Is that you?*

*Help me.* The voice answered inside my head. I remember the figure I had seen in the tunnel at Jessel. Was she with me now?

I picked up speed, moving blindly. I had no idea how I kept making myself move forward.

*Show me*, I said.

I felt a coldness on my neck, and this time, I moved to the left.

I began to panic. Was something—someone—controlling me? I was so unbearably scared. I had to breathe. I couldn't. Yellow dots swam in front of my eyes.

The pressure increased. I wanted to raise my hand and touch my neck but I couldn't; I didn't dare. I walked forward, kept walking. How, I didn't know.

*Because I have to*, I thought. *Because Julie needs me.*

And my racing mind pulled in the last thing Jane had said to me. It was a fluke; after my breakdown, I hadn't gone anywhere, done anything. I stayed away from everyone. But one night, I had finally left my house and gone running in the park, to get the oxygen in and the adrenaline down, and I'd stopped to stretch.

Jane had stepped from the shadows. She'd looked at me, didn't say hello, or say sorry—none of that. Her lip had curled back in a sneer and she'd said, "I can't believe you bailed, Lindsay.

You should have fought for Riley, if you liked him so much."

My mouth had dropped open. I just stared at her. I was stunned by her unbelievable gall.

"Having a breakdown is just a convenient way to bail," she'd gone on. "Everyone feels sorry for you, and you get to give up."

I couldn't bail now. I couldn't fall apart. So I finally forced myself to breathe and let the *thing* guide me though the black hole of the basement.

I pushed on yet another door. It swung open.

I shook my head. I didn't want to go through any more doors, any closed spaces. I began to freeze up. I couldn't move. I shook so hard the bones in my head ached.

No. I could do this. I could.

*Okay*, I thought, and started walking.

A horrible stench hit me—smoke and cooked, rotting meat. Dead things. I blinked back tears and hugged myself. I wanted to stop so many times.

I thought I heard more groans as I stepped through more ashes.

I stretched out my hands into empty space. I lifted my foot.

Stairs.

I began to climb through the blackness, bracing myself each time I took another step, thinking that I would collide with someone, or someone would jump at me and push me down to the bottom.

I could almost hear voices, but I didn't know if they were inside my head. Echoes and echoes of echoes, laughter. Through the smoke and kerosene, I smelled blood, and urine, and the terrible metallic odor of sheer fear. After I reached the top of the stairs, I stepped on something hard that cracked beneath my shoe, like bone. I bit the inside of my cheek and tried to breathe through my nose.

I did hear voices, and saw the bloom of light ahead of me. I had no idea how I kept going; more light flared against a black, shattered wall far ahead of me. I started going down at an angle; there was more light and I was able to make out my surroundings. I was walking onto a smashed sort of balcony littered with curved rods of metal and slats of rotted wood. It was like the horseshoe lecture hall for my lit class, only instead of individual desks in rows of semicircles, there were three balconies, and they had at one time ringed the entire the building.

Snow sprinkled down on me; I looked up, to see sections of the wall that had fallen in. The moon glowed overhead, until it disappeared from view.

And then I saw a silhouette against the blue moonlight and faint yellow lamplight. It was a girl's face, and she was turned away from me. I knew that face so well.

Julie.

She began to turn toward me, and I ducked down behind a pile of debris and peered over the side of it. I didn't know why, but in the next instant, I was glad I had: she wasn't alone. Mandy's head appeared beside her, as the glowing skeleton I had seen in the turret room floated over her living body. Its shroud-gown flapped in the real wind, and snowflakes fell on flowing dark hair that whipped around her like tattered sails on a tall ship. The shape of her head reminded me of Julie's white head in our room.

*I'll save you, Julie*, I promised, clenching my shaking fists. My heart was beating so fast I was afraid I was going to pass out. I looked around for more cover in case I needed it, and realized that if I leaned to the left and rested my weight on my hand, I would be better hidden from anyone coming the same way I had come. I carefully moved; my hand covered something soft, pushed into it. I almost screamed when I realized it was a freshly dead animal. I smelled the odor, felt the slime. I had to close my eyes for a second to pull myself together.

"What was that?" Mandy whispered. "Is she here?"

"I didn't hear anything." Julie's voice was calmer than I would have expected. And a little lower than normal.

"She'd better show," Mandy hissed.

"She will," Julie murmured.

Then someone behind me said, "Belle, we're finished. Come and see." It was Sangeeta.

A flashlight flared over Mandy's horrible face . . . and then hit Julie square on.

*No.*

Her eyes were black.

*No.*

And a white skull flared over her face, blurring as she stared into the flashlight. I saw her features clearly. I clamped my jaw so tightly I almost broke my teeth.

Mandy rose and started heading toward me. I ducked down and held my breath.

*Oh God, please, don't let them see me. Please.*

An ice-cold wind washed over me. Tears formed in my eyes. My lungs were aching. I couldn't breathe.

"They can't wait to show you," Sangeeta said.

"I'm sure they've done a fine job, sweet bee." Mandy's voice was behind me. "Can you believe it? I thought this day would never come."

Their voices faded. The flashlight bloom disappeared. Julie had been left behind. Were they so sure that she couldn't escape? Was she tied up?

There was silence for a few heartbeats. My arm was aching. I was so cold I had to fight to keep my teeth from chattering.

"Lindsay?" Julie whispered. Her voice was normal. "Lindsay, oh God, if you're here . . . please help me, *please*. They're going to kill me." She rose slowly, moving toward me; then she stumbled. "Caspi," she whispered, her voice breaking into deep, heavy sobs.

I didn't say anything. Her black eyes had frightened me. Was she Number Seven? Or . . .

Or was she a replacement for Kiyoko, who was dead? And if she was, then who really was Number Seven—the one they really wanted dead?

*Oh God . . .*

"Lindsay, come quick," she whispered. "*Please.* They're going to set this place on fire."

I didn't speak, didn't move. I would wait until she went past me and follow her. As she came up the aisle I shrank down, as best I could. I was numb. I felt as though my hair was frozen. Like Kiyoko's hair, that night.

*Don't call out. Save me. Hide me.* It was the voice inside me.

Julie was to my right, about five feet away from me, sobbing. She was hunched over, her arms crossed, young and defenseless. . . .

*Please, for the love of God . . .*

. . . And I knew who was Number Seven. The one who didn't belong. The only one who'd ever noticed the awful reflections, the blacked-out eyes. The only one who'd ever heard voices, smelled smoke.

Me.

*I was Number Seven.*

Then Julie stopped to my right. My lip quivered. I didn't want to look, didn't want to see.

But I did.

Julie was staring down at me. She opened her mouth.

"Julie," I whispered. "Julie, you . . . you're possessed. And you . . . you have to get out of here, *now.* I'll help you."

She took a breath.

And then she shouted at the top of her lungs, "She's here!"

# thirty-three

"Julie, no," I gasped, as she grabbed me. I slipped away from her easily and ran toward the darkness.

Just then, Mandy and Sangeeta stepped from it. And Alis, Lara, and Rose as well.

*One: Mandy.*

*Two: Lara.*

*Three: Julie*

*Four: Sangeeta.*

*Five: Alis.*

*Six: Rose .*

Alis was holding up a Coleman lantern. I heard the hiss of kerosene.

"So grand of you to accept my invitation," Mandy cooed, in her Southern accent. She grinned at me, and I could see the toothless jawbones of a skull.

She cocked her head; the skull seemed to be screaming. I saw rage in the white bones. Dread clamped down on me, squeezing my chest, lashing my jaw shut.

"Mandy," I said. "Mandy, this is crazy."

"You know that I'm not Mandy," she said, in her Southern accent. "You know who I am. I'm Belle Johnson."

I shook my head. "I don't know that name."

The smell of kerosene hit me in the face, so strong I gagged and covered my eyes. I shook my head and tried to bolt, but Lara and Rose darted at me and grabbed my arms. Their hands were icy and their bodies stank like rotten meat. My knees buckled and Rose chuckled.

"Stop pretending," Mandy—Belle—said.

Kerosene.

Smoke.

"You're going to pay." Belle gestured to Lara and Rose and they began to drag me back the way I had come.

"I'm not pretending," I told her. "Pay for what? I don't know why you're doing this."

"Don't play dumb," Lara said. "You know what's happening. And why."

We walked down the corridor, but not down the stairs I had taken. Instead, we continued down a hall draped with so many cobwebs it looked like a cocoon. My left hand was covered with blood and ooze, and I stared at it instead of the things gathered around me. Instead of the white-skull back of Julie's head, as she walked ahead of me, with Belle, arms around each other's waists.

I started to fuzz out, but I forced myself to stay focused. *Roast her alive.* Why?

"I haven't done anything to you," I said.

"Hush your mouth, child," Belle ordered me.

"Maybe it's not her." That was Julie, the merest bit of uncertainty in her tone.

"Julie, Julie, help me," I said, but Lara dug her nails into my wrist.

"You stop it," Lara demanded.

The lantern flared over the cobwebs, and then the gaping mouth of a doorless entryway. And then I saw it, whether it was real or in my imagination, I couldn't say. It was almost like a memory. But it was so real. . . .

*The men.*

*The operating table.*

*Strapped down.*

*Screaming until the chloroform knocks her out and then . . .*

*The ice pick.*

*Ice.*

*Ice.*

*Ice.*

*And then . . .*

*The blood and the—*

*Nothingness.*

*Must stop it, must stop it . . .*

I bent over and threw up.

"I can't go in there," I begged.

"Oh, yes, sweet bee," Belle hissed, whirling on me, grabbing up my hair and yanking back my head. Her skull glowed; her black eyes stared hard. "You remember. You know."

"I don't," I rasped.

"Come out, Celia. Damn you to hell for what you did," Belle said. "You come out and pay."

Then they were dragging me into a huge cavern. As we entered, snowflakes tumbled in the lantern light. The ground was covered with dead leaves and rubbish.

Ten feet ahead of us, a stack of trash and wood stood about five feet high. Newspaper surrounded the base. As I looked at it, Lara reached into the jacket of her parka and pulled out a pair of handcuffs. I had seen them in the photographs in Mandy's trunk.

Rose dug in her pocket and pulled out a small rectangular-shaped can. Lighter fluid.

Alis had a bottle of brandy.

Sangeeta had a box of kitchen matches.

"Get it out," Belle snapped at Julie, who was studying the pile. "Hurry."

Alis turned and Julie quickly unzipped her backpack. She pulled out the white head and held it up for all to see. A shining globe of white.

"Bring it," Belle ordered her.

Above the head, Julie's skull face stared straight at me. And then, for one second, her black eyes turned hazel, and she was Julie. Her lips parted in shock.

Then her eyes turned black again.

No one else seemed to have noticed. I kept my eyes fixed on Julie as Lara gathered up my wide, untamed hair and held tight. Alis took over, gripping my arm.

"Look," Belle said, holding the white head at my eye level. The thing that had been on my own windowsill night after night since Julie had found it.

"No," I whispered.

"Do it," Belle said. "Or we'll make you so sorry . . . "

I tried to close my eyes. Tried so hard.

*No. Stop. Don't. I beg of you.* It was as if a voice from inside me was crying out. "*Now*," Belle said. "Or after we're done with you, we'll kill little Julie."

The thing inside Julie smiled at me. But her eyes . . . despite the blackness, they looked . . . sorry?

*Julie,* I thought.

Belle moved the white head closer to my face.

*Don't look,* begged the voice inside me.

But I couldn't stop myself.

In my head, I saw . . . girls in hospital gowns . . . I heard . . .

*My love is like a red, red rose . . .*

*Dr. Abernathy. He's the butcher who mutilates you. . . .*

"I know you're afraid, Celia," Belle whispered in a crazy, seething voice. "You know the Devil's going to eat your soul for supper." She moved the white head, caressing it slowly with her finger, touching the forehead. Then she set it aside. "Because, dear little Number Seven, you are a mass murderess."

Sangeeta screamed, "Set her on fire!"

"Burn her!" Rose shook her fists at me.

"I felt the skin melt right off my face, before I died," Belle whispered, moving the head back and forth, back and forth, like a hypnotist.

*He straps you down.*

*Stop.*

"Julie, I'm so sorry," I said, as I felt myself dissolving. I was going away. Lindsay Cavanaugh 2.0 was falling apart, just like Lindsay 1.0 had.

"Don't worry. Your sweet little Julie's not here," Julie said.

"That's how she came to us, but after that idiot Kiyoko died . . . "

"I moved into this one," Julie said. I heard her, but I couldn't see her. Couldn't understand what she—it—was saying. My gaze was riveted to her, this non-Julie. This voice speaking *through* Julie. "My name is Pearl Magnusen," she went on. "I was born in 1874. I was sent here because I fell in love with the wrong boy. A farmhand."

Mandy-Belle sneered. "They called her sinful, promiscuous. My uncle . . . he tried to force himself on me." Her voice was strained. "And I fought back, retaining my honor. And they said I killed him because I was bedeviled. . . . " Her tone hardened. "So they sent me here. To die."

"Not me. I'm Lindsay," I whimpered.

"They said I was too strong-willed," Lara said. "Not ladylike."

"Come to me. Come to me," Belle whispered. "Breathe in, breathe out, become one of us."

"One of us." Lara took up the chant.

"One of us."

I felt myself responding. Felt my lungs filling, exhaling. The iciness on my neck.

*It happened that first day*, I thought. *When I was spying on them. I breathed it in. Breathed her in. I'm tied to this, to them. Somehow.*

"No, no," I pleaded. "I am Lindsay. I'm Lindsay Cavanaugh."

"I loved him," Julie-Pearl whispered. "My only crime."

"You killed us," Belle insisted.

"I didn't mean to," my voice said. But they weren't my words. "Please, Belle," the voice begged—the voice that was mine but not mine. "It wasn't my fault."

*I am Celia Reaves. I am Celia.* I was no longer Lindsay. Or was I? I didn't understand.

"She's here," Belle shrieked, rocking with glee and triumph. Her hatred burned her like a firestorm. "Let us proceed, my sweet girls. My sweet bees."

They dragged me forward; my legs gave way as Lydia and Martha ran ahead and poured liquids over the wood and trash and Anna and Henrietta dragged me toward the pyre. I knew what they were planning. They would restrain me and set the pile on fire, and watch me burn . . . Because I had let them die in the fire. It was my fault. It was all my fault. But I didn't know.

Smoke swirled around us; heat too intense to come from a lantern blistered my skin. Screams echoed through the theater: *"The door is locked! The door! Open the door!"* But no one was screaming. Yet.

Belle laughed, fingering the white head again. The model. The dummy. What they used to demonstrate the operations on.

I gazed across to Pearl, who could not be a party to this. Who would never knowingly harm anyone . . .

"Dear God," I begged. "For the love of God . . . "

"Burn, burn, burn!" Belle screamed, as Martha snapped the restraining device on my right wrist.

"No!" Pearl shouted.

It was a blur: Pearl ran forward, grabbed the white head out of Belle's hands, and crashed it down on Belle's head. As the others reacted in confusion, Pearl grabbed the other end of the restraining device. I couldn't keep control—

---

Julie Flew with me into the corridor; it was pitch-dark and I was unsure which way to go. *The right, theright, therightheright*—it was as if my heartbeat was talking to me. Julie was dragging me by the other end of the handcuffs; I was trying to catch up, she was shouting something at me but I couldn't understand it.

I smelled fresh smoke.

I heard screams.

We flew out of the theater and missed the stairs; I sailed into space and landed on my hands and knees in the snow. Something clicked; then I hurt so badly I saw yellow behind my eyes and acid rose into my throat. Julie jerked me to my feet and I started after her as she shrieked. Through flurries of snow, I saw the cold, blue moon, casting light on nothing but tree branches and rocks; it was as if someone had shoved them together to form a wall while we'd been held captive inside the operating theater.

"You bitch!" It was Belle, only her voice roared with fury. Demonic shrieking chased after us; heavy footfalls threw snow against the backs of my legs.

Julie sobbed as she fought to keep up with me.

"Julie," I said.

"I don't know what happened," she wept. "I wasn't myself. I don't know who I was, what I was doing."

We raced on; wind blasted through the trees and the branches sliced at my face. I ran on pure instinct, falling and rolling, as Julie forced me on. My throat was tight and dry. I couldn't scream no matter how hard I tried.

We crashed through the trees. The bonfire was blazing, so far away; I couldn't see the people. The lake spread below us, black and deadly.

And then I saw a rowboat tied up next to the NO TRESPASSING sign. That's where he'd wanted me to go. Why was there a boat there? "Julie," I begged. "Julie, where's Troy?"

She looked back at me as she ran down the incline, dragging me behind herself.

"Water puts us out," she said. "That's why . . . Kiyoko drowned. They can't get to you on the water."

She let go of the handcuffs. "Take that boat. Go as fast as you can."

"Please, come with me," I begged her.

She gestured to the bonfire with her glowing bony hand. "Go and get help."

"No! I'm not leaving you, Julie!"

"This is the best chance," she said.

"Kill her!" a voice shrieked on the wind.

"*Kill her, kill her, kill her.*"

The voices reverberated against the trees, sharp as axes, distorted and cunning. We separated, and as Julie—or had it been Pearl talking this whole time?—raced to my right, I scrabbled over rocks, falling again and again. If I stopped, I'd be dead. I ran on, hampered by my stupid skirt. By then I was so close I could read the letters on the No Trespassing sign, and I put on a fresh burst of speed. It was unnatural; there was no way I could run so fast after what I'd been through.

I saw the rope tied around the bottom of the sign, and raced to it. It was tied to a white rowboat bobbing in the water with Lakewood Academy painted in dark letters on the side. The boat was half-full of snow. I fell to my knees, fingers plucking at the rope, looking fearfully over my shoulder.

They were coming. Glowing white shapes elongated and distorted over the bodies of Mandy and the others as they ran toward me. The shapes grew, rising over their heads, blurring and spreading across the sky—skulls and bones and whirls of luminescent fog.

The rope was too tight; I couldn't find a loose piece. I briefly considered trying to break the signpost, but knew I couldn't. I ran to the boat and found the cleat the rope had been wound around, and started working on that.

The shapes expanded, riding the wind; they crashed forward like waves, like galloping horses. I kept unwinding. Belle was no more than twenty feet away. Beneath the glow of the skull, Mandy's face was crisscrossed with scratches. Her hands were bleeding. Her clothes had been half–ripped off.

And still she came. I could smell her—smoke, sweat, and blood—I saw her eye sockets.

And then the rope went slack. I had unfastened it from the cleat. I let it drop, shoved off, and leaped into the boat. I hit snow. I saw the oars. It took a lifetime to secure them into the oarlocks.

The boat rocked crazily as freezing water splashed me. I was panicking, unable to coordinate my rowing motions. Oh God, what if I drowned like Kiyoko?

Belle stood on the shore, not four feet away. "Damn you, Celia, come back!" she shrieked. She started forward.

"No," the blazing white skeleton beside her shouted, grabbing onto her. It was Lara—or whoever she *really* was. "Not in the water."

"Let go of me. I curse you to hell," Belle screamed at her. She slammed herself into Lara, who released her.

With a loud splash, Belle jumped into the water and started swimming. The ghostly image seeped into the water, lighting it . . . slithering toward the boat.

"Belle, no!" the others cried, as they massed on shore, shouting; but no one else jumped in. They were a blaze of glowing white, intertwining, thinning, undulating, blossoming.

Wind pushed against the stern of the boat. I rowed, sparing no more glances at the water or what was in it. I couldn't feel anything. Everything slid away. I was numb.

The moon beamed down on the shore. The white glow shrank as I put more and more water between the boat and land. The white in the water thinned, winked out.

*Thank you for this boat, Troy, thank you*, I thought, afraid for him.

I kept rowing, unable to feel my feet. Then I looked down, and realized that the snow was rising around my thighs.

I was taking on water. There was a hole in the boat.

*Trap*, I thought. *No, oh, please.* Had he done it?

Then, amazingly, my cell phone vibrated in my sopping jacket. I grabbed it.

It was Troy. I tried to press the connect button. My hands were shaking too badly. I tried again, yelling, "Troy!"

And then I dropped it, and it plunked into the water in the boat. I searched for it, my hand plunging into the ice water.

I had to let it go for now. The water was rising. I was exhausted, and so cold. I looked around. The moon was too weak to show me the shoreline; a vast expanse of ebony blackness stretched in all directions. I tried to stay calm. I had to think.

I had been a lifeguard. I could swim. But the water was freezing.

I had to get out. Maybe I could flip the boat and use it as a flotation device.

I would freeze to death.

I looked in the direction I had come. I couldn't see anything. Would they make their way to the other side of the lake?

I couldn't stay out here forever.

I closed my eyes for a brief moment and tried to find the phone. No luck. Then I rolled myself to the right hard, and knocked the boat on its side. It sank beneath me and I slid into the water.

My skirt was so heavy. I tried to get out of it but I couldn't.

I started doing the breaststroke, but the water pulled on me. I tried, so hard.

I lost time, so much time. I knew I went under the water a dozen times, a hundred.

*I'm dying*, I thought. *Will I see my mom?*

# thirty-four

**I couldn't move** and it was coming and it was here.

I was panting, screaming, clawing.

Sweat rolled off me. The back of my neck was cold but my forehead . . . my forehead, oh God. I couldn't move and it was crawling toward the bed; one hand was on the mattress oh—

Come to me come to me come to me come to me come to me.

It was on my chest, it was pressing down, it—

# thirty-five

**December 17**

I jerked awake with a cry.

On Jessel's porch.

My body ached with cold. I was sopping wet, and covered in mud and cuts. The sky was growing light.

"What?" I said aloud. What had happened? I'd dreamed . . . had I dreamed *everything*?

I broke down then. I cried because I couldn't do anything else—cried a river, cried a lake, wept and sobbed and tried to scream and cried some more.

I cried until I was dry as bones on the inside.

I got up, as the sun cast my shadow on the porch—me, solid; me with my wild, untamed hair and my destroyed wet clothes and my bruises and my puddles of tears. Wiping my face, I staggered to Grose and stumbled into the room I shared with Julie. All her things were gone, just as she'd said they'd be. She must have taken the head, too.

There was a note:

*Hey Lindsay,*

*I looked for you at the bonfire but I couldn't find you.
I went to a party with Mandy but I must have drunk too
much—I can't remember a thing. I got all scraped up in
the woods coming home. My parents'll kill me. I have to go.
My parents are here now. Troy asked me if I knew where
you were, and he told me about you guys. He also told me
that you wouldn't hang out with him until he broke up
with her. So . . . okay, I forgive you for that.*

*Mandy and I are going to go riding over the break. She
says her brother Miles is back and she can't wait for us to
meet.*

*I wish I understood what's going on with you. I do think
you need to get some help. I really, really like you a lot, but
I think that it might be better if we had some space for a
while. Maybe you will feel better after you talk to someone.
Please don't be hurt. I want to be your best friend but, no
offense, I'm just not sure who you are . . . and I don't think
you know, either.*

*Love ya (really!!!!!!!),*
*Julie xoxoxoxoxooxoxoxo*

Julie didn't remember what had happened.

Shaking, I went into the kitchen and tried to call Troy. I
couldn't remember his number. I touched the buttons, straining
to remember the pattern. I swallowed back tears. Tried again.

Did it.

His phone went straight to voicemail. I tried over and over
and over. Nothing.

And then the phone rang. I grabbed it.

"Hey, it's Spider," he said. "Have you seen Troy?"

I almost lost it then. I said, "What are you saying?"

"He didn't come back from the bonfire. They're searching the grounds."

"Oh God." I began to shake. Had he gone looking for me?

"I gotta go," he said. "I'll let you know when they find him."

I tried to make myself go into the bathroom. But I couldn't, I just couldn't. So I went into the kitchen and turned on the water, let it run as I stripped off my clothes and washed. I was covered with bruises. I looked at my face in the microwave glass. I had a couple scratches, but nothing major.

*It happened. It really happened.*

I finished and carried my clothes to my room. Changed into the sweats I had laid out for my ride home. I was still frozen solid. And scared, so scared.

"Oh, hello, dear," Ms. Krige said from the doorway. "All set?"

I couldn't respond.

"Have a nice break," she added, and left.

*I'll never see you again*, I thought. And then I wondered, would I ever see any of them again?

# epilogue

**December 20**

**possessions: me**

> i am Lindsay Cavanaugh. i have not bailed. i did not break. i am here. and i am strong. and i'm going to make it through this.
> i think.

> *haunted by:* nothing. NOTHING.
> *listening to:* my mom's favorite old records. "Bridge Over Troubled Water" by Simon and Garfunkel.
> *mood:* strong. resolved.

---

## I didn't tell anyone. What could I say?

When my dad and stepmom arrived, I let them think I had taken a tumble at the bonfire to explain the bruise on my chin. And that I was so emotional because I'd missed them so much.

And in a way, I had.

All the way home, I tried to make sense of it. I tried to figure it out . . . the operating theater, the fires, and the thing I had become, the voice that had spoken inside me . . . the one they'd all called . . . a murderess?

Should I be in a psych ward somewhere?

"You're so quiet," my dad said, looking at me in the rearview mirror. "Did you party hard?"

My stepmom smiled at me over her shoulder. I couldn't smile back.

"Yeah, I'm tired," I told them.

We got home. There was nothing in that night's news about a missing boy. Missing or found. But Troy didn't call, and my calls to his cell went to voicemail. I tried the Lakewood office number the next morning, but the secretary there wouldn't say anything, or give out his personal information. No one would tell me if he was all right.

I called Julie, who sounded pleased to hear from me, if a little guarded. She had just gotten back from riding with Mandy.

"I'm keeping her company," she said. "Being supportive. Troy's still missing."

I felt frozen. "Missing," I said.

"They're searching the woods." Her voice trailed off. "Miles offered to join the rescue party, but his parents said no. He's so *intense*."

I went cold. Did Miles know about me and Troy? Would he come after Troy? Had he already? What could I do?

"If you hear anything, please call me."

She paused. "Okay," she said finally. "I will."

I net-searched Marlwood Reformatory. There were no hits. Nothing about a fire. I read about lobotomies. They were horrible operations; doctors sometimes stuck an actual ice pick into your head to separate parts your brain. It was supposed to cure depression and uncontrollable rage. More often than not, the patients—the victims—became mindless vegetables. Some killed themselves.

The ghosts of Marlwood had not been mindless. And they hadn't killed themselves.

The ghosts of Marlwood.

Maybe I had gone crazy . . .

*No.*

I searched the net obsessively. Mandy Winters' face was everywhere. It was the bustling winter holidays, and the Winters were about to go on a ski trip with Prince Harry and the President of France. She didn't look worried about a missing boyfriend. She looked happy. In one picture, she posed next to Miles in front of a fountain. His arm was wrapped tightly around her waist, and his eyes seemed to bore into mine. *You hurt her*, he seemed to say. *You're next.*

**December 23**

Three days after I returned to San Diego, my parents gave me a new cell phone to replace the one I'd "lost" at school.

My first call was from my ex–best friend, Heather Sanchez. She said I sounded like my old self, and she invited me to go to the movies the next day. It had been our Christmas Eve tradition the last three years in a row. Heather told me Riley was single again, and quite likely would show at the movies, too. I had a feeling she was arranging a reunion. Maybe I could start over here, too. Lindsay 2.0 was home, and she was the version I'd live with for the rest of my life.

I was alive. I had thwarted them. But what about Troy? I tried not to think of Searle Lake, where Kiyoko had died.

I wondered if Kiyoko had really fallen, or if someone had pushed her in. I felt overcome with sadness and regret, mingled with the icy fear I felt whenever I remembered what it was like seeing her body out there on the shore. . . .

About an hour later, the phone rang again.

The caller ID was blocked, but I figured it was Heather, with more details about the movie. I took the call.

"He's here," someone whispered.

I sat upright. "Troy?" I shouted into the phone. "Troy, is that you?"

The line went dead. I hit callback. It didn't work. I called Julie.

Mandy, not Julie, answered.

"Hi, Lindsay," she said sweetly. "Julie's busy right now. Can I take a message?"

"Mandy," I said, "just tell me."

"Tell you . . . what?"

"Please." *Did your brother go after Troy? Are you really, truly possessed?*

"I'll tell Julie you called," she said, and hung up.

I disconnected and tried to stop shaking. I got into bed and pulled the covers up over my head.

Then my lids grew heavy, and I began to drift.

---

**They are coming,** *they never give up, they cannot die, they will get you . . .*

*Lindsay, Lindsay. Help me.*

It was cold where I was, and black as the grave, as death. An unending corridor that stank of kerosene.

*We used kerosene when we went camping and we used oily rags. He had a pile of oily rags in the shed, and when he went to get our fresh gowns for the operating theater, I saw the rags and I started to plot and I stole them.*

*The door.*

*The door.*

Fire blazed around the white head, shooting to the roof, spreading along the floor. The numbered sections glowed; in the center of the forehead, a bull's-eye was labeled with a thick, dark 7.

Ice pick. Right through the bull's-eye. Lobotomy. Kill the lust, the lack of submissiveness. Good young ladies.

In the operating theater, with the good young gentlemen leaning from the spectators' balconies with their blanching faces.

*Help me.*

*I didn't do it. He did it. My father, he did it. I am here and he is in Massachusetts, in the legislature, and he has told everyone I'm dead and I am here. They are killing us, one by one; they are stealing our souls through that hole in our foreheads; they are making us die for the rest of our lives.*

"Celia?"

*He's calling my name. The doctor's coming for me.*

*Hide me. For the love of God, hide me.*

The weight was on my chest, pressing me down. I couldn't breathe. There was someone in the room, bending over me; I could feel it. My skin prickled but I couldn't move, or scream, or breathe.

I was suffocating.

Then I bolted straight up with a gasp . . . and my terrified face was reflected back to me, in the oval oak mirror above my three-drawer dresser.

Only it wasn't my face.

It was the face from the window, staring at me. The face with the black eye sockets.

A terrible coldness welled inside me.

Inside me.

"No," I whispered, shaking my head. The head.

The head.

The head in the mirror did not shake. It stared straight at me.

"No way," I said more forcefully.

*Help me.*

My heart pumped. I licked my lips.

The image in my mirror did not.

She was the one they had been looking for. And she was still hiding, inside me.

Number Seven.

Possession: me. *I was possessed.*

"You can go now," I whispered. "You're free."

She stared at me for a long time; then slowly, very slowly, she shook her head. And deep inside myself, wrapped in the freezing endlessness of life inside the grave, I knew.

"No," I pleaded.

It wasn't over. Celia. She wasn't free. The spirit wasn't free. And neither was I.

A silvery tear welled at the bottom of her empty eye socket and slid down her cheek. Then it clung to the oak frame of the mirror, dangling like a hanged man, and plopped onto my dresser like a drop of water into a lake.

And I thought of more lines by Robert Frost, Memmy's favorite poet and mine:

> *The wood are lovely, dark and deep.*
> *But I have promises to keep,*
> *And miles to go before I sleep.*

*I* hadn't promised anyone anything.

"But I have," the reflection said, her voice echoing. Then she said, "*Troy.*"

And I knew she was bargaining with me, and I knew why.

*I had to go back.*

*"Yes, there's something the dead are keeping back."*
—Robert Frost,
*The Witch of Coös*

## Acknowledgments:

With deepest thanks to the fantastic Razorbill team, Ben Schrank and my wonderful editor, Lexa Hillyer. Thank you to my agent, Howard Morhaim, and his assistant, Katie Menick. Thank you to my friends and family: Lucy Walker, Anny Caya, Leslie Ackel, Amy Schricker, Pam Escobedo, Karen Hackett, Debbie Viguié, and my super-nice daughter, Belle.

Can't get enough books by Nancy Holder? Check
out this chapter from:

# PRETTY LITTLE DEVILS

# prologue

**Sylvia:** "Damn it, Carolyn, I can still hardly hear you. Thank God you only have one more month on that loser phone. It doesn't get any reception."

**Carolyn:** "I know. I cannot wait. Can you hear me now?"

**Sylvia:** "That might be funny if I actually *could* hear you."

**Megan:** "Same here. I thought three-way calling was supposed to make this *easier*."

**Sylvia:** "Moving on. Listen, Breona threw down again. At the mall. It was another Josh incident. She said he wants to go back to her, but he's staying with me because I 'put out.' 'Put out.' Who even talks like that?"

**Megan:** "You have got to be kidding me! What a slut! She is dead!"

**Carolyn:** "So dead. But you know she was lying, Sylvia. Josh would never say that."

**Megan:** "Totally lying."

**Sylvia:** "It was like she was begging me to lose it right there in the mall, you know? It was in the food court. I was standing in line at Boudin's and she just came over. She was smart to pick a public place. You guys know what I can do when I'm pushed."

**Carolyn:** "She's so déclassé."

**Megan:** "*Vraiment.* Did you talk to Josh yet?"

**Sylvia:** "*Excuse* me? There is nothing to talk to him about. She's lying!"

**Carolyn:** "God, Megan, you don't believe her, do you? You don't think Josh would actually say something like that about Sylvia?"

**Megan:** "It's just . . . I don't know, I wonder how she can lie like that in front of everybody. Josh should know she's lying about him to people."

**Sylvia:** "You have a point. Josh should know his reputation is in danger."

**Carolyn:** "Except . . . it'll look like you don't trust him if you talk to him about it."

**Megan:** "Then one of *us* should talk to him."

**Sylvia:** "Maybe Ellen should. She's so *nice.* By the way, Ellen is our second agenda item, after we take care of this."

**Megan:** "Yeah, because she was wearing that retarded outfit again—"

**Sylvia:** "Megan, *second* agenda item."

**Carolyn:** "Right. Back to the first. Breona is such a ho."

**Sylvia:** "Well, it's just stupid anyway. The way she deals with guys is dysfunctional. If I ever thought Josh really was staying with me because I—because we—"

**Megan:** "She's so wrong. How can she think she can get away with this?"

**Sylvia:** "That's my point. She can't. By the way, she talked about the *incident* too. You know which one I mean."

**Megan:** "Oh my God."

**Carolyn:** "That skank. She really is looking for trouble."

**Sylvia:** "Absolutely. But, as you say, no one will believe her. No one believed all the other gossip about your little entanglement. It died down over the summer. With the pictures."

**Megan:** "Was Stephan there when she mentioned it?"

**Carolyn:** "Megan, get over Stephan. He just brings it up to get a reaction out of you."

**Megan:** "Whatever. We need to discuss how we're getting back at Breona."

**Sylvia:** "Give me your best ideas tomorrow morning. Before school. We are seriously weakened as a group if Breona thinks she can just say whatever she wants without any repercussions. Now, on to the second item. Let's talk about Ellen."

**Megan:** "She's been a total humiliation lately. That dress—"

**Sylvia:** "One bad outfit I could forgive. But that hair . . . This is the beginning of junior year, ladies. We have to take ourselves seriously, or no one else will. When Ellen started falling all over that guy at the movies—"

**Carolyn:** "She does act a little dorky on occasion. . . ."

**Megan:** "A *little*? His friends were *laughing* at us. She didn't even notice."

**Sylvia:** "Ladies, ladies. I don't want to get rid of Ellen. She's been really loyal, and she's a good friend to all of us. But it is a bit of a problem."

**Megan:** "It's like you always say, Sylvia. We are known by the company we keep. If we hang with losers, *we're* losers. We've worked hard to get where we are. We all take pains to look good, to be popular. What we do reflects on all of us."

**Sylvia:** "No. No dumping Ellen. It is not an option. We don't want people saying we turn our backs on our friends. It would be terrible publicity. Breona would jump all over it. And she would probably invite Ellen into her group just to get to all our secrets."

**Carolyn:** "Ellen would rather die than betray us."

**Sylvia:** "Well, it's a situation, definitely. She's losing ground. Maybe she's working too hard, babysitting *too* much. We could cut back on her jobs. . . ."

**Megan:** "Then *we* would have to do them. I've already got tons of homework, and Mrs. Sprague said I have to get some more extracurriculars if I'm going to get into a decent college."

**Carolyn:** "Like your brother?"

**Megan:** "Back off, Carolyn!"

**Carolyn:** "God, Megan, what's your problem? Your brother goes to a serious school. Does that, like, freak you out or something?"

**Sylvia:** "Megan? Are you keeping something from us? Because friends share."

**Megan:** "No. It's nothing. I didn't understand what she meant."

**Carolyn:** "So you thought the worst?"

**Sylvia:** "Both of you chill out right now. My God. Do you even remember what we were talking about? I say it's time to ask a new girl in. That way we can dilute the Ellen factor."

**Megan:** "Are you serious? It's always been the four of us."

**Sylvia:** "Are you questioning me, Megan? Who has kept this group going all this time? Me. And what I say goes. Oh, look, Ellen's logged on. Let's go to the chat room, *mes petites*. Now remember, be kind. Ellen is still one of us."

---

## you have entered
## The Pretty Little Devils chat room
## this is a private chat room for invited members only

**Members in chat room:**

**PLDSLY**

**PLDEL**

**PLDCARO**

**PLDMEG**

**PLDSLY:** *Bonjour*, El! Home early?

**PLDEL:** Still at Hernandez. Using their laptop.

**PLDCARO:** *Bonjour, toutes!*

**PLDMEG:** *Bonjour!*

**PLDSLY:** Clever U, El. Don't forget 2 charge 4 lateness.

**PLDEL:** Suki warned me ahead of time might B late.

**PLDSLY:** Late = late. Suki agreed 2 7 PM. On schedule.

**PLDEL:** OK.

**PLDSLY:** We let 1 slide, they all do it.

**PLDEL:** Sorry. :(

**PLDSLY:** N/p. Listen, El, Breona attacked me at the mall. Re Josh. It was bad.

**PLDEL:** OMG, that's terrible! She hurt U? :(

**PLDSLY:** Not physically. Not a scratch. Though she did have her claws out. LOL.

**PLDEL:** What'd she say?

**PLDSLY:** SOS. Josh couldn't wait 4 me 2 go 2 France, only came back 2 me cuz I give him benefits.

**PLDEL:** OMG. UR kidding! :(

**PLDSLY:** No worries. I ripped her a new 1. She wuz crying by time I left. :)

**PLDEL:** Go, Sylvia!

**PLDSLY:** Of the past. We move on.

**PLDCARO:** But Josh needs 2 know she's lyin' about him. Some1 needs 2 tell him. Not Syl, cuz it'll look like she doesn't trust him.

**PLDEL:** Don't worry, Syl, I can do in Art2.

**PLDSLY:** GR8. I'll call U later, fill U in.

**PLDEL:** KK, but before 9 OK, cuz my dad.

**PLDCARO:** Just put cell phone on vibrate. More fun anyway, LOL.

**PLDEL:** LOL, but big trouble if he finds out.

**PLDMEG:** El, UR a wimp.

**PLDSLY:** Meggers, B nice. :(

**PLDMEG:** Sorry, S.

**PLDSLY:** N/p. El, I'll call B4 9. So, new school year goin' on. PLDs gotta look good. Love streaks, Meggies. New salon?

**PLDMEG:** Still at Tuberose.

**PLDCARO:** In the mall, right?

**PLDMEG:** Please. Who goes to mall 4 hair? White trash!

**PLDSLY:** El, UR place is in mall?

**PLDEL:** Yes.

**PLDMEG:** Oops. Sorry, El! My bad X2.

**PLDSLY:** El, mebbe try Meg's? Also, gel . . . over.

**PLDEL:** Hair not good?

**PLDSLY:** U've done better. Every1 remember, we R in spotlight. That dress Friday . . . *mais non, cherie.*

**PLDEL:** ?

**PLDMEG:** No offense, it makes U look fat.

**PLDEL:** OMG!

**PLDSLY:** We can't give Breona any reason 2 attack us. Solid fashions, solid rep. We R Pretty Little Devils!

**PLDMEG:** *Mais oui!*

**PLDCARO:** *Mais oui!*

**PLDEL:** OMG, Suki home. Gotta go.

**PLDSLY:** *Au revoir!*

**(PLDEL has left the chat room)**

**PLDMEG:** So, do you think she got it?

PERSONALBLOG
HAPPY2BME

SHE'S SUCH A STUPID BITCH. SHE THINKS SHE'S TOTALLY
HOT, BUT SHE'S GOT NO IDEA WHAT CONSEQUENCES
ARE. YEAH, WE'LL CHANGE THINGS. WE'LL SEE WHO
MAKES THE CUT. ONE BY ONE. THEY'LL ALL FEEL THE
BLADE. LAISSEZ LES BON TEMPS ROULER!

# one

By the end of the first week of school, everyone had their designated seats in the cafeteria. Hazel Stone's spot was at the third table from the diversity mural on the west side. There, the diffuse light from the thick windows cast a halo over the heads of her so-called friends—Lakshmi, Ginger, Jamie, and the embarrassingly named LaToya.

Friends . . . they were more like friends by default. Joy had been the one they had in common, and Joy had moved to San Jose during the summer. As soon as she'd left, Hazel had tried her hardest to break away. It hadn't taken.

She had gotten a job and steered clear of the phone, preferring to blog on her LiveJournal or watch *Osbournes* reruns with her little brother, Corey. Hazel had spent more time that summer with Corey than she had the rest of their lives combined, and if her parents had been the kind of people who actually commented on what was going on around them, they would have told her they were pleased.

They wouldn't have been pleased if they'd known what

else had happened during the summer, but she was not going there.

Lakshmi spotted Hazel and waved expectantly. Hazel cringed as the four girls smiled and beckoned her over, as if they had to invite her or something. It would never occur to them that she didn't want to sit with them. It didn't matter that Hazel had pretty much avoided them for the entire summer.

She had pretty much hidden herself away from everybody, feeling guilty and unsure about what she was doing. She would start to think, *Okay, I've made the break.* Then her mother would answer the phone and unknowingly accept an invitation from the Lakshmi contingent on Hazel's behalf. Her mother was clueless, as usual.

Unable to explain that she was trying to dump "those nice girls," Hazel would find herself at the movies or the mall. Thus she would be reconnected with Lakshmi's group, and all her careful isolation would be thrown out the window.

Hazel didn't feel she was asking for much. All she wanted were *real* friends—friends who were interesting and intelligent, friends who understood her. Lakshmi and the others were just treading water until they got out of school, content to stay in the background, idly worshiping the popular kids. Graduation was their only goal.

Hazel had bigger dreams—way bigger. She wanted high school to count for something. She wanted to be one of the girls people remembered when they opened their yearbooks. Not just some other "Who?" in a sea of unrecognizable faces. This was the year to make it happen. Senior year would be too late. The time was now.

And this was a defining moment. Or at least it felt that way. Here she was, halfway through October and still trapped. She knew she needed new friends. And not just good friends, but great ones. And if she worked it right with the right group, she might even have a shot at the object of her total desire, the new guy, Matty Vardeman.

She stole a glance at his table. Despite being new, he was already on the varsity football team, and he sat with some of the first-string guys, like Stephan Nylund, Brandon Wilde, and Josh Douglas.

Stephan was stocky, with red hair and a goatee. He was some kind of tackle or something. Brandon and Josh were the team quarterbacks—friendly rivals—and Josh was Sylvia Orly's boyfriend. He was tall, blond, and very wiry. He laughed a lot, and he was very smart. He would have to be, to keep up with Sylvia.

Brandon was bigger, with chestnut hair and a pair of very thick eyebrows. Unlike Josh, Brandon was a total jerk. Last year he had humiliated a girl in Hazel's geometry class by pretending to ask her out, then telling her he was kidding when she stammered out a yes—as if he would ever go out with someone so beneath him.

Hazel felt sorry for the girl. Then she felt sorry for herself. For her, Matty was just as unreachable.

*But God,* she thought, *he is hot.*

Matty Vardeman sat at the far end of the table, leaning back casually in his chair. He was wearing a gray sweater that looked thick and expensive, maybe hand-knit, and a pair of black jeans. He favored dark clothes, and he looked good in them. The other guys had on their green letter jackets and jeans. Matty usually just carried his jacket, but when he did wear it, his shoulders looked enormous.

She had noticed him on the first day of school. He was Matty, not Matt—and he was a miracle of quirks. Push the quirk meter one more click on the dial, and he would be ugly. But somehow, all of his face's strangenesses came together into one amazing picture. He had a long, straight nose, flaring cheekbones, and deep-set eyes that were dark chestnut in color. His eyebrows were heavy and also dark, like his wavy hair. No spiky tips for him; instead, it was a little long—more Ashton Kutcher than Chad Michael Murray, to use Lakshmi's fan-girl vocabulary.

He was smart, too, Hazel knew. His classes were all AP or honors. He carried a sketchbook wherever he went and sometimes spent study hall or lunch working on a drawing.

His birthday was March 16 and he was from Virginia. He had a soft southern accent that made Hazel smile.

His father was in the navy and his parents had moved to Japan. He had come to Brookhaven to live with his sister and finish out his junior and senior years. Hazel had heard he was really pissed off about having to leave Virginia, but whenever she saw him, his full lips were curled in a faint smile, as if everything secretly amused him.

He was a little reserved and still a little apart from the other guys. He sat at their table and hung with them, but Hazel could tell he wasn't one of them. Not yet.

Hazel had tried everything to get him to notice her. She had memorized his schedule and had "just happened" to wander by his classes so many times that one of the boys in his precalculus class had asked her what the homework was. Despite the fact that Hazel sucked at drawing, she'd taken to carrying a sketchbook as well. She hoped if she appeared to be into art, it might pique his interest. Nothing seemed to have any effect.

"Hazel!" Lakshmi shouted over the din, half rising from her chair as the others waited for her to come and sit down. LaToya gazed at her over her soda cup, sucking on a straw.

Hazel sighed. She just didn't know how to do it, how to go through with cutting them loose. Putting on a little smile, she made eye contact, walked steadily to the table, and put down her tray.

They all had on knockoffs of the current fashions: short blazers, white shirts, and light wash jeans. But somehow on them, it looked like trying too hard.

Hazel had gone preppy, with an oxford shirt, knee-length denim skirt, and black ankle boots. Blue went nicely with her auburn hair, which she'd added a tiny bit of henna to. She had blue eyes, and she knew she wasn't ugly. But looks weren't always enough.

"Hi," Lakshmi said, grinning at her as the others made a show of clearing a welcoming place. "Didn't you see us?"

"Oh, I—I . . ." Hazel stuttered. "I just got distracted for a sec. I thought I heard someone call my name."

"Guess what!" Lakshmi said. "Breona and Sylvia had a fight in the mall last night. The security guards had to come and pull them off each other. There's a deep scratch on Breona's cheek and she's going to sue Sylvia."

Jamie nodded. "She's going to get plastic surgery. Because of the disfigurement."

Hazel's attention immediately ticked to the cheerleader table, where Breona sat with her new, spiky haircut. Her brown sugar complexion was flawless; her dark almond eyes glittered as she talked with the other cheerleaders, all of them in tight kelly green sweaters and gold cheer skirts that showed off their skinny, muscular bodies. There was a Band-Aid on her cheek. But it hardly covered a plastic-surgery-worthy wound. Lakshmi was good for gossip, but sometimes she tended to overdramatize.

Not that the Breona-and-Sylvia war needed dramatization. The two queen bees had always hated each other. They were the two most popular girls in school, and the source of their conflict was always Josh.

The gossip went that last summer things had come to a head. Even though he was officially Sylvia's boyfriend, Josh had hooked up with Breona two weeks after Sylvia had gone to France with her family. Sylvia came back and Josh pretended everything was fine. But of course Sylvia found out the truth. From what Hazel had heard, Josh was lucky to be alive.

"It's all over the school," Lakshmi gushed as she plucked a couple of french fries off Hazel's plate. "Everybody's talking about it."

Hazel watched as Lakshmi popped the fries into her mouth and chewed.

Lakshmi had a skin problem. Hazel had tried to tell her not to eat greasy food, but Lakshmi was very fragile on the subject. She would start crying and insisting that Hazel thought she was ugly. She *wasn't* ugly, but her skin could definitely use some help.

Lowering her voice, Lakshmi leaned forward and added, "Sylvia's got to go to anger management classes. Court-ordered."

Lakshmi's face was flushed with excitement: the thrill of having serious information—the coup of being in the know—was almost too thrilling for her.

"Who told you all this? Your mom?" Hazel asked. Mrs. Sharma worked in the school's office and told Lakshmi all kinds of privileged information. It was wrong and tacky, but Lakshmi and her mom thought it was a way to raise Lakshmi's social Q, and it gave the rest of the group something to talk about.

Lakshmi nodded and Hazel shifted her attention to Sylvia's table.

There they were, the PLDs—the Pretty Little Devils—rivals of the cheerleaders as the most popular, stylish, lucky girls at Brookhaven. Party rumors aside, the PLDs *got it*. They talked about universities and internships and summers abroad. They made appearances at school events but weren't all "rah-rah" about it. They were just the right combination of interested and too-cool-to-care. Hazel would have given anything to be friends with them—if only she knew how.